MW01199543

A
BEACH TO
DIE
FOR

A SMILEY AND McBLYTHE MYSTERY

A
BEACH TO
DIE
FOR

A SMILEY AND MCBLYTHE MYSTERY

BRUCE
HAMMACK

1

"Is Leo sure this is a murder?" asked Heather.

Steve answered with a shrug.

She led him out of the muggy morning air into an upscale apartment in a gated complex within Houston's inner loop. The metal tip of his white cane swept back and forth across a floor of beige travertine. Once past the foyer, coat closet, and home office, the open floor plan gave her a view of a kitchen, dining area, and living room of substantial proportions.

She took in a full breath. "The kitchen counters are marble; the stove and ovens are professional grade." Heather turned to the dining room. "Dining room table and chairs for ten. All new and high end."

Steve responded with a grunt but no words.

"The stone floor ends where the living room begins. The carpet is what's called loop-cut-loop. It's tightly woven, has geometric patterns, and looks expensive. The room reminds me of one hit by a tornado. Broken lamps and vases, ripped couches and chairs, paintings thrown about willy-nilly, and a puddle of what I'm sure is drying blood by the coffee table."

Leo, Steve's former partner at Houston homicide, added, "It's blood. We tested it. The forensic crew bagged and tagged a fireplace poker with hair, skin, and blood on it."

Steve asked, "How much hair?"

"Some loose strands and what was in a clump of skin about the size of a dime."

"Are the loose strands of hair with or without roots?"

"With," said Leo.

"All of them?"

"Every one."

Steve issued a quick "Uh-huh" and rested both hands on the top of his cane. "How much blood?"

Heather and Leo traded glances before Leo said, "Too much for the victim to live and talk about it."

Steve huffed a note of impatience. "How much is too much?"

Heather came to Leo's aid. "That will be impossible to tell until the forensic crew cuts out the stained carpet and analyzes it."

"I know that," said Steve. "Give me your best guess."

"It depends on the pad underneath the carpet. The quality of the carpet tells me the pad has a moisture barrier. If we assume it does, I'd say four units, give or take one."

"Any blood splatter?"

Leo took over again. "None."

"Was there a blood trail?"

"No."

"What's the distance from the fireplace tools to the pool of blood?"

"Fifteen feet."

"Any trail of blood around the puddle?"

"None."

Silence prevailed for half a minute before Steve asked, "What did they take?"

Leo took his phone and read from notes. "Signs of burglary include: no wallet found in the apartment, indentations in the master bedroom's carpet show recent removal of a home safe, and no jewelry found." He looked up. "His phone was on the nightstand."

"So," said Steve. "You have no body but plenty of evidence of a burglary and a homicide." He lowered his voice. "Can anyone else hear us?"

Leo didn't bother reducing the volume of his words. "I sent everyone outside, including forensics."

Heather knew what was coming, and it sent a shiver down her spine. When Steve came to the location of a suspicious death, he had an advantage over others because of his special gift. Its proper name is associative chromesthesia. A small fraction of people can perceive colors when they are writing music, painting, or deeply immersed into a creative activity. Steve possessed the ability to "see" shades of red at homicides. Quite the trick for a blind man.

Steve lifted his chin. "Leo, what's his name?"

"Quinton Rush."

Heather locked her gaze on Steve. The odor of rusty metal found her as blood continued to dry in the puddle of eggplant-colored goo.

Steve took his time before announcing, "No red and no pink; you don't have a homicide."

"An insurance scam?"

"Uh-huh. Start with a financial check of Mr. Rush. Look for life insurance policies, especially those taken out in the last six months. I'm sure you'll find he has serious money problems."

Leo tapped notes into his phone as Steve continued, "There's too much physical evidence of a burglary; no reason to destroy paintings, lamps, and furniture. A fight would have resulted in splatter somewhere in the room."

Steve took off his sunglasses and rubbed his sightless eyes. "What's in the puddle belongs to Quinton Rush, but there's too much of it. He planned this for a long time, extracted his own blood, and stored it until he had enough."

"So much blood made me suspicious. I needed you to confirm it."

Steve continued, "You probably already thought of this, but the missing safe, wallet, and jewelry also speak of Mr. Rush wanting to keep things of value. Did you notice he was smart enough to leave his cell phone here?"

Heather spoke up. "All the hair samples having roots made me wonder. A blow from a poker would have broken some."

Steve summarized. "Look for Mr. Rush's love interest. Odds are she, or he, is the beneficiary named on the insurance policy and in his will."

"Anything else?" asked Leo.

"Two things. Mr. Rush will have a bandage on his head from where he or his partner gouged a chunk out of his scalp."

"Got it," said Leo. "Anything else?"

"Yeah. Where are we going for lunch?"

"Sorry. I'm breaking in a new detective who's wondering why I kicked her and everyone else out of the room when you arrived. Thanks for confirming what didn't seem right."

"It's a good thing you called me this week and not next."

Leo's eyebrows arched in a question. Heather explained. "We're flying to St. Croix for Bella and Adam's wedding."

Steve added, "I can't wait to sit under a palm tree listening to waves lap against the shore."

Leo snapped his fingers. "That's right. It's already August." He tilted his head and looked at Heather. "Speaking of marriages—"

Steve cut him off by cupping his hand and speaking in a loud pretend-whisper. "We don't talk about when she and Jack will tie the knot."

Heather placed her hands on her hips and gave an answer that sounded lame even to her. "How do you know we haven't already eloped?"

"Good try," said Steve. "I'd know it if you had."

She rose to the challenge. "How?"

"Experience. Maggie and I couldn't wait and got married during our last year in college. She worried until the following June that her parents would find out."

Heather felt her mouth hinge open as Leo said, "You old dog. I didn't know that. Where did you live?"

"In separate apartments. We each had roommates to save money. Her father made it clear that she'd be my responsibility the day we married. He must have said that twenty times after we got engaged. We had another full year of college and selected June for the church wedding her mother insisted on."

Steve's past seemed to come alive. "It came down to a lot of guilt over sin or holding back information. Being a fiancé with benefits wasn't an option for Maggie."

"But sneaking around was?" asked Heather.

Steve's grin threatened to stretch his face. "Maggie and I were both working and taking a full load of classes. Going public would have added another year before we graduated." A mischievous tone slipped into his words. "Her dad was an avid fisherman and had his eye on a new bass boat, which he couldn't afford as long as he was paying for college. He secretly hoped we'd elope. We did, but didn't tell him."

Leo nodded approval. "Smart move, but didn't it bother Maggie to hide the marriage from her father?"

"Not much. It was a great way to ease into living together. We barely made it through the big church wedding without busting out laughing, especially when Reverend Brown winked at us before we took our vows."

"You told the preacher?"

"Why not? He agreed with our decision. Coveting a bass boat was a bigger sin to him than two grown people getting married on the sly."

Leo looked toward the front door. "I need to get this crime scene processed." He gave Steve a firm pat on the shoulder. "Have a safe trip. Tell Bella and Adam I wish I could have come to their wedding."

Heather placed Steve's hand on her arm. "It's still a week away. All you have to do is ask, and I'll send my plane back for you."

"Six kids, school's starting, and the oldest is going off to college. My day in the sun and sand on a tropical island is about twelve years from now." He looked at the door. "Time for me to let the troops back in."

Frowning crime scene technicians covered their noses and mouths with blue masks and slipped back into the apartment.

Heather pushed a button on the key fob and her Mercedes SUV came to life on the far side of police tape. Steve lifted his head. "That sound means the air conditioner is on. We need to let you get back to work."

"Thanks again for making the trip. I'll talk to the captain and get this case transferred to fraud. That should earn me a gold star for the day."

"Don't be so sure this case is over. Once the beneficiary finds out the insurance company won't pay, Quinton Rush may be your next homicide. Hopefully, he'll choose an island other than St. Croix."

"Speaking of," said Heather. "I need to think about what I'm going to wear."

"And I need lunch," said Steve.

2

Once in the SUV, Heather asked, "Any preference on where you want to eat?"

A click sounded as Steve put on his seatbelt. "Something fast. I can tell Leo's call came at a bad time. You're not your normal cheerful self."

Heather wondered if she should mention the disappointing financial reports she received yesterday. She chose not to, and said, "We passed a sandwich shop a couple of blocks from here. Is that all right?"

"Fine. I'll get something worth eating. You can have your usual salad and tell me what's bothering you while we eat."

She didn't wait. "It's mainly a self-inflicted wound. We haven't had a case to work since January and here we are with summer slipping away. I've done nothing but work for seven straight months and several of my investments are slipping. I feel like I'm in a rut."

Steve nodded. "Stale is how I'd describe myself. I'm writing less and wasting my time listening to podcasts more and more." He took a breath. "How are things with Jack?"

"All right, I guess."

She realized her tone betrayed her. "Let me amend that. I think he's fine. I really haven't spent much time with him."

"Why not?"

"The way the economy is going, it's harder and harder to grow the business. I've tripled my domestic business trips and doubled the international ones. Overall, profits are flat-lining."

"That's good to hear."

She glanced to her right. "Why is that good?"

"I thought it was something serious, like your father's health, or Jack had been in an accident. Business is down all over the country and you're maintaining. Sometimes things are beyond your control. Not going backward is an impressive achievement."

"I don't like it."

"Would you like to stomp your feet and scream at the sky for a while?"

"I've already tried that. I bruised my heel."

Steve started chuckling, which rippled her way. She caught it. Like some irresistible force of nature, the laughter started and couldn't be contained. She barely made it into the parking lot before laughter-induced hiccups set in. She chose the first available spot, put the vehicle in park, and reached for a tissue to dry her leaky eyes. "Thanks. I didn't realize how tight I was wound until now."

"I know just what you need. Call your office, take the rest of the day off, and pretend we have a murder to solve."

"I have a better idea," said Heather. "I'll do what you said, except I'll think about St. Croix while I'm at the spa. An overhaul on everything from toenails to my hair's split ends is long overdue."

Her phone sounded the ring tone indicating it was Jack calling. She enabled the call and said, "Hello, handsome. Are you calling to ask me to dinner?"

A hesitation sounded in his voice. "Listen, something's come up."

Her back stiffened. "Please tell me it's not your mother."

"No," he said with urgency. "Mom's fine. It's something legal I have to take care of." He gave a strained laugh. "I'll be out of town for a few days."

"That's a change. I'm the one who's always saying that to you. Is it a big case?"

"Yeah. I need to go."

The call cut off and Heather slipped her phone in her purse.

Steve pulled the handle and the door popped open. "I'm getting potato salad with my sandwich. What are you having?"

"Some sort of salad. I want to look halfway decent in a bathing suit. Only another week before we leave and then a week until the wedding."

Steve was halfway finished with his meal when his phone announced a call from Adam, Bella's fianc. He placed the phone on the table so they both could hear. "Hello, Adam. I'm having lunch with Heather and she's listening."

A strained voice came back. "I'm calling to see if you and Heather can get here as soon as possible."

"Is everything all right?"

"No. No it's not. Bella's a wreck."

"That sounds like more than pre-wedding jitters. What's happened?"

"She found a man dead in the parking lot of her parents' resort."

"Take your time, and give us details."

"Bella found the body this morning. All she could say was, 'Call Steve and tell him the killer used a garrote.' The police are questioning her now."

"Do they suspect her?"

"They locked down the resort. I don't know who they suspect." An indistinguishable voice in the background preceded Adam saying, "The detective wants to talk to me next. I need to go."

A metallic click ended the conversation.

3

The next morning, the day's first rays of sunshine poked through the window of Heather's new twin-engine corporate jet. She'd chosen a seat at the front while Steve had moved to the rear of the ten-passenger plane, a step up from the five-seater she sold. This one gave her additional range for international flights and allowed her to travel from Conroe's regional airport to St. Croix direct.

She rose from her leather seat, took a couple of steps, and refilled her cup with strong coffee in the plane's compact galley. Despite the whine of the engines, Steve must have heard her stirring. He raised his seat back to a sitting position and pushed aside a fleece blanket. "I hope you made enough for everyone."

"There's plenty. You've been asleep for three hours. Are you ready to start your day?"

"Is it daylight?"

"The sun's peeking over the horizon."

"That means it's officially coffee time."

She filled his mug, went to the rear of the cabin, and took the seat facing him. He'd located and pulled a tray table from a hidden compartment to his left.

She stated the obvious. "Good, you figured out the table. Coffee is at your two o'clock."

His fingers inched forward until they touched the porcelain mug. "By the window is the logical place to find a hidden tray table. Besides, these seats are almost the same as those on your last plane." He yawned. "Thanks for the coffee. I was in and out of sleep. How many phone calls did you make?"

"Five. Two to Germany and one to England." She paused. "Those were the ones to Europe. The calls before them went to Japan and Vietnam."

He ran his fingers around the mug until he located the handle. "How long before you shift gears and relax?"

"Soon, I hope. If we have a murder to solve, that will take the place of work. I wish I could say I'm not worried about Bella."

"Try thinking about the possibility of us having a case to work on."

"I'm on to your ways, Detective Smiley. You couldn't stand not knowing, so you called Bella yesterday to get details on the homicide."

He didn't deny it. "The victim is Nate Johnson. He's a local hotel owner who was scheduled to purchase the Swenson's resort."

Heather's finger slipped off the edge of her mug and into hot coffee. "Purchase the resort? When did Bella's parents decide to sell?" She dried her finger with a napkin. "How long have you known about this?"

"A couple of weeks, and don't feel bad. It's been in the works for months and she didn't tell me, either. Bella's so focused on Adam and the wedding, I guess it slipped her mind."

"Why didn't you mention it to me before now?"

"Check your calendar. How many days have you been home in the last two months?" He paused. "The answer is three. I was afraid this would happen when you took in part of your over-sized office. Did you really need an efficiency apartment?"

He raised his mug but delayed taking a sip. "By the way, your cat isn't happy with you."

A stab of regret hit her. "Poor Max. He deserves a better mommy." She heaved a sigh. "Thanks for taking care of him."

"Do you miss him?"

"Absolutely!"

"Look under the blanket." Steve pointed to a curtain separating the main cabin from a storage area and the lavatory.

Heather jumped to her feet and threw back the curtain. She lifted the blanket from a pet carrier and tossed it aside. The black mound of fur didn't move. She sank to her knees. "Max? Are you all right?"

Panic filled her voice. "He's not moving."

Steve's voice remained calm. "Check again. I hear him snoring."

She opened the door, reached in, and stroked the fur that felt like warm sable. "Why isn't he coming out?"

"I took him to the vet. She suggested he'd be a happier cat if he slept through the flight. It took some sleight of hand to get him on board without you realizing it. Your pilots deserve a bonus."

"They'll get it. Are you sure he's all right? What about him staying at the resort? Bella's parents don't mind?"

"I cleared it with Lonnie and Ingrid. They know how crazy Bella is about him. Ingrid said she's missed Mike following her around since he went to doggie heaven." Steve took a sip of coffee. "Max will be the resident therapy cat for you and Bella."

"Brilliant. I'm moving his crate closer to us."

Times like these made Heather especially grateful for her friendship with the blind detective. It also made her realize how much she missed her beloved Maine Coon cat. It was as if someone had thrown a switch in her brain and it was time to reorganize her priorities. She sent a text to her personal assistant and told her to handle all the business calls. She then sent a text to her father, telling him the same.

Their similar replies came one after the other. "It's about time."

A loud meow sounded, and her gaze shifted to Max. She looked in the crate to see an arched back as he greeted her with a curled-tongue yawn. Seconds later, she had a lap overflowing with purring fur. Her world changed for the better as she leaned back and stroked his wide head.

———

HEATHER AWOKE WITH HER HAND RESTING ON MAX'S BACK and the plane touching down. He was still purring. "How long have I been out?"

"Over an hour. Once we're stopped, you'll need to put Max back in his crate. Bella and Adam are waiting for us."

"You talked to them this morning?"

Steve gave his head a single nod. "You were sound asleep."

She rubbed her eyes as the plane slowed to a stop. Max nudged her hand to keep stroking him. Gratitude pushed worry out of its way. "I'm so glad you brought him."

The engines decreased in volume, and the co-pilot came to the back of the cabin. "It's a post-card-perfect day in paradise. Of all the airports in the Caribbean, this is my favorite."

"Why's that?" asked Steve.

"It's big enough for large commercial planes, which means a smooth runway that's two miles long. But more than that, it's named after a native son, Henry E. Rohlsen. He was one of the Tuskegee Airmen of World War II. As a former air force pilot, I appreciate what those men overcame to serve our country."

The pilot looked down. "Is Max ready to get back in his crate?"

"Probably not," said Steve, "but that's where he has to go."

Heather placed him at the door of the crate. Forlorn eyes asked for a reprieve from the cage. He let out a huff, padded his way through the open gate, kneaded his blanket like it was dough, and eased down.

They exited the plane and stepped into bright sunshine. Heather squinted and reached into her purse for sunglasses. Distant palm trees, aided by warm trade winds, waved a greeting. A van pulled alongside the plane and the passenger door flew open. Bella hopped out and jogged toward them. The young woman who reminded Heather of a Nordic goddess enveloped Steve in a hug. As usual, she'd braided her thick blonde-white hair into a rope that hung down her back brushing her waist.

The wordless clench broke and Heather found herself in Bella's arms. "Thank you so much for coming, and I apologize for the short notice. It's a shame Jack couldn't come."

Heather tried to mask the disappointment in her voice. "Legal stuff to take care of. He'll arrive in a few days."

The co-pilot spoke from the open door. "We'll be along with the luggage and Max after we refuel and button up the plane."

Bella shook her head. "Max is going with us. We can also take the luggage."

Up to this point, Adam had stayed in the background. He stepped forward. "If you'll bring everything down, I'll load it in the back of the van."

Steve was the next to speak. "Adam, you're so quiet I thought Bella came by herself."

"It's good to have you both here."

Heather took a long look at Bella's future husband. He was more handsome than she remembered, yet quiet and unassuming. Dimples sunk deep into his cheeks when he smiled. His raven hair and olive skin were the perfect counterpoint to Bella's Scandinavian features. They always reminded her of the figurines standing atop wedding cakes.

With hosts, guests, luggage, and cat loaded in the van, they soon cleared the airport property. The road wound its way to the far side of the island, where rooms with a view of azure waters awaited them... as did a murder investigation.

4

After the initial gush of emotion at the airport, Steve found it interesting that an uncomfortable silence settled in on the trip to the resort. Long ago he'd made friends with silence. Adam also practiced an economy of words, but when he spoke, it was on point and worth listening to. Bella and Heather normally morphed into chatter-boxes when they got together, the way close sisters carry on. Silence for Bella was out of character unless she had something to be upset about. Finding a body two weeks before her wedding qualified as a traumatic event. With the initial glee of the reunion behind them, the silence told him the two women had each returned to their own land of worries, both large and small.

Pretending nothing was wrong seemed a waste of time and mental energy. Gathering information about the murder, however, was something he could pursue. If he put Bella's agile mind to work, it might pull her out of her funk. He raised his voice to be heard over the noisy van. "Bella. Tell us about the victim."

He could tell by the direction her voice came from that she'd swiveled in her seat to face him. "I still can't believe he's dead. His name is Nate Johnson. My parents have known him forever."

"Describe him to me. Begin with physical, and then what he was like as a person."

"Not a big man, about five foot six, a hundred and fifty pounds. He was a descendant of slaves, so his skin was very dark and he kept his hair short."

"Age?"

"Mid-forties." The pace of her words picked up. "Nate was a hard worker. A long time ago, he bought a small run-down hotel in town. He fixed it up and made constant improvements. I don't know how, but he hand-dug the hole for the swimming pool. There was enough land for him to add ten very cute bungalows. He was a certified dive instructor and offered free lessons to anyone who stayed at his hotel. That's the niche he tapped into, and he partnered with locals who do diving excursions. Dad jokes that Nate never slept."

"What about his family?"

"Never married and no kids. Mom says he worked so hard he couldn't take time off to court a woman, let alone bother with a wedding or a honeymoon."

The mischievous streak in Steve wanted to say something to Heather about working so much Jack would have to choose between a wedding or a honeymoon. She wouldn't have time for both.

Steve dismissed the passing thought. Instead, he asked, "Did Nate have any enemies?"

"None," said Bella with certainty. "Everyone says he was born with a smile. It made him happy to work and serve others."

"Strange that someone killed him. Could the murder have been a case of mistaken identity?"

"Not likely. He was an island native. Everyone who lives here full time knew him and thought the world of him. I don't think it was in him to have a bad thought, let alone to speak a harsh word."

Steve spoke in a loud whisper. "Yet someone killed him in one of the most brutal ways possible."

Bella's voice caught as she responded. "It was horrible. So much blood from the wire that cut into his throat."

"Did the police find the murder weapon?"

"No," said Adam. "They're still looking."

Heather gave Steve a tap on the leg and said, "Let's move on. Tell us what the police have done so far."

The sound of Bella's soft sobs reached Steve, and he realized why Heather had nudged him. Adam fielded the question. "Interviews and searches. They secured the area of the parking lot where Bella found his body, locked down the resort, and didn't finish interviewing staff until after midnight."

Bella sniffled and said, "They spent a lot of time with me. Kept asking the same questions over and over."

Adam asked, "Should we read anything into them spending so much time grilling Bella?"

"Not at all," said Steve. "The emphasis at the beginning of an investigation is on physical evidence and witness statements. They're after facts that they can use to paint a picture of what happened. Don't let it surprise you if they interview you again."

The van suddenly dipped. Everything inside shifted violently, and it sounded like the dash was coming apart. Adam announced, "Sorry. Some roads on the island need attention. I forgot about that monster pot hole."

A meow of protest came from the back of the van. Heather said, "It's all right, Max. We'll be there in a few more minutes, and I'll order a nice fish dinner for you."

The jolt from the pothole and Max's complaint took away the desire to speak of the murder, especially from Heather. In an effort to shift the conversation, she asked, "How are the wedding preparations going?"

"Fine until yesterday morning," said Adam. "Everyone's still getting over the fact that something so horrible happened at one of the most peaceful places in the world. The police seem to be struggling with motive."

After hearing Bella's description of Nate Johnson, Steve had to rearrange his ideas concerning motive. The case wasn't getting any easier. Or was it? It didn't seem likely that the killing was spur of the moment, or revenge, or because of passion gone off the rails. He wasn't ready yet to take those cards off the table, but they moved to the bottom of his list. There must be another reason for such a good-natured, hardworking man to die such a horrible death.

Bella announced from the front seat. "We're here. The crime scene tape is still up in this parking lot, so we'll go around to the lobby."

Steve wanted one more bit of information before they arrived. "How did you find the body?"

"There's a sweet lady named Judith Tovar staying here. She likes to go on early morning walks because she uses a walker. The best place and best time for her to do that is at first light in the parking lot. I've gotten into the habit of going with her. I happened to glance between cars and saw the body. At first, I thought it was someone who partied too hard and couldn't get back to their room. It was horrible, but at least I was able to divert Mrs. Tovar before she saw anything. She'd lagged a few steps behind me. I told her to go back inside and tell Dad to come to me."

"Who called the police?"

"I had my cell phone and called them."

Steve cut her off before she could say anything else. "I get the picture."

The van came to a stop and Adam spoke. "This wasn't the conversation we planned on having when you arrived, but I'm glad we did. You don't know how your being here puts Bella's mind at ease. And mine."

"Amen to that," said Bella. "Let's get you inside and settled."

"Meow!" came from the back of the van.

Steve said, "I believe Max is ready for his breakfast and a trip to the biggest sandy beach he's ever been on."

Heather protested. "I can't let him run wild on the beach."

"You don't have to," said Steve. "I bought him a harness and one of those retractable leashes. We've been practicing taking walks."

Bella chuckled, which was the first sign of the happy young woman he knew and loved. "Knowing Max, he'll catch his own meal."

5

Heather couldn't wait to get Max out of his crate, but Bella beat her to the back of the van and even located his harness and leash. The future bride had Max thoroughly hugged and hooked up before Adam unloaded the rest of the luggage onto a cart.

"I'm taking this tubby boy for a long walk on the beach," announced Bella.

"Good idea," said Steve. "When you're through with him, you can take me. I've been dreaming about listening to the waves rolling to shore and digging my toes in the sand ever since you and Adam announced your engagement. I'd have been very disappointed if you got married anywhere else."

Lonnie Swenson, Bella's father, arrived with a warm word of welcome. He instructed the porter to take Steve and Heather's luggage to their rooms.

"Same room as last time?" asked Steve.

"Of course," said Lonnie. "Facing the ocean with a balcony so you can hear the waves."

"A dream come true," said Steve. "Is Ingrid with you?"

"She's waiting inside. I thought we might have a word with you and Heather, unless you're too tired from your trip."

Heather answered. "Steve slept halfway, and Max and I took a nap after he woke. We're ready to help in any way we can."

"Let's hope that won't be necessary," said Lonnie as she took in his features. He was as she remembered him, a tall, lanky man with large hands who went about his duties with calm confidence. His years of hospitality formed him into a man who knew when to stand back and when to confront customers with soft words that set hard boundaries.

Adam stepped forward. "Lonnie, do you need me to help you with anything?"

"Thank you, no."

"I'll be in my room if you do. Only four more hours until the markets in New York close."

Heather asked, "How's the day trading?"

A smile showed off his dimples. "Volatile markets are feeding times for traders like me. We make money if stocks go up or come down."

"Perhaps I should follow your lead, or at least diversify more."

"Let's talk about it while you're here."

Lonnie held out his hand toward the door to show the curbside financial conference needed to end and that Heather was to lead Steve and follow him. It was the closest she'd ever seen Lonnie to being firm, so subtle that most people would have missed it. Murders have a way of draining joy, even out of paradise.

Steve piped up. "Thanks for the ride, Adam. I'd like to spend some time with you, too. Bella's been secretive about your future plans."

Adam stopped at the van door. "I don't know why. We'll start off by splitting our time between Houston and Puerto Rico."

Lonnie chimed in. "We'll follow them as soon as we get this property sold. It will take longer than we thought since we lost our buyer yesterday."

Steve's gait slowed. Heather knew him well enough to tell

when something turned a gear in his mind. He'd heard a snippet that meant nothing to her but was a piece of the puzzle he'd turn and twist until it fit into a bigger picture.

Lonnie walked at a good pace while Heather lagged enough so she could whisper to Steve. "What did you hear?"

"I'll tell you later."

They went a short distance down a long hallway and turned into an office with a sign on the door that read STAFF ONLY.

Lonnie held the door then closed it behind them. Ingrid, an older version of Bella, stood, rounded a desk, and greeted both of them with a warm hug. "It's so wonderful to see you again." She looked at the door. "Is your fiancé not with you, Heather?"

Lonnie broke in before Heather could answer. "Sorry, Ingrid. I was supposed to relay a message to you from Bella. Jack couldn't make it today. He'll be along in plenty of time for the wedding."

Heather flicked her wrist and quipped, "It's what happens when you put together a business owner and a defense attorney. A crisis always interrupts our plans. I'm sure you know all about dealing with last-minute surprises."

Ingrid's eyes were as blue as the water in the horseshoe cove in front of the hotel. Her smile rose all the way into the tiny wisdom lines that radiated from those striking eyes. "Surprises are a way of life for us. The event that happened yesterday was the second worst day of our lives. The first, of course, was when that man kidnapped Bella as a child."

Steve broke in. "That worked out, and so will this."

Ingrid gave her head a nod. "You being here gives us hope it will."

Steve asked, "Do you want us to investigate?"

Lonnie and Ingrid looked at each other. He answered. "We do, but the police don't want you to. I'm afraid Bella told them you'd be here today. Detective Nohr made it clear this was a police matter and he won't tolerate interference."

Steve nodded. "I can't say I blame him. In fact, I acted the same way when I was a homicide detective in Houston."

Heather broke in. "Do you know if they're close to an arrest or have a suspect?"

Ingrid and Lonnie traded glances and shook their heads. Ingrid said, "Up to now, we've answered questions and turned over our financial records to them. Detective Nohr is a sullen sort of man who asks questions but divulges nothing. The communication has been decidedly one-sided."

Steve nodded. "How many guests were here yesterday?"

"About two hundred, including children.

"Remind me," said Steve. "How many rooms do you have?"

"Two-hundred here in the main building. The remaining forty are in the four-plexes and two honeymoon cottages."

"Do you have security cameras?"

"They cover the common areas and hotel hallways."

Ingrid added, "Don't forget the front entrance to the property, the front desk, and the pools."

Heather said, "I'll do a review of your coverage and look for blind spots. I brought some extra cameras with me."

"I'll get Bella to go with you." A mother's concern seasoned her words. "She loves it when you include her. I worry about her involvement, but she needs something to get her mind off what happened."

Steve cleared his throat. "We tried to stop her from helping with our last case and look what happened. She not only helped solve the case but scored a fiancé."

The levity helped relax everyone's shoulders. Lonnie allowed a hint of a smile to cross his face. He added, "And a fine young man he is. I've tried to find faults in him, but I'm not having much luck. He wants to train me to be a day trader like him after we move."

A knock on the door caused Lonnie's smile to disappear. "I told them we weren't to be disturbed."

He opened the door and spoke in a firm tone. "I'm sorry, we're in a meeting. Someone at the desk can help you."

A woman brushed past Lonnie and stationed herself in front of Steve. She wasn't over five foot tall, with long, straight hair so black it had a shimmer of blue. She issued a slight bow to Steve. "Are you Detectives Smiley and McBlythe?"

"That's us," said Steve.

"My name is Li Jing. I need to hire you."

"Why?"

"The police will arrest me today. I am innocent of killing Mr. Nate Johnson."

6

Lonnie and Ingrid excused themselves, leaving Steve with Heather and Li Jing in the office. He listened carefully as Li Jing eased into a chair and spoke with hasty, coherent words. "I doubt we'll have much time. Like I said, I didn't kill Nate Johnson."

"Then why are you sure of your imminent arrest?"

"I found a blood-stained garrote under the mattress of my bed this morning. Someone is trying to frame me for the murder. My passport shows me to be Chinese, but that's not my nationality. I know it looks suspicious, but I can't tell you anything else at this time."

Steve gave his head a nod of affirmation that he understood. He then ran through a few reasons why she couldn't reveal her identity. The list was short. "Can I assume the passport is a forgery?"

"By the time the police discover it is, I'll be out on bond. Hopefully by then you'll know who killed Mr. Johnson."

Steve pursed his lips as he considered how the police would react. "You're right about the passport. That will be enough for them to arrest you."

"Where is the garrote?"

"I hid it," she said in a measured, calm voice. "I'm not who or what the police think me to be." Her voice pleaded for understanding. "I can't divulge more."

Steve leaned forward. "We work with the police, not against them."

"I'm familiar with your reputations. That's why I'm trusting you. You should start with two guests staying here who go by the names Chip and Roxy Smith."

It was time to make the first major decision of the case. Should he risk running afoul of the law by withholding evidence? He mentally looked for a way to walk the narrow line between keeping silent and possibly committing a crime, or trusting a woman he'd just met. He thought he knew why she'd have a fake passport, but wasn't sure.

"If the police ask us for help in solving the murder, we'll assist them. As for your claim about someone placing the garrote under your mattress, we won't mention it unless they ask us."

Skepticism filled Heather's words "We won't?"

"Not now."

"By helping the police solve the murder, you'll be helping me. That's sufficient."

Soft footfalls and the click of the door opening told him Li Jing had nothing more to say. A man's voice sounded from the hallway. "Li Jing. I'm Detective Nohr. You're under arrest for possession of a false government document and suspicion of murder."

Clicks of handcuffs tightening reached Steve's ears prior to footfalls fading down the hall.

Heather went to the door and closed it. "What are you doing? That garrote is evidence that could cost me my law license."

Steve nodded. "I believe we're swimming in deep, shark-infested waters."

Steve and Heather stayed in the office, discussing the strange turn of events until a knock sounded, followed by Bella entering. Max made his presence known by issuing a soft purr.

"Are you two hungry? The dining room's open for lunch."

Heather walked past him. "You two go without me. I'm long overdue for a nap with Max." She took Max's leash and strode down the hall to get her room key.

Bella sidled beside him and placed his hand on her arm the way he'd taught her. "Find us a table away from inquisitive guests."

They walked through the lobby, then down a different hallway. Bella said, "I don't know if you remember, but this takes us to the indoor dining room."

"I remember it having a door leading to a veranda and outdoor seating with a bar."

"Good recall. There are several ways to get to the covered patio. One is through the main dining room. There's another path from the villas."

"Is the dining room quieter than the patio?"

"Uh-huh. The patio overlooks the pools and the beach. Guests with children rarely eat lunch indoors."

He tapped his cane on what sounded like ceramic tile until Bella pulled up short. "Here we are. I picked a table as far away from the windows as I could get. No one is near us, but we probably should keep our voices down. Noise carries in here."

Steve did as she recommended and dropped the volume of his voice to something softer. "Tell me about Chip and Roxy Smith."

"Physical description first or what they're like?"

"Start with physical."

Bella took her time, apparently arranging her thoughts. "I'll start with Chip. I'd say he's between forty and forty-five with wide shoulders and a barrel chest. He has a crooked nose and his left ear looks like a run-over beer can. It's all still there, but it lacks the definition that the other has."

Steve nodded. "He must have spent time in the ring or on the mat."

"Huh?"

"It's called a cauliflower ear. Get hit hard enough and long enough and the bruising eventually breaks down the ear's cartilage. It's common among boxers. Wrestlers suffer the same fate because their heads are constantly grinding together."

Bella said, "I'm betting he was a boxer. His eyebrows have scars, and his hands look like small anvils."

"Anything else?"

"He's not the sharpest hook in the tackle box. I guess that's not uncommon for people who put on padded gloves and beat the brains out of each other."

Steve nodded. "Not uncommon at all. What about Roxy?"

"She's big in a different sort of way. Top-heavy in two big ways, if you know what I mean."

"Ah, yeah. I do know what you mean." He moved on. "They sound like an interesting couple. What are they like?"

"Predictable. They follow the same routine every day: sleep late, go to the dining room at noon, he drinks three Bloody Marys, and they eat lunch. They stay in their room until it's time for supper." She paused. "Oh yeah, they have a bottle of gin delivered to their room every day and want us to keep their refrigerator stocked with Sprite and limes."

He needed clarification on one point. "You said he drinks three Bloody Marys and they eat lunch. How much does she drink?"

"If she drinks at all, it's only one when she comes in the dining room."

Steve filed the nugget of information away. "What do they do here at the resort?"

"When they first arrived, they spent a lot of time away from the resort. Now they mostly stay in their room."

Steve could almost picture them, but not quite. "How old is Roxy?"

"It's sort of hard to tell."

"Why?"

"She's one of those women you can't imagine as a girl. It's like she's always been wise to the ways of the world. Know what I mean? She's probably mid-thirties, but could be in her forties."

His imagination played a five-second clip of what Bella described. He dragged a hand down his face to remove the image. "Yeah. I dealt with lots of women like Roxy when I was a cop."

Unfazed, Bella continued, "Her skin is very fair and she has brassy, red hair."

Descriptions ceased when Bella said, "They just came in. Do you want us to sit with them?"

"Go tell the bartender to mix me a Virgin Mary. Tell him I'll switch to Sprite made to look like a mixed drink. Make sure he understands he's not to put alcohol in anything for me, but put an extra shot in the Smith's drinks."

"I thought you didn't like tomato juice."

"It's an old trick detectives use. Get people lubricated, and more information will slide out of them."

Bella's chair scraped as she pushed away from the table. "I'll be right back."

Steve's hunger came to life as aromas wafted his way. He identified steak on a grill and fresh bread baking. It took self-discipline to stay focused. He had an interview to complete; food would have to wait.

Footsteps approached as Bella returned from her errand. He stood with cane in hand. "Introduce me to the Smiths. I'll take it from there."

7

Bella walked at a steady pace as they wove their way through tables and chairs that his cane brushed against. They slowed, and his guide spoke in her bright, airy voice. "Hi, Mr. and Mrs. Smith. Did Ralph take your order for Bloody Marys yet?"

A woman's raspy voice replied. "Hi-ya, Bella. Yeah. Ralph's on it today."

The male voice asked, "Did ya' get a new bartender? My drink has a good kick to it. Who's your friend?"

"This is Steve Smiley. Next to Adam and my dad, he's the most important man in my life. He and his business partner are here for my wedding."

Bella kept speaking before they could respond. "Steve and Heather found my parents. When I was a small child, a man kidnapped me and raised me as his adopted daughter."

"Ya' don't say. That's a story I'd like to hear. Join us, if ya' can. Skip and I ain't got nothing better to do today than hear a good story about kidnappin'."

The sandpaper voice of the man said, "Yeah. Youse guys join us."

The accents were thicker than expected. In his imagination,

Steve saw a bulky former boxer and street fighter from the blue-collar side of the Hudson River. "Pleased to meet you. Your accents tell me you hail from New Jersey."

"That's us," said Roxy. "All the way from Hoboken."

Bella announced, "Here's Ralph with your drink, Steve. I'm putting it right in front of you. Do you want me to get rid of the celery stick?"

"Please. Those stringy things always get caught in my teeth." He allowed enough time for Bella to take out the stalk before picking up the glass and downing half of it. He settled it on the table and issued an "Ahh" of satisfaction. "I can't think of a better way to start a day."

"You're talking my language," said Skip.

From the sound of ice clinking in his glass, Steve believed Skip had downed everything but the vegetables and the ice.

"Bottoms up, Steve. I hate to drink alone."

Bella took care of ordering a second round. As they waited for Ralph to deliver round two of what promised to be many, Roxy waved off a second drink.

Steve needed to keep things light and get them comfortable. People usually loved to talk about themselves. "Is this your first trip to St. Croix?"

A hesitation preceded Roxy's response. "We try to get out of Jersey now and then."

He made a mental note that she didn't come close to answering his question, so he took up where she left off. "It's my second time to come to this slice of paradise. There's nothing like sitting on the balcony of my room, sipping something tall and cool all afternoon, and listening to the waves and birds."

Skip spoke again. "Squeeze a wedge of lime in it, and you can listen to the waves until midnight."

Steve tilted his head toward Bella. "Is it afternoon yet?"

"Three minutes after."

"Good. I feel a third round coming on."

"Make mine gin and Sprite," said Skip.

Round after round of drinks arrived at the table. Skip drank doubles while Roxy switched to water. Steve made a point of avoiding direct questions. He and Bella took turns recounting how a well-known hunter-television personality kidnapped her from the beach beyond the swimming pools.

Bella showed she could find the good in almost any situation by stating, "I was angry at first, but I'm okay now with how things turned out, even though I was seventeen before Steve and Heather reunited me with Mom and Dad." Her voice cracked, but only for a second. "I have Blake Brumley to thank for making me into a television personality."

Roxy asked, "What kind of show did you have?"

"Hunting," said Bella in her chipper voice. "I went all over the world filming with the man I called Daddy. We killed so many animals."

"Like what?" asked Skip.

"I killed a cape buffalo when I was seven."

Steve added, "She's telling the truth. The old episodes are hard to find, but they're still out there. Search for Bella Brumley and follow the thread."

"Brumley?" said Skip, with mistrust in his voice. "Your parents' name ain't Brumley."

"Everyone in show business advised I keep Brumley instead of my legal name. I'm glad I did. It made the transition from hunting to fishing shows and modeling easy. I use Swenson here on the island."

Roxy asked, "Do you still do fishing shows?"

"I had a show for several years. We filmed here in the Caribbean. Now I appear as a guest on other shows. There's plenty of offers coming in. Also, I model sportswear."

"You're still doing that?" asked Steve.

"Yeah, but I'm being a lot more selective with the products I endorse."

"Honey," said Roxy. "You got everything in all the right places. You're drippin' with innocence, and that makes men drool." She ran her finger around the rim of her glass. "Few girls are smart enough to keep the best parts hidden away. It's curiosity that keeps the customers coming back."

Steve was getting a good read on Skip and Roxy, but he wanted to see if he could mine something more specific. He heard Bella shift in her chair. When she didn't reply to Roxy's statement, he figured she was uncomfortable or embarrassed by it, so he asked the couple, "How long did you say you two have been here in St. Croix?"

"A couple of weeks, this time," said Skip.

Steve took a long drink of sweet soda and set the glass down again. "I'm looking for a new adventure while I'm on vacation, but I have limited options. What would you recommend, Skip?"

"I dunno."

Steve spoke as if he had a flash of inspiration. "Let's me and you go parasailing."

"Para-what?"

Bella explained. "It's like water skiing, but instead of sliding across the water on skis, you strap on a parachute, and a boat with a long rope snatches you off a pier or the beach. You go up, up, and away. It's a blast."

"There're two things wrong with your idea, Steve," said Roxy. "Skip doesn't go near the ocean, and he's not fond of heights."

Skip countered with, "Heights ain't too bad, but I'll leave the water to the fishes."

Steve intentionally slurred his words. "It took me a while to go back in the water after a double homicide I worked. We dragged a couple of guys out of the Houston Ship Channel. There wasn't enough left of them to get a positive ID. Forensics got lucky with dental records. It turned out to be a gang killing."

Roxy didn't react, an indication she knew quite a bit about him and Heather. He wasn't so sure about Skip.

The drinks were having their effect on Skip. He responded with a chilling chuckle. "Yeah. Ain't nothin' like cement shoes and a dip in the Hudson."

This gave Steve all the information needed to get started on investigating the couple from New Jersey. He ended the conversation by turning to Bella and saying, "I've been awake since two this morning. Take me to my room?"

"What about lunch?" asked Bella.

"I drank it."

This earned a hearty laugh from Skip. He added, "You're a fun guy. Let's drink our lunch again sometime."

"Yeah. Then we can go parasailing."

"That'll take more than we drank today," Skip slurred.

Steve reached for his cane and pretended it fell in Bella's lap. She played along. "Let's get you to your room."

He leaned heavily on her until she whispered, "They can't hear us. We're almost in the hall."

"I know. The floor changed textures." They took a few more steps, and Steve corrected his posture. "That's better."

"Do you want to go to your room?"

"Please. I need something to soak up all the Sprite. A cheeseburger and fries from room service should do the trick. Then, I'll dictate my notes from our chat with Skip and Roxy and email them to Heather. Remind me later that I have a job for you."

8

They stepped into the elevator, and the doors were closing when a small voice said, "Wait for me."

The doors whisked open again, and the same small voice asked, "Mister, why do you have a white stick?"

"Because I can't see. The stick helps me not run into things."

"You can't see anything?"

"Not with my eyes, but that doesn't mean I can't tell where you've been or what you've been doing."

"How can you do that if you're blind?"

Instead of answering, Steve said, "You've been swimming in the ocean. You're wearing a bathing suit, water shoes, and a T-shirt. You also kicked a dead fish with your right foot."

"I didn't kick it. I stepped on it."

"You also picked it up then wiped your hands on your shirt."

The door slid open. "I also wiped 'em on my bathing suit. You're smart for someone who can't see."

All three stepped into the hall. "Do you want me to tell you where you got those shoes you're wearing?"

"Yeah."

"Right now, you got them in the hallway."

The boy complained as Steve laughed. "You tricked me. I thought you meant where my mom bought them."

"Words are tricky. They can mean more than one thing." Steve reached out with his cane. "You can use that joke on your parents and friends."

"I will, but I'll have to wait to trick my mom. It's just me and Dad here. They're getting a divorce. I think it stinks."

"Worse than that fish you picked up?"

"Yeah. A lot worse." He paused. "I'll see ya' around." Squishy shoes padded down the hall.

Once inside Steve's room, Bella said, "You'd have made a great dad."

"Not me. I was tied to my job and would have messed up a perfectly good kid." He took in a deep breath. "I don't want you to worry or say anything, but I have a sinking feeling about Heather and Jack."

He heard the concern in Bella's voice. "Are you sure?"

"No, but him not coming with us is out of character." He gathered his thoughts. "The only reason I'm mentioning it is so you don't get blindsided if he doesn't show up."

"Thanks. I was going to ask Heather what's going on. What should I do?"

"There's not much anyone can do. We'll have to let things play out. She doesn't want to say or do anything that she thinks will upset you this close to your wedding."

"Have you tried to find out what's going on?"

He answered her question with one of his own. "If the situation was reversed and you and Adam were going through a rough patch, would you want me butting into your private life?"

"Not until I asked you."

"Exactly. She hasn't asked."

"How should I treat her?"

"Ask her questions about the case. Give her your perspective on the interview today. Tell her about your plans to live in Puerto Rico and Houston."

"It will probably be near you, north of Houston."

"I'd like that."

"In other words, you want me to talk about anything but Jack."

"Unless she brings it up, that's my plan."

"I understand." She hesitated a tick of the clock. "What do you think about Skip and Roxy?"

Steve didn't hesitate. "They're up to no good."

"Do you think they're responsible for Nate's murder?"

"Ask me again a week from now. For now, I'll give Heather something to think about besides Jack not coming with us."

"You don't want me to collect background information on them?"

Steve shook his head. "You have a wedding to concentrate on. If Jack doesn't show up in a week, I'll need your help."

Bella wasn't one to give up so easy. "Mom's coordinated so many weddings, she can do it in her sleep. What if I duplicate what Heather's doing, just for practice? Who knows, I might accidentally turn up something she misses."

"If you do anything, keep it on the down-low. The only person you can tell is Adam. Get used to sharing things like this with him." He slipped the key in the lock of his door. "Your parents and Heather will feed me to the fish if they find out I have you working on a case this close to your wedding."

Bella placed her hand on his arm. "Mom and Dad were really looking forward to selling this resort. Who will want to buy it now?"

"It will be interesting to see who shows interest."

9

Heather stabbed the red icon with her finger, threw her phone on the bed, and walked to the sliding glass door that opened to her balcony. She stared without paying much attention to the people frolicking in the pool. Beyond that noisy group, she noted the small waves that scurried to shore and retreated just as fast. They reminded her of a young child who bravely approached the tiny waves, only to run back to their mother when the next one threatened.

Her thoughts were back in Conroe, Texas, where Jack lived and practiced law. She turned and gave her phone one more hateful look. It had betrayed her by not being able to connect with her betrothed. Deep down, she knew it was childish nonsense to think her phone was the culprit, but just like a child, she wanted something, or someone, to blame.

"Snap out of it," she said to herself. The words came out sounding as hollow as a drained coconut. Disgusted with herself, she spoke out loud. "I'm a successful woman, not given to flights of fancy or irrational thoughts. Pull yourself together and do something constructive. Call Steve and see what progress he's made." Li Jing's face came into her mind. "At least I'm not sitting in jail with a murder charge hanging over my head."

She picked up the house phone and called Steve's room. He answered on the fourth ring. She didn't give him a chance to speak. "Are you in your room?"

He chuckled. "You used the hotel phone."

The palm of her left hand struck her forehead. "Sorry. Are you sleeping?"

"I'm good at sleeping and talking, but not at the same time."

"Please don't make fun of me. I just woke from a bad dream."

"I'll open the door. Bella and I had a long talk with Skip and Roxy Smith. I'll fill you in."

Heather scooped up her phone, told Max to come with her, and made for the door. The chubby cat didn't move until she spoke in a voice that brought to mind the stern headmistress of one of her boarding schools. "Max! Get up! We're going next door to see Steve." That roused him, and he jumped off the bed.

The two arrived, and Max announced himself by rubbing against Steve's leg on his way to the king-size bed.

Steve's return greeting came with a hint of camaraderie. "Make yourself at home, Max. It feels like nap time for me, too."

Heather went straight for the couch. She kicked off her sandals and sat with her legs tucked under her. Steve took a club chair sitting at a forty-five-degree angle from her.

"Do you want to go first?" he asked.

"I tried three times to call Jack with the same result each time. All calls are going to voice mail. I also called his office. Another recorded message. I can't imagine why his mother doesn't answer. She has caller ID and knows it's me."

"You're assuming she's there. There are a thousand reasons for her to be gone."

Heather wasn't in the mood for a logical response. "Jack's supposed to be here with me, and his mother was looking forward to reworking her files without so many interruptions." She released a huff of frustration.

"Uh-huh," said Steve, which meant absolutely nothing other than he heard what she said and acknowledged it. "You sound like a frustrated executive. I suggest you take off your business hat and put on a fedora with a pulled down brim. It's time to think like a detective."

As usual, Steve was right. The romantic vacation wasn't cancelled, only delayed.

Instead of asking anything more about Jack or his mother, Steve launched into a monologue that began with, "Bella and I made progress at lunch. I pretended to get tipsy by downing eight virgin mixed drinks while Skip stayed up with me, swilling double shots of the hard stuff. It loosed his tongue enough for us to find out some interesting tidbits."

"Like what?"

"They've been here for two weeks." Playfulness crept into his voice. "They're up to mischief and malfeasance."

"What kind?"

"I'm not sure yet, but they have all the makings of a madam and her bouncer. Perhaps they're looking for a new hotel or resort to ply their trade."

"Are you sure?"

"They're from Hoboken, New Jersey and were on the island earlier this year. Bella says they spent the first few days since their arrival going to town. Every morning they'd leave and not come home until evening. For the past week and a half, they've stayed here, spending most of the day in their room. I need you to do a complete background check on them. You still have old college buddies in the State Department, don't you?"

"Plenty of Princeton graduates end up there. So?"

Steve let out a huff of frustration. "Do I have to spell it out for you? We need intel on Li Jing. Who is she? Who does she work for? Does she have hotshot attorneys trying to get her out of jail? If so, who's paying the tab?"

Heather stood and paced a path from the couch to the patio door. She made two laps and stopped. "Sorry. I'm having a hard time shifting gears."

His words came out seasoned with determination. "I'm

trying to find someone to help me with a murder investigation. If you can't, I'll ask Bella."

"You can't do that." Her voice held all the charm of a snapping turtle.

She shook a finger at him. "Don't overplay your hand."

"If you want to waste your time, that's up to you," said Steve in a marginally less combative tone. "By the way, I have one more job for you."

"You do it. My dance card is full."

His response came back with staccato words, much quicker than his normal cadence. "I would if I could, but I can't, so I won't."

She chuckled. "I haven't heard that since I came back from a summer session in Switzerland when I was fourteen."

"Fifth grade for me," he said with a sly smile. "We peasants must have been ahead of the aristocracy with stupid sayings."

"Enough," said Heather with a laugh. "Tell me what you need me to do."

"Find Judith Tovar, and take her on a walk tomorrow morning."

Heather wondered why she hadn't thought to do it without Steve's prompt. "She's the woman who was with Bella when they found the body."

"Bella told me she's been at the resort all summer. Find out why and anything else you can get her to divulge."

Heather went back to the couch but didn't sit. In a mocking tone, she asked, "And what will you do while I'm working my fingers to the bone?"

"Lonnie emailed me a list of four other people who've been here longer than four weeks. I'll complete background checks on them."

"Is that all?"

"No. Leave Max here. We both need a nap to shake off the effects of jet lag."

Heather huffed. "I can't spend a full day with my cat?"

"We both need our beauty sleep, and he's recovering from a drug overdose."

The banter with Steve acted like a shot of B-12. It was good to smile and to have action replace emotions. This was therapy from the grind of high-stakes business that came at no cost.

Once back in her room, she put her phone on the desk and asked it nicely to ring extra loud if Jack called. She did her best to put thoughts of him away and made a list of the tasks Steve asked her to complete. Her first call went to Bella.

"Heather. What's up?"

"Were you planning to walk with Judith Tovar in the morning?"

"She called me five minutes ago. I told her the police tape was coming down and we could get back to normal if she wanted. She said our walks started her days off right."

"Can you come up with an excuse for me to take your place tomorrow? Steve wants me to find out what I can for him."

"Why didn't he ask me?" Her voice had a tinge of hurt to it.

Heather contemplated telling a half-truth, but this was Bella. Their relationship was based on trust. "Steve knows I'm having trouble shifting from business to detective. He's keeping me busy with a list of things to do. Interviewing Judith Tovar is one of them."

"Now I understand," said Bella, as if she'd solved a great mystery. "Steve's filling your day so you won't worry. I'll tell Mrs. Tovar I can't come, but I've found a replacement."

"What time and where do I meet her?"

"In the lobby at first light. She'll want to have a cup of tea. It's a ritual with her."

"Before you go," said Heather. "How about you and Adam having dinner with me and Steve tonight?"

"Sounds great. Adam knocks off as soon as the stock market closes in New York. I'll go out and catch something for supper. Do you have any preference for the type of fish?"

"Now you have me drooling on my computer. Are you sure you can catch something?"

Her laugh sounded like the tinkle of a small bell. "Don't you remember? I had a fishing show. If they don't bite what's on the hook, I'll put on flippers and a mask and go after them with a spear gun. The reef at the mouth of the cove is our fish market. It stays fully stocked and open all day."

Heather let out a sigh. "I can't believe your parents want to leave this place."

"They need to," said Bella. "After having to rebuild after two Cat 5 hurricanes over the years, I don't think they could stand to do it again." She paused and added, "Sometimes things aren't as perfect as they appear."

Heather swallowed hard, told Bella she had other calls to make, and bid her good luck fishing. She picked up her phone and searched the contacts for the name of an old Princeton buddy. Ten minutes later, she disconnected the call after receiving a commitment to call back in a day or two with information on Li Jing.

She looked in the mirror and didn't like the image looking back at her. Her right hand brought a sample of her auburn hair around to where she could inspect it. As suspected, the split ends hadn't snipped themselves. She leaned into the mirror. Her eyebrows needed plucking, and her nails reminded her of a crab's claws. Her body could use a complete overhaul. Grabbing the guest services book, she removed the hotel phone's receiver and punched in the numbers for the spa. A cheerful voice gave the response Heather wanted to hear. "Yes, Ms. McBlythe, Bella told us we might hear from you and you're in luck today. We can fit you in this afternoon. That's a massage, facial, manicure, pedicure, and haircut. Anything else?"

"If I missed anything, I'll come back for it tomorrow."

"We look forward to serving you, Ms. McBlythe."

Heather placed the receiver back in the phone's cradle. "Bella read me like I was a children's book. She knew I needed pampering. Let's see if it gets me out of this mindset of work I've been in."

The ringing of her phone sent her scampering to answer it. Partial disappointment followed her eager expectation. She engaged the phone's speaker and said, "Hello, Father."

"With that flat tone, you must be in the middle of something unpleasant. Should I call back?"

"Sorry. I thought you were Jack."

"He's not with you? I thought you were flying to St. Croix together."

"Steve and I came a week early. Knowing Jack, he's filled his calendar with appointments."

A pause followed. She broke the silence by saying, "This probably won't come as a shock to you, but there's been a murder here at the resort."

Her father's first response was, "Oh, dear." He moved on quickly. "I'm always amazed at how you and Steve sniff out homicides. It's like you have some sort of magnetic attraction to them. Is there anything I can do to help?"

Heather wracked her brain, and a thought bubbled to the surface. "Do you still have that private detective from New York on retainer?"

"Of course. She's saved me millions over the years. You know how important it is to do thorough background checks on people before entering into business agreements. Who do you want information on?"

"There's a couple staying here at the resort. Steve had a long lunch with them today and believes they're up to something nefarious. Their names are Skip and Roxy Smith, and they claim to be from Hoboken. That's likely an alias last name, but Roxy and Skip should ring a bell with someone on the west side of the Hudson."

"Do you have a physical description?"

"I haven't met them yet. Steve described her as a madam and him as her bouncer."

Her father let out an uncharacteristic laugh. "Leave it up to you and Steve to find colorful characters. I'll get on this immediately."

"Not so fast, Father. Was there a reason for your call?"

"How foolish of me. I was so caught up in your world of cops and robbers that I forgot to tell you to check and see if Bella would mind if I could pay a visit to the resort. There's a rumor floating around that her parents are selling. Are you looking to buy it?"

"I wasn't aware it was for sale until yesterday. I think I'll take your advice about not doing business with people I have close emotional ties with."

Heather only waited long enough to take a breath before she said, "Why don't I talk to her parents and get back to you? The prospective purchaser of the resort is the victim of the homicide we're investigating. If they're open to other bids, when do you want to come?"

"How does mid-week sound? I'd like to spend some time with you, if you're not too busy."

"That should work out fine. If no room is available, I'll book you into another hotel on the island."

"Speaking of rooms, I'll need three."

"I thought your pilots always shared a room."

"They do. The other room is for Zhang Min, my new personal assistant."

A knot formed in the spot right above her stomach. "When did you get a female personal assistant?"

"She's a recent addition. I thought I told you."

After some parting words and promises to accomplish tasks from both of them, the call ended. She picked up a framed photo of Jack and spoke to it. "I might as well be a bat the way I'm being kept in the dark. First you, and now Father. I wonder what Steve's not telling me?"

10

The combination of the pampering, an excellent meal of freshly caught fish, light conversation with Steve, and seeing Bella and Adam so desperately in love had Heather in a better mood. Steve stated the obvious. "The spa made an almost new woman out of you."

The server removed her plate, which held only the skeletal remains of Bella's ability to put food on the table. Heather pulled her glass of white wine toward her but didn't lift it. The relaxed atmosphere made small talk easy. "The masseuse had hands like padded vice grips. She said a troop of boy scouts must have practiced tying knots in my back and shoulders."

"She's the best," said Bella. "I go to her at least once a week."

Adam added, "Twice a week for me, every Wednesday and Friday. After staring at computer screens and making quick decisions all day, I know all about knots in shoulders."

Heather saw Bella's right hand move under the table, no doubt resting on Adam's thigh. His left hand disappeared. A passing thought of Jack came to mind.

Steve spoke next. "I'm still not sure how you make such a good living day trading."

Adam sat up a little straighter. "It all boils down to knowing how to read financial charts and trusting in percentages. Programs based on algorithms do most trades. I trained my mind to think like a computer programmer. It's all about making decisions based on probabilities."

"It sounds like counting cards at a blackjack table."

"Same principle, but I have better odds. If I read the charts right and don't get greedy, there's a seventy-five percent chance I'll make money on my trades. History may not repeat itself exactly, but it comes amazingly close."

Heather didn't know why, but that thought stuck in her mind. She shrugged it off and kept listening.

Steve asked, "How many trades do you make in a day?"

"It varies, but not more than a couple dozen. I study the charts, make an educated guess as to the probability of a stock making a significant move up or down and either go long, go short, or don't put in an order."

"You lost me," said Steve.

"Stocks are in an almost constant state of flux. I look, with the help of sophisticated computer programs, for big potential swings either up or down in value."

"How long do you hold on to a stock?"

"As long as the charts tell me to. Sometimes, I unload them after only a few minutes. I program my computer to put in buy and sell orders. If a stock I own dips below a certain point, it automatically sells. I take the profit and minimize my loss."

"Can you program it to buy a stock?"

"Sure. That's a buy order. The human element comes into play when I decide how much risk I want to take. I'm fairly risk-averse, so I'd rather make a bunch of small gains than shoot for the moon on one or two stocks. That's how people lose their shirts. My investment strategy is to get in, take a small gain, suffer a minimal loss, and not count the money until the end of the day."

Once again, something about Adam's statement struck a

chord. It was off-key and grated on her soul. She shook it off and asked, "What about selling short?"

"That increases your risk because it's a leveraged investment. I always have a conservative stop order in place. The first rule is to not lose more than you're prepared to lose." Adam gave her a quizzical look. "You know about day trading. Have you ever tried it?"

She forced a smile. "As far as investments go, I'm more comfortable with tangible assets."

Steve put a quick end to talk of finances when he looked at Heather and asked, "Did you take care of getting the ball rolling on the things I asked you to do?"

Heather finished taking a sip of wine. "My friend in the State Department is getting us information on Li Jing, Bella set up a walk-and-talk with me and Judith Tovar early tomorrow morning, and I spoke with Father this afternoon."

Steve asked, "How's Dad?"

"You can ask him in a few days. He's coming with his new personal assistant."

Steve tilted his head. "There's disdain in your voice."

She knew better than to deny it. "Her name is Zhang Min."

"Ah."

"Yeah. 'Ah,' is right." She filled her mouth with wine.

Bella challenged her with, "So what? It makes sense for your dad to have a competent woman as a personal assistant."

She didn't have an adequate answer, only a feeling of resentment. After all, her mother had been dead for less than a year.

Steve came to her rescue. "What else did your father have to say?"

"He heard through the grapevine that this resort is for sale, and he wants to meet with Lonnie and Ingrid."

"That's great," said Bella. "Can he come for the wedding? I know I should have invited him, but assumed he was too busy. He's so sweet."

"Shrewd and sweet begin with the same letter," said Heather with a voice intended to convey caution.

Still reeling from the thought of her father in such close proximity with another woman, Heather changed the conversation. "Steve, I put Father to work on another task."

"Oh?"

"He's contacting a PI in New York City that he's used for years." She motioned for Bella and Adam to lean forward then whispered, "Father's asking her to find information on Skip and Roxy."

Steve lifted his chin and made his volume match hers. "Good thinking. There's something fishy about the Smiths staying here indefinitely. I could see them wanting to escape a cold winter, but not August. It'll be interesting to find out who they really are and what they're doing here."

"What makes you say that?" asked Adam.

Bella answered before either she or Steve could. "They never leave their room, except to eat lunch. Why come to a resort known for sun, snorkeling, and fun if you're going to stay in your room?"

Steve added, "I look at crime the way Adam looks at investments."

"How so?"

"Probabilities. You'll understand when you meet them. Everything about them screams big city hustlers, but here they are on a tiny island. The permanent population of St. Croix could fit into a couple of city blocks where they come from."

Adam's dark eyebrows arched to form a question. "What's their reason for being here?"

Steve shrugged. "That's one of the questions we need an answer to."

"Surely you have an educated guess."

Steve hooked his finger into the handle of his coffee cup. "They're running *from* something illegal or *to* something illegal. Either way, it spells trouble."

"Are you sure?"

"As sure as you were on your last trade of the day. About seventy-five percent."

The unexpected hand on Heather's shoulder preceded a soft yelp. She spun in her seat, hoping to see Jack. Instead, a man from her past looked down at her.

11

"Hello, Heather. Remember me?"

Her hope that the hand belonged to Jack dissolved faster than a sugar cube in a pot of boiling water. "How could anyone forget you, Jim?" She composed herself and passed out introductions. She hadn't seen Jim McCloud in years.

After they exchanged names, she added details about how they knew each other. "Jim is an entrepreneur I've had dealings with."

"Heather's too modest," said Jim. "She beat me to the punch on a hot deal in Florida three years ago. In fact, she has a habit of either beating me to the finish line or driving the price up and making me pay more than I should."

Heather didn't correct his half-truth. She'd won most deals by outworking him, offering a fair price, and sealing the deals before he could counter her offers. The second part was mostly true. She enjoyed seeing him pay a fair price. Jim McCloud was a bottom feeder, always looking for the next big deal and to get it cheap. Her mind swirled with reasons why he was at the resort. Two possibilities came to her, and she didn't like either of them.

All this was running through her mind when he said, "I don't want to interrupt your evening. Perhaps we could have breakfast tomorrow and catch up. I hear you're getting married. Congratulations." He counted the chairs and stated the obvious as a question. "Your fiancé isn't here?"

She put on her best smile. "Thanks, Jim. Breakfast would be fine. I'll meet you here at eight."

He gave her a wolfish grin. "It's a date." He paused only for a tick of the clock. "Sorry. Just a figure of speech."

She issued a nod of dismissal. He took the not-so-subtle hint to leave and gave a parting smile. She monitored him out of the corner of her eye as he walked to the door, opened it, and joined the festivities at the outdoor bar.

"That's interesting," said Steve.

Bella spoke up. "I don't trust him."

"You're an excellent judge of character," said Heather.

"Why did you agree to have breakfast with him?"

Steve answered for her. "It's no coincidence he's here. Heather needs to find out why."

"I don't understand," said Adam.

Heather leaned forward again. "There are two properties for sale on this island that he might be interested in." She looked out the window toward the bar on the patio. "He's an opportunist in every sense of the word. You can bet he's looking to scoop up one of them below value. I need to find out which one he's looking to steal. Sorry, I should have said purchase."

Bella spoke with confidence. "It won't be this one." She looked at Adam. "Come on. We're going to warn Mom and Dad there's a snake on the island."

The young couple pushed back their chairs. Bella gave Steve a kiss on his cheek, then Adam took her hand and led her out of the dining room.

He waited until they were out of earshot before saying, "I hope she doesn't outgrow doing that."

Heather considered how little physical contact Steve received. It also occurred to her that he hadn't mentioned Kate.

Had something happened with their relationship? If so, how could she bring up the subject and make it sound natural? She engaged in small talk about the quality of the dinner until she felt enough words had passed before she broke the seal on a new conversation. "By the way, Steve, how's Kate?"

"I fired her."

"What?"

Her memory went back to Miami where they first met Kate, a successful author, when she and Steve spoke at a writer's convention and also solved a murder. Steve and Kate had a chemistry of sorts, and he became interested in writing about some of his experiences as a homicide detective in a fiction format. At the end of the conference, Kate offered to mentor him. A few months later she invited him to South Padre Island, Texas for a working retreat and it seemed a romantic relationship was in the cards. It began like a romance novel until someone murdered Kate's abusive ex-husband and the police arrested her. Steve solved the case, but what should have been a storybook vacation left Kate traumatized. They'd agreed to go their separate ways.

When Heather's mother died suddenly in Boston and she had to leave in the middle of a case, Steve asked Kate to be his 'eyes' so he could finish the case. Heather thought the two of them might be able to regain a more personal relationship during that week, but again Kate left town and returned to Florida. Things had been status quo with them ever since.

A chuckle brought her back to the present, and told her she'd fallen for one of Steve's favorite tricks. He'd say something so outlandish that it caused her to overreact. She pushed her glass of wine away and folded her hands on the tablecloth. "Now that you've had your fun, tell me what's going on with Kate."

"Not that much to say. You and I were in a drought of cases to work, and Kate's schedule filled up. She didn't have time to give me feedback on my writing. When I said I fired her, I was only half kidding. I joined a writer's group of guys like me who used to be cops. I'm looking for a new editor and writing coach."

Heather realized again how busy she'd become in trying to maintain profits with her various business pursuits. She also believed there was more to the story of Steve and Kate than he told her. What could have caused a rift in what seemed like such a perfect match? She took a stab in the dark. "Is Kate dating someone else?"

Steve cleared his throat. "You're still very good at reading people. How did you know?"

"It was a wild guess." She paused. "Are you all right?"

"It's been a couple of months since she told me. I still have my memories of Maggie, and that's the happy place I go to. Kate and I were having a junior high romance compared to what Maggie and I had for over twenty years."

Heather swallowed a lump. "I'm sorry I wasn't there to talk to."

"Max is a good listener."

Another thought sped through her mind like a bottle rocket zooming skyward. "Is Kate coming to Bella's wedding?"

"That would be awkward for her and her new husband."

The gasp that exploded caused heads to turn. She was too stunned to speak until she heard Steve laughing.

"Got you again." He leaned forward. "Kate's dating a fellow editor, but I don't think she'll ever marry again. I'm happy for her. She and I parted as friends. Sometimes that's what life gives you."

She wasted a perfectly good glare on him as he continued to chuckle. Finally, she managed to eke out, "You can stop with the shock treatments. I get what you're trying to tell me. Life goes on no matter what happens."

He nodded. "Let's you and me solve a murder. What do you say?"

"I like the sound of that. If Jack dumps me for some hot

blond, I'll still have Max, my business, and the occasional murder to solve."

"Speaking of the murder to solve, do you have questions lined up to ask Judith tomorrow morning?"

"Not yet. Let's brainstorm."

12

The alarm caused Max's ears to twitch, but he didn't lift his head from the pillow. Heather pulled a hand down his back, to his ample rump. "Sorry about the rude noise. Mama has work to do." She closed the bathroom door behind her before turning on the light. Her pre-dawn preparation included cleaning her teeth, brushing the tangles out of her hair, securing it with a scrunchy, and slapping on just enough makeup that her eyes didn't resemble a raccoon.

She left the bathroom door cracked open to give her light to find her new yoga outfit, socks, and tennis shoes. It was still dark when the door to her room closed behind her. She trod down the hall and took the stairs to the lobby. A bleary-eyed desk clerk wished her a good morning and invited her to partake of coffee or tea on the table in an alcove. Cookies were also available, but it was much too early for something so filled with calories.

With a to-go cup of coffee in hand, she made her way to a chair that allowed her to see the elevators and a full view out of an east-facing bank of windows. The first rays of sunshine split the starry night, chasing the celestial fireflies away. She had to admit that a brisk walk was a delightful way to start her day.

A loud ding from the elevator interrupted her enjoyment of

the hot cup of dark roast and the world coming to life. She stood. The metallic sound of a walker's wheels accompanied a woman she judged to be in her late forties. Bella's brief description had missed the mark. She might be sweet, but wasn't the seventy-something Heather had in mind.

The woman wore a billowing moo-moo that covered her from throat to pink tennis shoes. Taller than expected, Judith Tovar walked upright with better-than-average posture.

"Mrs. Tovar?" asked Heather.

"It's Judith, and you must be Heather McBlythe. Bella told me you'd be here bright and early." She studied Heather with keen gray eyes. "She wasn't kidding when she said you're a beautiful woman. What I'd give to have a mane of auburn hair like yours."

"Don't look too close. I found the first weed of gray creeping into the garden and uprooted it without mercy."

This earned a laugh, followed by Heather saying, "Bella tells me you start your day with a cup of tea. I'll be glad to get it for you."

"Keep looking at the streaks of daylight. I'm particular about the amount of cream and sugar I put in it." The teeth revealed by her smile looked like they should belong to someone much younger. "I guess that makes me a fussy old woman."

Judith left her walker at the end of the couch and walked slowly to the table holding hot beverages. She returned to the couch and put down her cup. She offered a word of explanation. "I need surgery, but I don't trust doctors. The walker is handy for taking long strolls. I can hobble around all right as long as it's not far. And I've found this thing is handy for being assured I have a place to sit. Most people these days are still quite courteous to someone with a walker."

"It also has a nice bag attached with pockets," said Heather. "That must come in handy."

"Yes, I brought us each a bottle of water." She settled in a chair and took a tentative sip from the steaming cup.

Heather knew better than to ask probing questions too quickly, so she waited for Judith to speak. It didn't take long.

"Bella talks about you and Steve often. She's very fond of you both. I feel like I already know you."

"She's a very special young lady."

"That's what she says about you. I didn't believe her, so I got online and did some checking. McBlythe Enterprises is quite the organization. Bella says you're a genius businesswoman." Judith took a breath. "And you're a former police detective and an attorney."

"You know all about me."

"Not everything, but more than enough to admire your accomplishments."

"I was fortunate to come from a wealthy Boston family. Business is in my blood."

Heather needed to change the conversation. "How long have you been here at the resort?" It was a question she already had the answer to.

"Several weeks."

Judith's answer was technically accurate but truncated and not precise. Heather let it slide and didn't press her. Instead, she asked, "Where do you call home?"

"I'm a world traveler." She took another sip of tea. "My husband died four years ago. His work took us all over, and I developed a severe case of wanderlust."

"I know what you mean. My businesses keep me globe-trotting. It's fascinating to experience other cultures."

Judith looked around the room before her gaze settled on the view out the window. "Have you ever seen such a perfect cove?"

"Too bad there isn't a dock to provide services to yachts and sailboats."

Judith shifted her gaze from the view to Heather. "The reason there are no sailboats of any size is the barrier reef at the mouth of the bay."

A nod of her head showed Heather understood. "Hmm.

Yes. If the barrier reef were gone, and larger boats were allowed in, that would spoil the feeling you'd landed on a deserted island."

"You can't help it, can you?"

"Help what?"

"Thinking of ways to make money. You imagined blue-water sailboats in the bay. Like you said, it's in your blood."

Heather considered her response before speaking. "It's a blessing and a curse, but this resort isn't one of my projects."

"Why not? It's an open secret that Lonnie and Ingrid are going to sell. In fact, they all but had it sold to a local man—the one killed in the parking lot." She shivered. "I'm glad the police caught the culprit so quickly. I don't think I could sleep knowing a killer was among us."

Heather finished her coffee and noticed Judith's cup was empty. "Are you ready for our walk?"

"It will be more of a stroll than anything approaching a cardio workout."

"Perfect. I'm on vacation."

Judith's squinting eyes told Heather the woman didn't believe her last statement. She was right. There was a murder to solve.

The walk went as Heather expected, a slow and relatively quiet stroll around the parking lot. With wheels on the front legs of the walker and plastic slides on the back it glided across the pavement with only a slight rattle.

Heather slowed to a stop when they reached the spot where Nate Johnson breathed his last. Police had attempted to remove the puddle of blood, but the bleach water left a telltale shadow on the asphalt. "Such a shame," said Heather as she looked down.

"What's a shame?"

Heather pointed. "This is where Nate Johnson died. Don't you recognize it?"

"I didn't get this far." She pointed. "Bella saw him first and told me to get back."

"Did you notice anything else? People remember little things after the shock wears off."

Judith shook her head. "It was a morning like so many others. The weather was perfect with a gentle breeze, and the sun looked like a big red ball rising in the east. I knew when Bella told me to get her dad that something was wrong. The police questioned me, but I couldn't tell them anything."

The response seemed genuine. As Heather and the woman continued on the circuit of the parking lot, Judith became more verbal. "Did you notice the scratch on the car door in the space next to where they found the body? It amazes me how careless people can be."

Heather nodded. "Rust is forming in it. That means it's nothing recent."

Judith stopped and looked at her. "I can see why you're a good investigator. You looked past the marks and noticed the rust. It must take a detail-oriented person to be a good detective."

Judith continued walking and switched to rambling on about the flora and fauna of the island and the resort in particular. She had an encyclopedic knowledge of plants and carried the conversation. Heather tuned her out as they rounded the last row and headed back to the hotel. Her mind had already switched to questions she'd ask Jim McCloud.

As they approached the hotel's entrance, Jim came jogging toward them. "Perfect timing," he said. "I'm staying in one of the fourplexes." His eyes made a quick sweep of her tight yoga outfit. She wished she'd brought a windbreaker.

He brought his gaze back to eye level. "Who's your friend, Heather?"

"Judith Tovar, this is Jim McCloud."

Jim was quick to respond. "If you're a friend of Heather's, you must be here on business."

Judith responded with a matronly laugh. "Goodness, no. I'm here to soak in the sun and pamper myself with the occasional restorative dip in the warm waters." She pointed toward the cove. "Between the warm salt water and the excellent pool, I'm feeling ten years younger." She lowered her voice. "Of course, I'm not senile enough yet to believe it makes me look any younger."

"Nonsense. I bet the men at the country club swoon every time you pass."

She played along. "Where were you twenty years ago when I could dance all night and be ready for whatever the day brought?"

An awkward silence followed that Heather broke by asking Judith to join them for breakfast.

"Thanks, but no. I take far too long making my face into something that doesn't cause children to cry. I'll bid both of you a good day and retire to my room. Try the egg white omelets. They're delicious."

She picked up her walker and repositioned it to point toward the door. Off she went at a good pace, much quicker than the walk in the parking lot.

Jim held out a hand like a theater usher. "Shall we?"

"You go on and order me coffee and orange juice. I'll join you in just a few minutes. Silly me. I forgot to bring my phone."

He stuck out his bottom lip. "Your phone. That means you'll be checking emails. I was hoping we could have a quiet conversation. You're such a worker, I doubt we'll be able to talk if you have your phone."

"All calls go to voice mail, and I won't check emails."

"Promise?"

She made an X over her heart, which gave Jim the excuse to shift his gaze down. She turned before he completely undressed her with his eyes and made for her room.

13

J uice and coffee awaited Heather as she joined Jim at the
table. She zipped her windbreaker and smoothed it over her
hips before choosing a seat that gave her a view of the
room. Instead of launching into questions, she glanced around
and noticed Steve tapping his way toward them. "I'll be right
back," she said to Jim's questioning countenance. He saw the
reason for her sudden departure and let out a sigh of disappointment.

She approached Steve and in a mocking tone asked, "Are you
checking on me?"

"I dreamed of waffles and bacon last night and woke up
chewing my pillow."

"We'd better feed your tapeworm. Jim McCloud and I just sat
down. You haven't missed anything."

"Good. You can tell me about your walk with Judith later."

Jim rose to his feet and put on his most convincing salesman's
face. "Good morning. Join us. We haven't ordered yet."

"Are you sure I'm not interrupting some sort of big deal you
two are negotiating?"

"In my dreams," said Jim as he glanced at her.

Heather didn't want to wait too long before she threw Jim a

curveball, but not yet. She'd let him toss out the first pitch. He wasted no time.

"Tell me, Heather, what projects are you working on?"

It was a question she expected him to ask. "We're finishing up with the development at Lake LBJ in Texas. Construction permits for infrastructure on the golf course in Belize came through last week."

"Did you ever get permission to build a hotel?"

"It took longer than expected but we broke ground on a hotel and the clubhouse."

"Anything else?"

"Not much. The mine in Montana is still producing decent returns of gold, silver, and other minerals we weren't expecting to find. I also sold a property on South Padre Island in Texas."

"That can't be all."

"Everything else is international and top secret."

They traded smiles and she asked, "What about you? I haven't heard your name mentioned lately."

"I've had a run of bad luck." He held up his hands. "Nothing serious, but not the returns I was expecting."

The server cleared his throat, which caused the conversation to come to a quick stop. Heather took Judith's recommendation and ordered the egg white omelet stuffed with grilled vegetables. She splurged and added a bagel with lox. Jim had eggs over easy, ham, and toast, while Steve held true and ordered the breakfast he'd dreamed about.

With that task out of the way, Steve took over. "It's a shame Lonnie and Ingrid lost their buyer for the resort. They've invested so much blood, sweat, and tears into this place. I guess they'll have to take what they can get and move on."

"That's not what I hear," said Jim.

"Oh?" asked Heather.

"You can quit play-acting. Anyone can see you have your eyes on this place. It would be perfect for your portfolio."

She looked him straight in the eye. "I don't risk close friendships to make deals. There's too much to lose."

Steve charged ahead with his next comment. "Heather and I are up to our necks trying to solve a murder. I need her help. She's been dancing around the question that has both of us wondering. Are you interested in buying this property?"

Jim's gaze dipped to the cup of coffee in front of him. "I can't. If I could turn back the clock three years, those high-rise office buildings in New York and California would belong to someone else." He shrugged. "My crystal ball must have been defective. I'm having to sell them at a tremendous loss."

"Are things that bad?" asked Heather, with more sympathy in her voice than she thought possible.

He looked up. "I'm not starting over from scratch, but I'm one of those guys who's using the phrase 'the good old days' more than I thought I would."

At that moment, Heather knew that if Jim was telling the truth, he was interested in only one property on the island and that was Nate Johnson's hotel in town. It was a big *if* as to whether Jim was telling the truth. She'd discuss it with Steve.

The meal ended and they parted company from the entrepreneur on a somber note. As Heather led the way across the lobby to the elevators, she came to a sudden stop. Detective Nohr waited for them. He didn't look happy.

14

William Nohr stated his name and confirmed theirs. Heather noted that he glanced around the room, frowning. "Is there someplace private we could talk?"

Steve took the lead. "My room has a sitting area with a couch and chairs. Heather's cat will want to join us, but he's specially trained not to divulge anything he hears."

He replied with a brusk, "Your room will do."

Everyone remained silent as they boarded the elevator. The brief trip gave Heather a chance to catalog the detective's appearance. Sandy, thin hair topped a narrow face with sharp angles. He appeared lean and athletic, without the bulk of muscles attributed to lifting weights. He reminded her of a stereotypical European bicycle rider. Because of the last name, she guessed him to be of Dutch descent, which made sense since St. Croix began as a Dutch colony. Worry lines radiated from blue eyes in a suntanned face. His hands spoke of some sort of hobby that produced callouses. His voice was soft, albeit rather brusk so far, and he seemed to be a man of few words.

They arrived at Steve's door, and he asked, "Would you prefer coffee or tea this morning?"

"Tea, if it's not too much trouble."

Steve chuckled. "All it takes is a phone call, and things appear like magic from the kitchen."

Heather retrieved Max, brought his food and water bowls, and returned to Steve's room. Max sniffed the air as soon as he entered. He scanned the room and locked suspicious eyes on the stranger. A soft hiss preceded him scurrying under the bed and letting out a low growl.

"Don't pay any attention to Max's poor manners. He'll be in your lap once he gets used to you."

Detective Nohr's eyebrows came together. "I'm not sure I have enough lap. I've never seen such a big cat. What kind is he?"

"Fat."

At least the detective's voice was losing some of its edge. Maybe he was a cat person. Heather responded to Steve's comment in a terse voice. "Hush. You'll hurt his feelings." She turned to their visitor. "He's a Maine Coon. They're an exceptionally large breed, but Max is bigger than most."

Steve got down to business. "How is Li Jing adjusting to jail?"

Detective Nohr stopped the question in its tracks and sighed. "Before we talk about Li Jing, I'd like to apologize for the way I spoke to you two. It was very unprofessional."

Steve waved away the apology.

"No," said the detective. "Acting in such a manner is not a minor thing with me. This has been a very hard case for me and unfortunately, others have borne the brunt of my anger."

Heather took over. "We understand you and Nate were very close friends."

Grief filled the detective's response. "Nate was like an older brother. No matter how busy we both were, we went diving once a week. He was a wizard at fixing anything and everything. He taught me so much about construction and maintenance."

"That explains the callouses on your hands."

Detective Nohr looked at his palms. "Souvenirs of long hours and good times working together."

With two simple words, Steve changed the tone of the conversation. "Apology accepted." He kept talking. "We're on vacation. Would it bother you if we dropped the formalities when we're by ourselves. I understand William is your first name."

"That's correct, and I'm not normally so uptight. Homicides on St. Croix are virtually unheard of, much less ones involving my friends."

Heather moved on with a question. "How much grief is Li Jing's attorney giving you?"

"Plenty, and it's attorneys. Two of them. They're seasoned, smart, and the best money can buy. The bond hearing is this afternoon, and the judge is under tremendous pressure to release her pending trial. They've filed a flurry of complaints about jail conditions, including the property she may keep in her cell."

"Is she here on St. Croix or St. Thomas?" asked Steve.

"St. Thomas. That's the capital of the U.S. Virgin Islands."

Heather took her turn. "What are her attorneys demanding?"

"To name a few, they say she must have her makeup as well as a supply of masks to protect her from diseases. They're also asking for extra exercise time, longer visits, and a special diet reflective of her culture."

"That's all part of their strategy. They're willing to lose a few minor skirmishes, but they'll save the big ammunition to hit the judge with this afternoon. Have they brought up racial profiling yet?"

"Not yet, but I'm expecting it."

She rose to answer a knock on the door and spoke over her shoulder. "I don't think you have to worry about her absconding. It's automatic that she surrenders her passport if released on bond, so she can't fly out."

"True, but Li Jing is a ghost. We know from her passport that she's a Chinese National, but that's where the information ends."

She barely heard Steve's reaction of "Interesting."

The server wheeled in a cart, which put the conversation on

hold but didn't stop Heather from wondering why Steve had responded with that word. She concluded her business partner had heard something of significance. Sometimes he told her what it was, but not always. She suspected this would be one of the latter. He'd file the detail away, would continue asking questions, and observe with his remaining senses that were honed to a razor's edge.

As Heather checked the cart to be sure they had everything they needed, Steve surprised her again. "Did you call your buddy at the State Department to see what they can find out about Li Jing?"

Heather upped the ante. "Yes. I think I'll also call a friend at the CIA. He owes me favors."

William's eyes opened wide. "Who are you people?"

Steve spoke with a rural twang. "Just a couple of former detectives who like to play cops and killers."

Heather placed a tea bag in the pot of steaming water and let the hinged lid fall with the clink of metal on metal. "If they release Li Jing on bond, will she have to stay on St. Thomas, or can she come back here?"

"That will be up to the judge, but we're hoping she comes back here. We'll want to monitor her movements, which will be much easier to do from here. All the cruise ships dock in St. Thomas, and it would be very easy for her to get lost in a crowd."

She poured Steve a cup of steaming coffee and put it on the table in front of him with a word of warning. "Let it cool for a while."

He didn't respond to her word of warning. "William, if Li Jing is allowed to return here, do you have a plan for keeping tabs on her?"

The detective sighed. "Not yet."

"We can help. That is, if you want us to."

"How do you propose to do that?"

Steve reached for his coffee but drew back his hand after touching the side of the cup. "I'll get with Lonnie, Ingrid, and

Bella this morning. We'll set up a plan to keep tabs on Li Jing if she comes back to the resort. They have a small, loyal army of servers, cleaners, lifeguards, groundskeepers, and other staff who can monitor her."

Heather added, "You may not know this, but Li Jing believes Steve and I are working for her. She was arrested before we could officially sign a contract."

William ran a hand across a smooth chin. "Did she tell you she didn't kill Nate?"

"Yes."

"Do you believe her?"

Steve answered William's question with one of his own. "What's the primary job of a detective?"

Detective Nohr took in a deep breath and let it out slowly. "I know what you're asking and why. You want to see if my mind is closed to the possibility of Li Jing being innocent. I've thought a lot about that very thing since we last met."

"And?"

"The job of a detective is to discover the truth. If the facts lead away from Li Jing, then I'll change my mind about her guilt."

"Do you care who discovers the truth?"

"Not anymore. That's the second part of my apology. I let my emotions get away with me. I know you two solved Bella's kidnapping. By the way, the book was so much better than the movie."

Heather said, "Call Senior Homicide Detective Leo Vega with Houston P.D. if you have any lingering doubts about us. Steve trained him, and he knows almost all of Steve's secrets."

Steve picked up his coffee cup. "You can find Heather with an internet search, but be ready for a long read."

Enough time had passed for the tea to have properly brewed. Heather filled cups for William and herself while Steve returned his cup to the table. "I don't know what kind of coffee they have here, but I'm taking some home with me, even if I have to smuggle it into the country."

William smiled. "Some of the smoothest in the world."

Any distrust that existed before the meeting washed out on the tide. It wasn't long before Steve was asking questions about Nate Johnson's hotel and who would inherit it.

"Funny you should ask." With a sheepish look at Heather, he said, "He left it to me."

"Now that is interesting. Has anyone approached you about buying it?"

Heather looked on with her senses fully tuned in. She sensed the answer was of great significance.

"Not yet, but I don't imagine anyone knows. I didn't know until Nate's attorney called me yesterday."

Steve leaned forward. "We need you to trust us to do something."

"I can't agree or disagree until I hear what it is."

Steve sat back and folded his hands in his lap. "I think it's possible that someone killed Nate in order to purchase his hotel at a reduced price. It's possible they stayed there recently to check it out."

The muscles in William's jaw flexed. "I've been wracking my brain trying to find a motive. That could be it."

"Are you wanting to keep your inheritance a secret?"

A puzzled look crossed William's face. "Should I?"

"Perhaps." Steve took his time before moving on. "Do you have time this morning to go to the hotel and get a list of all the guests for the last three months?"

"I'll make time."

Max chose that moment to walk a figure eight around William's legs, rubbing and purring as he went. With grace and agility that belied his bulk, the feline launched himself into William's lap. The reaction from the detective mimicked that of so many others who'd received Max's special treatment. "This is the softest fur I've ever felt."

Heather responded with a smile while Steve chuckled. "Email the list to us when you get it. Heather keeps her ear to the ground for investments. She might recognize a name or two of people who like to buy under market value. In fact, one person known for buying at rock bottom is staying here at the resort. His name is Jim McCloud." He reached for his coffee again. "Until then, let's keep it quiet that you're the new owner."

Heather took over where Steve had left off. "Tell us about the hotel. Would it be a prudent investment?"

"For the right person it will produce a nice return. It's more like an oversized bed-and-breakfast than a hotel. The pool is the key feature and attracts those wanting to learn to dive. That was a passion for Nate and me, and he developed a great marketing scheme."

Heather took a sip of tea. "Are you tempted to quit the force and become a hotelier?"

He shook his head. "I'm more tempted to sell it and put myself in a position where I could buy a first-class dive boat and start my own business. I can't tell you how many times Nate threatened to sell the hotel so we could go into business together."

Steve asked, "Do you think you could take us on a tour of Nate's hotel tomorrow?" He paused. "I should refer to it as your hotel."

"Not until the will goes through probate. As for going to the hotel, I'll be glad to show you around tomorrow." He rolled his eyes. "What am I thinking? Everything depends on what happens this afternoon in court. If Li Jing stays in jail, I can go. If she's released, there's no telling what I'll have to do."

"We'll play it by ear. Let us know how things turn out. Our schedules are flexible."

William slapped his leg in a self-loathing way. "My mind is made of sand. You don't need me to show you around the hotel. I'll tell Connie you're coming. She's been Nate's back up for years."

The detective stood and thanked them for the tea, conversation, and giving him a place to start his investigation. "I'll call you and let you know what happens today. Since I need to go to Nate's hotel, can you arrange to have Li Jing monitored?"

Heather answered this one. "Bella loves to play private investigator, and she's pretty darn good at it. I think she's getting nervous about the wedding, and with her mother in charge, there's nothing for her to do. Setting up and supervising a team to snoop on Li Jing will get her out of her mother's hair and calm her nerves at the same time."

After good-byes, the door clicked shut behind the detective, and Heather looked around for her phone. "I'll be back to talk more about the case after I retrieve my phone." She wanted to kick herself for being absentminded. After all, Jack might have called.

15

With quick steps, she traveled the short distance to her room and opened it with a metal key. There on her bed sat the device that kept her life in order. As usual, multiple icons flashed at her, indicating emails, text messages, and calls missed. She ignored all but one missed call.

"Hi, beautiful. Mom told me if I didn't call she'd disown me and quit being my secretary. Sorry, but something came up I didn't expect." The next words came out slow and strained. "I don't know what to do about the mess I'm in, but I can't discuss it long distance. It took every bit of my courage to call you this morning."

False levity entered his voice. "I guess you're out doing something fun, and a voice message isn't the best way to say what I have to say. By the time you get this, I'll be in the air. My trip involves a circuitous route." A long pause followed. "I'll be there for the wedding."

The call ended, and she stared at the phone, her emotions not knowing which direction to fly. "Steve," she said to her empty room. "He'll know what to do." She hoped it was true.

STEVE KNEW SOMETHING WAS WRONG BY THE WAY HEATHER entered his room. The insistent knocks on the door came faster and harder than usual. Max leaped from his lap. His sharp nails made scratching sounds on the tile floor as he scurried to a spot under the bed.

Instead of asking what was wrong, he opened the door and walked back to the seating area without a word. Heather passed him, and the spring-loaded door swung closed with a resounding slam. She was already seated by the time he lowered himself into the club chair.

He could tell by the way her yoga pants made a soft scratching noise that she'd crossed her legs and was swinging the top one with vigor. Again, he waited. It wasn't long until he heard her phone announce, "You have one saved message... First saved message... beep..." Jack's voice came on, and Steve listened to each word and nuance with extra care. He pursed his lips together when the phone clicked, replaced by silence.

"Well?" demanded Heather in a no-nonsense tone. "What do you make of it?"

Fingers laced together on his lap. "It's reassuring in one way and troubling in others."

Heather snapped back. "Pardon me if I don't join you in feeling reassured. What did he mean by being in a mess, and what's all that about having to take a circuitous route to get to St. Croix? He said he'd be here for the wedding, but not before." She raised her voice. He could see in his mind's eye her holding up a single index finger. "One day. It only takes one day to get from Houston to St. Croix. You might have to change planes in either Miami, San Juan, or St. Thomas, but one day is all it takes. Not two, and certainly not over a week and a half. Isn't that right?" She had to take a breath, but it was a quick one. "Furthermore, I can send my plane. He knows that and didn't ask for it."

Steve waited until he was sure she'd spewed all she was going to for the time being. "Let's look at the positive first."

"I heard nothing positive."

"Stop it! You now know he's not injured or dead, and his mother is all right. Be thankful for that much. I also didn't hear that he absolutely wouldn't finish his task early and come join you. Did you think he might want to surprise you with an early arrival?"

She grumbled under her breath but didn't contradict him. He allowed silence and the rebuke to have its full effect. He'd learned a long time ago that silence could be a wonderful friend when emotions ran high. Time and silence.

Her voice moderated a little. "What do you think he meant by being in a mess?"

"No idea."

"And the circuitous route?"

He didn't know any more than she did, so he didn't guess.

"I'm going to find out," she said with determination.

"Can I ask you something?" It was a rhetorical question, but her answer would give the opportunity for her to think more clearly.

"Go ahead, ask away."

"If the roles were reversed, what would you want Jack to do?"

"I wouldn't leave a message that made no sense."

"Are you sure?"

"What are you getting at?"

Steve took in a deep breath. "How many times in the last six months have you two talked for over ten minutes?"

She groaned. "You wouldn't have asked if you didn't already know. You also know I've been so busy that I've allowed our relationship to suffer... again!"

"Don't dodge the question, counselor. How many times?"

Anger and frustration flavored her response. "None. Zero. Goose egg. Nada. Are you happy now that I've answered your question?" She took in a breath and continued, "You win. I admit it. I'm guilty of being a workaholic. Point me to the nearest twelve-step program!"

Steve didn't argue with her on that point. Once again, he

allowed silence to fill in the gaps of what he left unsaid. She rose and began pacing to the patio door and back, which lasted at least three full minutes.

When she sat back down, he knew she was ready to listen without acting like a barracuda attacking a bait fish.

She blurted out, "My emotions are telling me to go to my room, get on my phone, and find out what airline he's on and where he's going."

"Then what would you do?"

"Once I found him, I'd have him followed to where he's staying and with whom."

He allowed the proverbial dust to settle before he lowered the pace and volume of his words. "I don't think another woman is involved."

"What makes you say that?"

"Call it my cop's intuition."

"Perhaps not, but he's in some sort of serious trouble or he wouldn't have said he was in a mess."

"I'll give you half a point on that one. If Jack says it's a mess, then we should take him at his word, but we don't have any idea what kind of mess it is. It may or may not be as serious as you think."

She let out a quick burst of air that told him she wasn't buying what he was trying to sell her. She followed it with, "My cop's intuition tells me it's serious."

Steve reached for the coffeepot, but made a point not to find it. He wanted to give her something to do, even if it was a menial task, like pouring a cup of coffee for a blind man. Right on cue, she said, "I'll get that."

"Thanks."

With cup in hand, he continued. "I'm back to my original question: If the roles were reversed, what would you want Jack to do? Hire a private investigator and track you down? Before you answer this time, give it some thought. Let's say something beyond your control popped up and completely blindsided you.

Would you want to handle it face to face, or send him a text, or tell him over the phone?"

Her voice came out in a loud whisper. "Do you know how aggravating you can be when you're so calm and rational?"

He grinned. "I used to drive Maggie up the wall and around the bend. She'd usually throw pillows at me." He let out a sigh. "Then she'd calm down, and we'd make the best decision available."

"Right now, I think it would be an excellent decision to have Jack tracked."

He shook his head. "It's your choice, but if you have him followed, you may or may not find out what his mess is."

"I know you're leading me to say something that's excruciatingly practical. You want me to wait and let him tell me face to face." She mumbled, "I may need a straight-jacket and a padded room if I have to wait that long."

He took a sip of coffee before answering. "Waiting is an acquired skill. Most people aren't very good at it."

She let out a sigh of resignation. "I guess if the roles were reversed, I'd get peeved if he sent a gumshoe to spy on me."

He gave a nod of approval. "It's not like we don't have plenty to keep us busy. Detective Nohr will send you an email with the names of who stayed in Nate's hotel, and you need to rattle the chain of your buddies at the State Department and the CIA. Here's another. We don't have a decent motive for Nate's death. There may be some truth to what I came up with, but there's more to the story."

"What will you do while I chew my fingernails to the bone?"

"I need to get with Lonnie, Ingrid, and Bella. Something tells me Li Jing is coming back to the resort."

Heather's phone came to life with a text. She read it and let out a moan. "It's from Father. He and his new girlfriend will be here Thursday. One more straw on the camel's back. Let's hope I'm not meeting my future stepmother."

Steve placed his cup on the coffee table. "If I drink any more of this delicious coffee, I'm going to float. Let's go down and talk to Ingrid, Lonnie, and Bella."

16

When they arrived in the lobby, Bella was checking out a family of four. Another worker was shadowing her, watching her every move. Heather stood close enough to determine the man was a new hire and still learning the trade. Bella said, "Check out is simple. All you do is tell the customer we've charged any remaining balance to their card, print out their receipt, and take their room key. If they lost it or left it in their room, don't worry. Some people keep them as souvenirs."

The employee seemed proficient with computers and communicated clearly and efficiently with the customers. Heather concluded he'd make a pleasant addition to the staff.

"Who's the new team member?" asked Steve in a friendly voice.

"Good morning," said Bella while flashing a model's smile. "This is Frank Jones. He and his wife, Mary, are a godsend. Frank, these are my two favorite people in the world, Heather McBlythe and Steve Smiley."

Steve extended a hand. "Pleased to meet you, Frank. Correct me if I'm wrong. Did I detect a Texas accent?"

"You're not wrong, Mr. Smiley."

Heather judged the man to be in his mid-thirties. He looked

trim, was well groomed, and had a friendly smile. A good addition to the resort.

"My wife and I quit the rat race and decided St. Croix was the perfect place to work and play."

Bella added, "Mary started with us three months ago. Frank had some things to clear up in Dallas before he could join her. We're lucky to have them."

Heather looked at Bella and asked, "Are your parents busy?"

"Not any more than usual. They're in the office."

An attractive young woman in her late twenties joined Bella and Frank behind the counter. Once again, Bella took care of introductions. "This is Mary, Frank's wife."

After cordial introductions and a few lines of small talk by Steve, Heather got down to business. "We need to talk to your parents and you, if you have time."

"Time and sunshine are two commodities we have plenty of in St. Croix. Come down the hall to their office."

On the way, Heather heard Steve issue something between a laugh and a snicker. "What's so funny?"

His cane swept back and forth across the tile. "Nothing important. I was listening to Bella train Frank Jones. It reminded me of Leo training his new partner and how he kicked her out of the crime scene. I was wondering how he explained it to her."

"I doubt he did. How do you explain a blind man determining if someone was murdered?"

He chuckled again, then changed the subject. "You take the lead with Lonnie and Ingrid."

"Are you trying to get my mind off Jack?"

"I am, and I intend to continue."

The door to Lonnie and Ingrid's office opened after Bella knocked. Once seated, Ingrid offered coffee or tea. Heather shook her head and spoke for her business partner. "If Steve has any more coffee, he'll need to go through a detox program."

"What can we do for you?" asked Lonnie.

"There's a very good chance Li Jing will return this afternoon or evening. We'd like for Bella to organize some of your staff to monitor her movements. Detective Nohr doesn't have the resources. He stopped by this morning and enlisted our help."

Bella squealed with delight.

Lonnie ignored her excitement and asked, "Do you think Li Jing is dangerous?"

Ingrid's level of trust exceeded her husband's. "We'll help, and please put Bella to work. There's nothing more jittery than a bride before her wedding."

"Back to my question," said Lonnie. "Is Li Jing a threat to the guests or staff?"

"Steve and I don't think so. She's a bit of a mystery woman, but she came to us asking for our help in clearing her name. That's not the actions of a killer. I'm hoping to get information about her from high-ranking government officials. If there's anything that makes us believe she could be a danger to anyone, we'll do something about it."

Ingrid and Lonnie looked at each other and nodded in agreement the way couples who've been married for so many years do. Ingrid gave words to what was unspoken. "We wouldn't have Bella if it wasn't for you two. Tell us what you need us to do."

When Steve didn't respond, Heather took over. "It's simple. Choose some of your most trustworthy staff, those who aren't prone to gossip, and tell them to monitor Li Jing's movements here at the resort. We'll need to know immediately if she leaves the resort."

Steve nodded while Heather continued. "Cameras are always helpful. I have some in my airplane for outdoor use. I'll send my pilots to get them."

Steve issued a word of caution. "Think of this as a covert operation. That means observe and report. No snooping or asking questions. The workers are to go about their normal duties while keeping an eye on Li Jing."

"Don't worry," said Bella. "I know the ones to choose."

Heather's gaze rested on Bella. "Have them report only to

you. Don't use our names. The only people who know the reason for us keeping an eye on her are in this room and Detective Nohr. Let's keep it that way."

"Do you want to know who I choose?"

"No need. You're in charge of this operation. Let us know if your people detect anything suspicious and notify us immediately if she goes missing."

"You can count on me."

Heather and Steve stood, received hugs from Bella, and left. They made it to the lobby when Heather slowed to a stop. "What is it?" whispered Steve.

"It's Judith. She's talking to a young man with two suitcases. They're walking to the counter. It looks like he's checking in."

"Describe him."

"Let's get farther away so they won't hear us."

Heather guided him to a spot near the front door. "He looks to be in his mid-twenties. Dark hair and complexion. A little less than six feet tall and trim. His clothes have a South American cut to them. Expensive, and I'd say the watch is a Rolex."

"Handsome or ugly?"

"Very handsome in a roguish sort of way."

"Go to the counter and see what else you can find out. I'll wait for you here."

Heather did so and stood behind Judith with her walker. The young man was signing in. She noticed the passport he used for identification.

Judith turned to her. "Hello, Heather." She let loose with a wide smile. "I'm here to welcome my stepson."

The man turned and lifted black eyebrows in a way that conveyed interest.

Judith pressed on. "This is Juan Tovar. Juan, this is Heather McBlythe."

Heather issued her response in Spanish, which resulted in a wide smile.

After a few pleasantries, Mary Jones, the desk clerk, asked, "Is there something I can help you with, Ms. McBlythe?"

"I was wondering what tonight's entertainment might be."

"I'll check in just a moment."

"No need; you're busy. I'll let it be a surprise."

Heather returned to Steve. "Are you ready to go back to your room?"

"Let's go. I want to change and dig my toes into the sand before it gets too hot."

When the elevator doors closed behind them, she gave her report. "His name is Juan Tovar, his passport is from Colombia, the Rolex is real, and he's Judith's stepson."

Steve nodded, which meant he'd filed the information away. Instead of any follow-up questions, he lifted his hand and read the braille on the elevator's control panel. "I'm interested in the names Detective Nohr is gathering for us. Let me know when you get them."

"What will you do the rest of the day?"

"What I came here to do. Sit under a palm tree and listen to the waves roll in. I'll not let another day go by without enjoying the beach."

"Good idea. I'll put on my bathing suit, grab my laptop and phone, and go with you."

"You can take me and bring me back, but I don't want to be anywhere near a phone. It's time for me to think and listen."

"Listen to what?"

"Nothing but the waves."

17

"Would you like to eat supper on the patio or inside?" asked Heather as she and Steve approached the dining room.

"Inside. I had plenty of the great outdoors. In fact, a little too much. The palm tree you put me under must have had some fronds missing."

"I thought you slathered on enough sun-block."

"Almost. The only place that cooked was my right foot."

Heather looked down at his sandals. "I can't trust you to do anything. The left foot is fine, but there are red streaks on your right ankle and foot. Is the aloe vera helping?"

"I'll keep applying it tonight. It's not a terrible burn and should stop stinging by tomorrow." The pain must have brought back a memory, because he reminisced. "Every year Maggie and I would go to Galveston to celebrate the beginning of summer. She'd warn me about the sun, but I was young and indestructible. I'd come home cooked to medium-rare."

Voices of patrons rose and fell as they followed a hostess to the table. The clangs and clinks associated with a busy dining room reminded her of an orchestra warming up for a concert. Heather took in the aromas and wondered how many more smells Steve could identify. It was fun when she challenged him to identify what the patrons at the nearest table were eating.

They took their seats and Steve located his silverware and napkin. He tucked the corner of the napkin under the top button of his shirt. This allowed it to cover his entire midsection and saved his shirts from the inevitable spills and drips.

While she studied the menu, he asked, "How loud can I talk without being heard?"

Heather glanced at the surrounding tables. "Keep it to a three or four." It was a code they'd worked out: One was a whisper in the ear, whereas ten involved hands cupped into a megaphone to maximize a shout.

"Got it. Did you hear from your pal at the State Department?"

"I did, but there's nothing to report. The relations between the United States and China aren't particularly close these days. It raises red flags every time someone makes an inquiry. Besides the extra scrutiny, the two countries appear to be in competition to see which has the most inefficient bureaucracy."

"Doesn't surprise me. It could be many days before you hear anything of value." He sighed. "Oh well, what about your contact with the CIA?"

"Nothing yet."

"And I thought the bureaucracy was bad at Houston P.D."

The server came and took drink orders. Heather ordered a glass of white wine while Steve had his usual iced tea. He smoothed the napkin over his midsection. "What about the investigator your father hired? Any word from him?"

"From her. Nothing yet on Skip and Roxy Smith, but Father may wait until he gets here to give us the report in person." She hesitated before saying, "Along with his personal assistant."

Steve sometimes took delight in goading her. "The way you say it, I'm expecting her to have an engagement ring."

Heather looked down at her left hand. It may have been her imagination, but the diamond solitaire on her finger had lost some of its sparkle. She buried her hand in her lap. "Let's not talk about me being a stepdaughter."

Before Steve could respond, a soft voice floated from over her shoulder. The words carried an accent from the far east. "Pardon for interrupting."

Heather twisted in her seat. "Li Jing. Please join us. I'm glad you're in a more comfortable environ."

The murder suspect pulled out a chair and seemed to float into it. "I don't want to interrupt your evening, so I'll only stay a moment. As you can see, they have released me on bond. Thank you for speaking with Detective Nohr. It seems he's open to considering other suspects."

Steve leaned forward with forearms on the table. "He and Nate Johnson were very close friends. All he needed was to allow his initial grief to pass, and he saw things more clearly."

"You're being modest, Mr. Smiley."

Heather asked, "Did the amount of bail seem excessive to you?"

"It was high, but not unreasonable. The conditions pose no hardship. I'm restricted to this island, and they took my passport. They did not require me to wear an electronic monitoring device. As you know, the reef guarding the bay means only Zodiac type boats can enter, and there's only one airport on the island. An attempt at escape would be foolish." She issued a sly smile. "It also doesn't surprise me that members of the hotel staff are keeping tabs on me."

"You can blame us for the surveillance. Them watching you is helping the prosecuting attorney and the magistrate sleep at night."

Li Jing stood. "If you'll excuse me, I'm going to my room for a long, hot shower. The jail was not a sanitary accommodation."

Heather stopped her from leaving with an upraised hand. "Could you meet us for breakfast tomorrow morning and share thoughts related to the case?"

"That would be lovely. Let's say eight o'clock?"

Steve said, "At least one of us will be here."

Li Jing gave a bow, turned, and seemed to float away. Once the mystery woman was out of earshot, Heather turned back to Steve. "I don't know how she walks with such grace."

"Practice. Like the diction and pace of her words, it took a lot of practice."

The server appeared at her elbow. "Are you ready to order?"

She focused on the menu and quickly abandoned it. "I'll trust the chef with his choice of grilled fish. Include a salad and fresh vegetables. No starches. Also, tell the wine steward to pair an excellent wine with the meal."

"Of course. And for you, sir?"

"Dinner salad with blue cheese dressing, steak medium rare, and baked potato. Be sure to cut the steak into bite-sized pieces in the kitchen."

Heather shook her head and mumbled, "You're hopeless."

"I've had fish twice a day since we arrived. At least I didn't order a lunch-meat sandwich."

Heather had no response, but Steve had another question for her. "Did you receive the list of guests at Nate's hotel?"

"Connie sent it to me this afternoon. It seems Skip and Roxy Smith stayed there two months ago. Recently, they visited during the day, even though they were staying here. Connie said Roxy asked copious questions."

Steve seemed to absorb the information slowly before asking, "Anyone else?"

"Jim McCloud stayed there a month ago. That didn't surprise me. He has a special knack for hearing about properties coming on the market."

Steve pulled his hands onto his lap. "We need to expand the search at Nate's hotel. Go back a full year and see if anyone that was here at the time of the murder stayed there."

Heather leaned forward. Her words came out peppered with suspicion. "I know you're intent on keeping my mind off Jack, but don't you think a full year is too long? Lonnie and Ingrid decided to sell only six months ago."

"I can't help but think there's at least one or two more people with eyes on this resort and possibly Nate's." He then gave her a more direct answer. "Start with six months. If you don't find anyone else, then keep looking."

"Nine months is my limit."

"It's a deal. Let's talk about your buddy, Jim McCloud. He interests me."

"I've known him for years." She paused. "Let me be more specific. I knew him at Princeton. We're the same age and came from similar stock. We palled around for a while, but went our own ways in the last year of college. I became an idealist, and he liked to gamble."

"Las Vegas or investments?"

"Both. He was a venture capitalist shortly after it came in vogue. Success came before we graduated. I had that big falling out with my father and became a cop until I had access to the trust my grandparents left me. His parents died and left him too much money for any twenty-one-year-old. Over the years, it's been booms and busts for Jim. He's in a bust cycle now, but I'm expecting him to make another comeback. He's too smart and hard-working not to claw his way back."

"He doesn't sound like a killer."

The server arrived with a basket of bread. Heather took a dinner roll and buttered it for him. "Bread at ten-o'clock." She continued the conversation. "If what Jim told me is accurate, I've never known him to be this far down. Father may have more information about him. We can ask when he arrives tomorrow."

"Do you think Jim is interested in Nate's hotel or this resort?"

"This resort is much more his speed, but I'm not sure he has the wherewithal to make a decent offer. I'll call my P.A. tonight. She'll get my research team looking into Jim's solvency."

Steve summed up the state of the investigation. "With all

these hooks in the water, we should catch some useful information in the next few days."

Heather checked her phone, just in case a text came in. A light blinked at her. She mentally kicked herself for putting the notifications on silent. She brought the device to life and read a text.

"Well?" asked Steve.

"It's from my personal assistant, not Jack," she replied with disgust. "I'll reply when I get back to my room."

Steve changed the subject back to the case. "I want you to call William and tell him to meet you at Nate's hotel first thing tomorrow morning. Your father may show up earlier than you think. You need to plan for that eventuality. I'll meet with Li Jing for breakfast."

Her salad arrived. She stabbed at it with her fork in an attempt to take out some frustration. The main course arrived and the meal seemed to drag on. Steve ate at his normal pace. It mercifully ended when he didn't order dessert and suggested they get a good night's sleep because of the busy morning that awaited them.

A group of guests filed out the door leading to the outdoor patio. Music and laughter flooded in until the door swung shut. Instead of a night with her handsome fiancé, she'd return to her room and change into a baggy T-shirt and cotton sleep shorts.

She rose from her seat and led Steve through the tables. They came to an abrupt halt. Into the dining room stumbled Jim McCloud, bloodied and battered. He took two steps and collapsed.

18

A couple of screams from guests preceded a cacophony of voices. Heather narrated for Steve. "It's Jim McCloud. He's hurt. Stand here. You're out of the way."

Heather was the first to reach Jim. He moaned and looked up at her through glassy eyes. "Lay still, Jim."

He spoke in a weak voice. "I'll be all right." Blood flowed from his nose onto his white shirt.

A woman's voice came from over Heather's shoulder. "I'm an ER nurse. Let me look at him."

Heather stood and took a couple of steps back. The nurse looked up from her kneeling position. "You'd better call an ambulance."

"No ambulance," said Jim in a stronger voice. "This is nothing compared to playing rugby."

The nurse took a long look at Jim's eyes. "The pupils have equal dilation. That's a good sign, but I need a flashlight."

Lonnie spoke over her shoulder. "I have one in the office."

Questions related to time, date, place, and short and long-term memory came from the nurse. Jim gave appropriate answers to each. He asked if he could sit up.

"Not yet."

Lonnie arrived with the flashlight. It didn't take long before the nurse said, "His pupils are responding appropriately."

Jim tried to push up with his elbows.

The nurse gently, but firmly told him to lie back down. "Any dizziness?"

"Not much."

Lonnie moved to kneel behind Jim.

"I'm spoiling everyone's meal. Can we go somewhere else?"

The nurse looked at Lonnie. "Stay behind him." She then cut her eyes to look at Heather. "Take his left arm, and I'll grab the right. Be ready to lower him gently back to the floor if his knees buckle." She then announced, "We lift on three. One, two, up gently."

Ingrid arrived as Jim made it to his feet. Concern etched her face, but she said nothing.

The nurse had her gaze locked on Jim, as did everyone in the dining room. "Let's take a few steps."

"I'm still a little wobbly, but I believe the worst is over."

"Take him to the office," said Ingrid.

The nurse agreed, but with conditions. "We go slow, just as we are. One person on each side and one behind."

Ingrid cast her gaze to Heather. "I'll bring Steve."

Progress was slow, but that was to be expected. Jim didn't stumble, only shuffled his feet.

Once in the office, they helped lower him onto the couch. The nurse again peppered him with questions, shined the flashlight in his eyes, had him follow her finger with his gaze, and checked reflexes. "He seems to be all right, but I still recommend a physician check him out."

"No doctors. All I need is a glass of water and an ice pack."

Bella and Adam arrived in time to hear Jim say what he needed.

The nurse asked, "Can you tolerate over-the-counter pain medications?"

"Sure. And before you ask, no known allergies."

The nurse smiled for the first time. "You're a quick healer." She then lost the smile. "You'll need someone to check your eyes every two hours throughout the night. Acetaminophen for pain. No aspirin."

Heather said, "I can do it. I'm familiar with what to look for."

The nurse gave a nod. "If there's no sign of concussion by morning, take it easy for the next day or two. No strenuous physical activity." She paused. "Brain injuries sometimes take a while to manifest."

Based on Jim's improving condition, Heather doubted that would happen.

Bella and Adam scurried away to get water, ice, and something for pain. The nurse followed them out after receiving thanks from Lonnie and Ingrid.

While all this was going on, Ingrid had placed Steve in the executive chair behind the desk. "Jim, where were you attacked?"

"On the path, about halfway between the hotel and my room in the fourplex. Someone blindsided me."

Steve took out his phone and spoke to it. "Call William Nohr."

The room went silent as everyone heard one side of the conversation. "Detective Nohr, I need you to come to the resort. Someone assaulted a guest."

It surprised Heather that the call was exceptionally short and cryptic. Steve refrained from discussing any details, preferring to say, "Bring your camera. Heather and I will wait until you get here to interview the victim. She'll be available to help you process the crime scene."

Steve put his phone back in the pocket of his slacks. "Waiting for Detective Nohr will save Jim from having to tell his story multiple times." He lifted his chin. "Heather, let's go to the lobby and wait there for the police."

It seemed like a strange request, but she rounded the desk and led him out of the room, down a hall, and into the lobby.

They settled in chairs on the far side of the lobby, near the front door.

Steve asked, "Is anyone listening?"

"Mary Jones is working the desk, but we're far enough away that she can't hear us."

"Good," said Steve. "Something's not right. I have a feeling Nate's murder is just the tip of an iceberg."

"Do you think the attack on Jim is related?"

"We'll know more after the interview. For now, I want to sit here in silence and try to make sense of what we know so far. Leave me here, and you go back and check on Jim."

"Are you sure there's nothing you need to tell me?"

He shook his head. "It would sound like a word-salad. Nothing's fitting together. William and I will join you in the office as soon as he arrives. Send Bella and Adam to stand guard on either end of the path to his room. I'd hate for someone to contaminate the crime scene."

"Good idea. I'm glad you're still thinking clearly." She took in a deep breath. "I need to apologize for being so distracted."

Steve mumbled something about there being no need. He'd already pulled himself inside his dark world of deep thoughts.

Jim was nursing a bottle of water while holding a bag of ice over the bridge of his nose when Heather returned to the office. Bella and Adam listened with care as she said, "Go to Jim's fourplex. Take flashlights and stay on the path. If you see anything but gravel, don't touch it or step on it. One of you go to the door of Jim's room and wait outside. The other stay where the gravel path meets concrete near the hotel. Don't let anyone pass you." She trained her gaze on Bella. "When Detective Nohr arrives, he and Steve will do a preliminary interview with Jim. After that, we'll meet you on the path."

"Can I help you search?" asked Bella.

"Detective Nohr is in charge. More than likely, he'll want me to assist."

Adam squared his shoulders. "We'll stay out of the way unless he wants our help. I'd hate to mess up an investigation."

"Rats. I was hoping I could search for a clue."

Once they cleared the door, Jim turned to Ingrid and Lonnie. "What do Bella and Adam think about you selling the resort?"

Ingrid handled the question. "She was upset at first, but she was brought up as a world traveler. I think she understands we would like some freedom from being tied to one place. I have a feeling she and Adam will be nomads."

"What about you and Lonnie?"

"We're looking for a simpler life. I'm afraid we're spoiled by a warm climate, so we'll try splitting our time between Puerto Rico and Texas."

Lonnie issued words of clarification. "That's assuming we get a good price for the resort. Its reputation is taking a beating with the murder and now an assault."

Heather thought she noticed the left side of Jim's mouth quirk for a split second, but it could have been a shadow from the bag of ice partially covering his face.

Small talk continued until Detective Nohr led Steve through the door. Once Steve returned to the chair behind the desk, the policeman focused on Jim. "Are you sure you're up to answering a few questions?"

19

Heather noted that the bleeding to Jim's nose had completely stopped. Detective Nohr spoke with even unrushed words. "Take your time, Mr. McCloud. Did someone come to your room?"

"He was waiting on the path."

"He?"

"If it was a woman, she punched like a pro boxer. All I saw was something coming at me followed by white dots."

"Let's not get ahead of ourselves. Back up and tell us what you were doing before the sun went down."

"I spent the afternoon sleeping in a lounge chair and snorkeling. It was awesome. I came back to my room, showered, shaved, and took another nap. I dressed for the evening and left my room. The bar on the patio was my next stop. Three beers later, I realized I'd left my phone in my room. By then, it was dark. I walked to my room, unlocked the door, grabbed my phone, and headed back to the bar."

Heather interrupted. "Are you sure you locked the door to your room?"

Jim tilted his head. "Now that you mention it, I'm not sure. I remember it closing." He lifted his eyebrows. "I was hungry, had a bit of a buzz going."

"Go on," said Detective Nohr.

"On the way back to the hotel, I was on the path, checking emails. As you know, the plants and trees are pretty thick along the walkway. What felt like a baseball bat hit me in the nose." He removed the ice bag. "Right here." He continued his narrative. "I went down like a sack of potatoes. The only other thing I remember is staggering into the dining room."

Steve broke in again. "Did you smell anything unusual in your room?"

"Like what?"

"Cologne, aftershave, cigarette smoke, body odor?"

Jim gave a slow shake of his head, then looked up. "Now that you mention it, there was an odd smell."

"Did you recognize it?"

"I hate to admit it, but I did. It's a memory from college and concerts. Someone was smoking a joint."

"In your room," asked Detective Nohr.

Jim checked his nose for blood. "Along the path, not in my room."

"Do you have any idea how long you were out?"

"I don't think I ever was. Just stunned, looking at white spots."

He raised his left wrist. "Oh, no!"

"What is it?" asked Detective Nohr.

"My Rolex. It's gone."

Steve was the next to speak. "Did anyone help you get to the dining room?"

"Not that I remember."

"Do you have your room key on you?"

"I don't know. Let me check." He reached into the pocket of his shorts, withdrew a metal key, and handed it to Detective Nohr.

"That's all for now, Mr. McCloud. We need to process your

room and search the path." He looked at Lonnie. "Is there another room available for him?"

Heather spoke up. "He can go to my room for tonight. I'll need to check his eyes every couple of hours until tomorrow morning."

Ingrid took a step toward him. "Come with us, Mr. McCloud. Lonnie and I will see you to Heather's room. I'll stay with you until she returns."

"Is that really necessary?"

"No arguments," said Heather as the group dispersed.

The night air seemed unusually thick. Clouds clung together, giving only occasional glimpses of moonlight. It was as if nature had conspired with the evening's events to obscure and confuse. Who could have assaulted Jim McCloud? Why? Was it a simple robbery for his watch? Could it have something to do with Nate Johnson's murder? Did the robber smoke a joint to bolster courage? Too many questions.

Heather glanced at Steve, who loosely gripped her arm as they approached the path with solar-powered lamps dimly illuminating the gravel pathway to Jim's two-story fourplex. She passed Steve off to Bella and directed her question to Detective Nohr. "Is it all right if Bella and Steve stay behind us? She brought a flashlight and might spot something we miss."

"They can come as long as they stay well behind us and touch nothing."

They scoured the path and found a couple of cigarette butts, but no signs of marijuana. Drops of what looked like blood dotted blades of a bush overhanging the path. Detective Nohr took photos before plucking off a couple leaves and placing them in a bag separate from the remains of cigarettes.

They reached the upstairs room where Detective Nohr took the key, clicked the lock, and turned the handle. Light flooded onto the balcony. Adam and Bella stayed outside, but not Steve. "Put me inside, out of the way."

Heather complied and placed Steve next to a chest of drawers. He took in three quick sniffs. "Jim was partially right. Someone smoked pot in here, not on the path."

"I can't smell anything," said Detective Nohr.

"Steve can. Bloodhounds are envious of him."

Heather scanned the room. It was smaller than she expected, with a lone king-size bed, a desk with chair, a single club chair, and the chest of drawers. Bella must have read her thoughts from outside the room with its door open. "These fourplexes were all that was here when my parents bought the property. They built the hotel and everything that makes this a resort after my kidnapping. It was their way of dealing with losing me. As you can see, these are for our more budget-conscious guests."

The search began. Detective Nohr snapped photos from multiple angles while Heather cataloged Jim's possessions. With the tasks completed, Bella and Adam joined them and gathered in front of the bed.

"Everything looks neat and tidy," said Bella.

"Too tidy?" asked Steve.

Detective Nohr took his turn. "Perhaps. One thing's for sure. The room wasn't tossed like I was expecting. The person who attacked Mr. McCloud must not have had time to search for valuables."

"Maybe he was only after the Rolex," said Bella with little conviction in her voice.

"Are the curtains open or closed?" asked Steve.

"Closed," said Heather.

"Anything else of interest?"

"Nothing."

"Then let's go."

Detective Nohr waited to ask Steve a question until the door was locked behind them. "Do you want to talk to Mr. McCloud again tonight?"

"Let's take a step back and digest what we have so far."

20

Heather squinted as a ray of sunshine peeked through a small gap in her curtains. It was only a sliver of light, but it seemed bright as a welder plying his trade. She issued a deep moan of complaint about the interruption of a nonsensical dream and scooted over on the couch to a place where her eyes weren't being singed.

Looking through crusty eyelids, she noticed the covers on the bed Jim had slept in were thrown back. There was no sign of him. She then recalled rousing her patient every two hours and checking to make sure the pupils contracted to light. Once satisfied, she'd return to the couch. It was just enough activity to bring her fully awake and not able to sleep again for at least an hour.

She now knew how it felt to be a Yo-Yo. Up and down, back and forth, on and off the couch, she'd traveled throughout the night. Thoughts pinballed between the assault on Jim, the murder of Nate Johnson, and the imminent arrival of her father with his new personal assistant. Expectations of a much-needed break from work and a peaceful vacation with Jack lay dashed against the coral reef at the entrance of the bay.

With phone in hand, she told it to call Steve so she could confess her inadequacy of keeping track of Jim.

"Good morning," he said, with a voice that told her he'd experienced a night of peaceful slumber. "Jim tells me you moan in your sleep."

"How would he know? He barely wiggled when I checked his eyes." She took a page out of her cat's book of stretching after rising from sleep. Her eyes were still having trouble staying open. "I take it you've seen him this morning?"

"We're having breakfast. Want to join us?"

"What time is it?"

"A little after seven."

A yawn preceded her words. "It's going to take a lot of coffee this morning."

"Go back to sleep. I have plenty to keep me busy."

"Like what?"

"If I told you, you'd have one more thing to worry about. I'll check in with you this afternoon."

The phone went dead, so she rolled over, facing the back of the couch where the sunshine couldn't reach her. Sleep overtook her in near-record time.

When the phone rang, she didn't know how long she'd slept. She pushed a green icon and put the device to her ear. It didn't sound like her voice when she croaked, "Hello?"

"Are you still asleep?"

The voice belonged to her father. "It was a long, sleepless night. What time is it?"

"Almost eight. Steve called and told me about you taking care of Jim McCloud. You should have hired a nurse."

"It seemed like the thing to do."

"I'm bringing information on Skip and Roxy Smith. By the way, those aren't their real names."

"I figured as much. Wait until you get here to tell me more. My brain feels like it's a plate of cold spaghetti. I'll be fully awake by the time you get here."

"Solve the murder and you'll be back in the pink."

"Not this time. Solving a murder may prove to be the simple part of this vacation."

"That's not what Steve says. You may have spaghetti brain, but he said the murder has his twisted like a pretzel. This must be a tough case. He also told me about Jim's assault. Tell me you're not in any danger."

"All right. I'm not in any danger."

"Don't be flippant."

"Sorry. If I thought we were in danger, I'd hire bodyguards or at least get my pistol out of the airplane." She took a breath. "Jim wasn't seriously hurt last night. It appears to be a simple robbery."

"Simple? That's not a word I associate with you and Steve or the cases you attract."

A yawn gave her a few seconds to think and come up with a reason to put her father off. "I really need to shower and dress for the day. I'm scheduled for fun in the sun."

"Ha! I doubt there's much chance of that. You're too much like me. I never give you the full story of what I'm doing, and you're the proverbial chip off the block."

Heather spoke before she thought. "It keeps things interesting between us."

"That it does. I'll see you in the dining room tomorrow morning."

"Tomorrow? I thought you weren't coming until Thursday."

"You're not the only one who could benefit from fun in the sun."

With the call ended, her thoughts rested on her father and the assistant that would accompany him tomorrow. She managed to stand with wobbling legs and looked down at her bare feet. "Start walking. There's a lot to do today."

STEVE ASKED JIM TO BUTTER A PIECE OF TOAST FOR HIM. THE victim of last night's assault complied and said, "I'm glad you were here this morning. I didn't want to eat alone again."

"Heather says you're smart, handsome, and financially well off. I have a hard time believing you have trouble finding someone to share breakfast with you."

"I'm between marriages and on a quest to discover the next woman I'm not suited for. Any advice?"

It was good to hear there were no residual effects to Jim's assault. Concussions didn't lend themselves to self-deprecating humor. Steve countered his levity with, "Plenty of advice, and it's worth what it will cost you... nothing."

"That's what I should have paid the therapists for all the good they did."

"Perhaps you're trying too hard. Heather thinks that's what's wrong with your business dealings."

"Did she say that?"

He made the sign of an X over his chest. "Cross my heart."

The sounds of shuffling feet reached Steve's ears. He estimated a family of two adults, two teens, and a child walked past their table.

Jim's voice took on a serious tone. "Is it possible to try too hard?"

He wondered if Jim really wanted an answer. Instead of giving him a one-word reply, he'd give him something to consider. "What do you think about Heather's businesses?"

The response came back with speed. "She's brilliant, well diversified, and seems to have the world by the tail."

"She's miserable. For the past six months she's worked herself into the ground. This economic downturn is bigger than anything she's ever faced, and she can't stand the thought of her fortune decreasing, or even staying the same."

"I don't have to worry about that happening. Mine already has." Jim lowered his volume a few decibels. "So far, I've lost over half my net worth, and there's a good possibility I'll lose another twenty-five percent. I need a miracle."

"Let's say you did lose another twenty-five percent. Would you still be in the top one percent?"

"Barely."

Steve took a bite of toast and chewed slowly, allowing time to consider Jim's words and for him to do the same. After swallowing and taking a drink of coffee, he asked, "Why do you think someone attacked and robbed you last night?"

"I don't know. Perhaps they saw my watch and wanted it."

"They didn't take any cash?"

"I guess they got scared and didn't take my wallet or the key to my room."

"They, he, or she?"

"I'd say he. All I know is the person hit me with something that felt like an anvil."

Steve leaned forward. "Who knows that you're interested in purchasing the hotel in town?"

Jim didn't deny the fact that he wanted Nate's hotel, but lowered his voice even more. "It's not the sort of thing you go around talking about. I mentioned it to a few people. I also told Heather."

"Why aren't you staying there to check it out?"

"They're booked up with people wanting to learn to dive. That woman named Connie is pulling double-duty and doing a great job. It seems like a good investment."

Jim had done everything but answer the question truthfully. Even with a budget room, he could enjoy the upscale amenities of the resort.

Deception had a sound of its own that Steve had trained himself to identify. Jim hadn't made reservations at Nate's hotel because he liked the life of a high-roller. What else was he lying about?

Steve allowed about fifteen seconds to pass before he

broached the heart of what he wanted to know. It was his practice to allow silence to heighten curiosity. Fifteen seconds of silence seemed longer when it interrupted the pace of a conversation. "Did the person who assaulted you also warn you not to put in an offer on Nate's hotel? I'm guessing he left a note with you."

He heard Jim swallow. "How did you know?"

"I didn't know for sure until now. Did they really steal your Rolex?"

Jim issued a nervous laugh. "Heather told me it was useless to hide anything from you."

"When did she say that?"

"In the wee hours of the morning. She woke me up last night to check my eyes. I pretended to be too groggy to talk to her. She said you'd interview me today, and I'd better tell you everything about me coming to St. Croix and that you'd know if I was holding back or lying. I wanted to test you."

"That was foolish. I'm not a mind reader, but it only takes a few seconds to take cash out of a wallet. You were stunned and unable to fight back." Steve took another sip of coffee. "Where's your watch?"

"In my pocket. Am I in trouble?"

"Not enough to worry about, but if you smoke dope in your room, don't lie about it." He paused. "You also need to stop lying about buying Nate's hotel. You're here to purchase it for someone else."

"Jeez," said Jim. "Nothing gets past you. What happens now?"

Steve pulled his napkin from the front of his shirt. "Do you want to get beat up again, or possibly killed?"

"I'd prefer not to."

"You have two options. First, you can catch the first available flight off the island and forget about the hotel."

Jim interrupted, "I don't like that one."

"I didn't think you would. Your second choice is to stay at this resort until we find out who assaulted you and put them in jail." Steve held up a hand of warning. "If you choose that option, you must tell the people you're representing that you're here to relax and not purchase real estate. If you've made some sort of agreement with them, break it. I'd suggest you fill every waking minute of your day with recreation and your nights pursuing the elusive perfect wife."

Steve held up a hand to signal he had something else to say. "I have to warn you, this choice comes with risks to your safety. Take precautions."

"It may be difficult to court beautiful women with this busted snoz. As for the daytime activities, the afternoon sun is brutal. Can you think of anything else I might do to while away the day?"

Steve rubbed his chin, hoping a burst of revelation came. He tapped his fingers on the table. "What do you know about day trading?"

"I know it's a good way to lose money if you don't know what you're doing."

"Bella's fiancé, Adam, is a day trading expert. He says he's not nervous about the wedding, but I'm pretty sure he could use a diversion. I'll call and see if he'll take you under his wing. You can watch how he earns a living. It will keep you out of sight and him from thinking about the wedding."

Steve took out his phone and told it to call Adam Webber.

"Good morning," said Steve. "Are you working yet?"

"I'm looking at the overnight activity in the markets, but I won't start trading for another hour."

"I have a favor to ask you."

The conversation progressed, and Adam was more than willing to teach Jim the ins and outs of day trading. Steve thanked him and hung up.

"That's all set. Adam will ease you into the waters with paper trading until you get the hang of it. He'll contact you this afternoon."

Jim rose and pushed his chair in. "Sounds good."

The server removed their plates, and Steve told her he'd like another cup of coffee. He'd been right about Jim wanting to purchase Nate's hotel. Mr. McBlythe would arrive with the report from the private investigator containing information about Skip and Roxy Smith days earlier than expected. The investigation was finally progressing.

21

It was the morning her father would arrive. Heather vacillated between taking the time to wash her hair or putting it into a ponytail and slapping on a baseball cap. The thought of meeting her father's personal assistant brought out the vanity in her, and she lathered up the thick auburn mane and scrubbed away. It seemed to take forever for the blow dryer to complete its task. She then put on extra makeup reserved for special occasions. Today qualified, but she didn't know why.

The thought wouldn't go away, so she repeated the question. No answer. She couldn't decide what to wear. A sundress of exceptionally bright colors won the flip of a coin. Should she wear the floppy brimmed straw hat. What was the use of washing her hair if she covered it?

After checking herself one more time in a full-length mirror, she exited her room and rode the elevator to the lobby. From there, she went to the dining room and found Steve sitting by himself.

He spoke in a kidding-serious sort of way. "It's about time you came out of hibernation." With chin lifted, he sniffed. "No wonder it took you so long. You washed your hair and put on perfume. A little extra makeup, too?"

"Hush. Father and his new P.A. are walking this way."

"Nervous about meeting her?"

She ignored the question.

Her father's warm embrace took her by surprise, but he soon pulled away to arm's length. "The way you sounded this morning, I was expecting to see you in pajamas with your hair buried under a baseball cap." He didn't wait for her to respond. "Heather and Steve, I'd like to introduce you to Zhang Min. This is my daughter, Heather, and her business partner, Steve Smiley."

Heather inspected the woman. She was of short stature, with occasional strands of gray in raven hair. Her eyes spoke of an oriental ancestry. Without thinking, Heather gave a half bow.

The woman returned the gesture and spoke in perfect English, yet with an accent. "Your names are forever on my employer's lips. It is an honor to meet both of you."

Heather wanted to believe the woman's relationship with her father was that of her employer and nothing else. Did Zhang Min speak the truth, or was it a ploy to pretend to be a mere employee? After all, she knew her father often concealed things from her. The woman's countenance revealed nothing.

It wasn't long before Steve asked, "Have you had breakfast?"

"Not yet," said her father.

"Nor have I," said Heather. "I'm sure you're both ready for something after having to rise so early."

"No earlier than usual, Daughter."

"If you'll excuse me," said Zhang Min. "I must unpack Mr. McBlythe's belongings and set up our workstations."

"No breakfast?" asked Heather.

"I brought my own and ate on the way." She removed a file folder from a valise and handed it to her father. Then she bowed, took steps back, and turned. Short, elegant steps took her away as if she glided on ice skates rather than walked.

Heather waited until Zhang Min cleared the dining room. "She seems extremely competent."

"More than competent. She has the gift of anticipating what I need. She speaks seven languages fluently and can read people like a book. There's a lot we can learn from people of the Far East."

Heather wasn't in the mood to consider all the things her father might learn from this exotic creature. It was enough that she was putting his underwear and socks in a drawer. She shook off the irrational feeling of betrayal and asked, "Is that the file from your private investigator?"

"Let's order and we'll discuss it."

"When did you receive it?" asked Steve.

"This morning at the airport. My investigator stayed up all night completing it, and it reads like a scene from a gangster movie."

The server came and stood with pad and pen in hand. Heather spoke first. "I'll have the buffet, coffee, and cranberry juice." Her father nodded. "The same."

The suntanned woman with a tattoo of a dolphin on her right wrist held out her hand in the direction of a buffet offering hot and cold foods. "Help yourself whenever you're ready."

Heather waited for her father to begin the conversation. A note of concern etched his words. "You're looking tired, dear."

Steve broke in. "She's still catching up from playing nurse and chief of hotel security."

"That accounts for the bloodshot eyes but not the worry creases on your forehead." He focused on the area above her eyebrows. "That's how your mother could tell you had something of consequence bothering you. I never noticed it until she pointed it out to me."

Heather didn't want the conversation bogged down by her list of woes. She and Steve needed to work on the case; but how to pacify her father? "I'll make a deal with you, Father. You tell us what's in the file, and I'll give you all the sordid details that are causing my worry lines."

"When will you tell me?"

"Soon."

"Not good enough. I want to hear it all by noon today."

"I need to help Steve this morning. I probably won't be here at noon." She cast her gaze to her partner. Her father did the same.

"Why do I suddenly feel like I'm the third person on a date? You two work this out between yourselves."

Her father kept his gaze on Steve. "Do you really need Heather's help this morning?"

"It would make the job faster, but Bella has already agreed to help me at Nate Johnson's hotel."

Steve had the annoying habit of giving non-committal answers when he felt mischievous. The ball was back in Heather's court, and she wanted to buy time before telling her father details of how Jack was acting so out of character. She lowered her voice to a somber tone and looked at her father. "I'll tell you one thing that has me concerned now. The rest I'll spread out to give you a chance to think about them and give me advice."

He pursed his lips together and gave his head a nod. "I'll consider it a down payment and expect a second installment tonight after supper. Start talking."

"Very well. I'm worried about my business. It's hit a plateau and nothing I try is working." She expounded on the topic as he asked for occasional points of clarification.

"You remind me of the man who went to the doctor with a sore leg and said, 'Doctor, every day I walk ten miles and my leg hurts.' The doctor told him to walk five miles. If it still ached after five, he was to walk only one mile. If that didn't help, the man was to buy a comfortable folding chair and go fishing."

"Said the man who works seventy to eighty hours a week."

Her father shook his head. "Not in this economy. Only fifty hours, and I plan on cutting back."

Concern entered her thoughts. "My turn for a medical question. Is there something you've kept hidden from me? I've never known you to work so little."

"Perfect health, other than the normal aches and pains associated with the last third of my life." He put his hand over hers. "It's not a question of desire or stamina. It's the simple fact that there are so few bargains. Significant downturns happen every forty years. Things go in cycles, and now it's best to take most of your chips off the table and watch others work themselves silly and still lose." His steely gray eyes bore into her. "I keep track of your companies and your investments. I recommend you unload some of your under-performing assets while you still can. Park your money where it's safe and wait. For the time being, breaking even is the best outcome we can hope for."

Heather didn't like what he was saying but realized he'd lived his entire life buying and selling through peaks and valleys. Still, it rankled her. He could see the future so clearly while she believed she could tweak her portfolio and keep her company growing.

Her father surprised her when he said, "Take Jim McCloud, for example. Jim lost a good portion of his wealth and learned nothing. He's here looking to scoop up a bargain and recoup some of his losses. He'd be much better off sitting in a lounge chair."

"Are you saying that the hotel in town and this resort are overpriced?"

He raised his shoulders and let them fall. "I don't have an opinion on those properties because I haven't studied them yet. This much I know: unless I can purchase a property today well below its true value and sell it tomorrow for a profit, I'm not interested." He looked toward the buffet. "I'm also saying it's time to eat."

She pushed herself up. "Steve, do you want me to bring you anything?"

He waved a hand to show a negative response.

As was her custom, Heather restricted her breakfast to a few selections. She bypassed pancakes, waffles, and the crepe station in favor of yogurt, a fruit cup, and a bowl of bran cereal with almond milk. She walked with her father back to the table where Steve sat nursing a cup of coffee.

Coming toward their table was Judith Tovar, accompanied by the metallic sound of her walker gliding across the tile floor.

22

Judith slowed to a stop beside their table. "I'm so sorry to interrupt you, Ms. McBlythe, but the resort is abuzz with rumors. Is it true that someone assaulted a guest?"

It surprised Heather that Judith acted like she didn't already know. Not wanting to add fuel to the rumor fire, she minimized the event. "The man wasn't seriously hurt. I'd equate it to more of a snatch-and-grab." She remained seated while her father rose. "Father, let me introduce you to Mrs. Judith Tovar and her stepson, Juan."

She was going to finish the formalities by stating her father's full name and introducing Steve, but Juan broke into the conversation. "How did you know my name?"

Judith placed her hand lightly on Juan's arm. "Ms. McBlythe and Mr. Smiley are private detectives. Unless I miss my guess, the local police have asked for their help in finding the person responsible for the recent murder. It wouldn't surprise me if they're helping with the assault, too."

Instead of focusing on Mrs. Tovar, Heather locked her gaze on Juan and his reaction to his stepmother's disclosure. He was an exceptionally handsome man and could easily be cast as a leading actor in a Mexican soap opera. The revelation of her and

Steve's unusual business partnership brought a sneer from the man. His countenance changed when his gaze swept over her. It reminded her of a hungry person examining a choice steak.

Juan switched his gaze to his stepmother. "A murder and now a robbery? Are you sure this is a safe resort?"

"Of course, it's safe. Two unrelated incidents."

Judith looked at Heather's father and issued a wide grin. "It's nice to meet you, Mr. McBlythe, and it's good to see you again, Mr. Smiley."

Juan continued to stare at her, mainly at the real estate below the chin. Heather countered this by asking, "Other than spending time with your stepmother, what brings you to St. Croix?"

"Scuba diving. The reef guarding the cove is one of the best-kept secrets in the Eastern Caribbean. Do you dive?"

"I'm fully certified, but unless something changes, there won't be time."

If there was one thing she didn't want, it was to have this Latino Adonis gawking at her in water so clear he could scrutinize her every curve.

Steve broke into the conversation. "I'd go with you, Juan, but the view wouldn't impress me."

Judith let out a laugh that mixed a bray with a cackle. "Oh, Mr. Smiley, it's so refreshing to find a kindred spirit. I refer to my walker as my chariot, and sometimes as my hot-rod. I believe gallows humor is a wonderful coping mechanism when life kicks us in the teeth."

Steve gave his head a firm nod. "Well said. Levity takes some of the sting out of life's tragedies. I lost my sight when a street mugger attacked me. How did a young woman like you earn a walker?"

"A spinal injury." She gave no further explanation. As quick as a heartbeat, she changed the conversation. "Come, Juan. We need to get you fed if you're going to spend the day diving."

"All day?" asked Heather.

Juan issued a sultry smile. "It is but one of my passions."

She had no desire to hear what his other passions might be. Judith gripped the handles of her walker, and led her stepson to a table on the far side of the room.

Heather's father was the next to speak. "That was interesting. What do you make of them, Heather?"

"I believe she qualifies as the town crier who takes in gossip by the truckload. As for Juan, my opinion is less charitable. I think he's the type of man who'd—"

Steve interrupted her before she could finish her sentence. "We could tell what kind of man he is."

Heather placed her napkin in her lap and took a large bite of yogurt to ensure she wouldn't blurt out something she'd regret. She was diving into her fruit cup when she noticed Li Jing make her way across the room and join Judith and Juan at their table.

She swallowed and leaned toward Steve. "Li Jing joined mother and stepson. She's wearing a cover-up over a bathing suit. I think she's sporting a diving watch."

Steve tilted his head. "Check with Bella and find out if Juan and Li Jing got together last night. It sounded like the band on the back patio had the place jumping."

"What are you thinking?"

His first reaction came out in a soft voice, as if he was speaking only to himself. "I'm questioning my decision about telling Detective Nohr about the garrote."

Steve shook his head. "No. Forget I said that. Either Juan is a fast operator, or he and Li Jing knew each other before they came here. Call Detective Nohr and let him know Li Jing will be diving with Juan today. Tell him I want to give her some rope and not to arrest her again for leaving the compound."

Heather turned to her father. "This is what a murder investigation is like. Chasing down leads that probably mean nothing."

"It reminds me so much of seeking prudent investments. Needles in haystacks." He cut into a serving of eggs Benedict and exclaimed. "Cooked to perfection. This is going to be a wonderful vacation."

The breakfast progressed. Bella arrived as the dishes were bussed from the table. "Good morning," she said in a flat tone. "I'll be leaving soon to carry out my assignment."

Steve leaned back. "What's that hint of worry I hear in your voice?"

"Several people are checking out early. Dad thinks it's because of the murder and the assault."

"Tell him and your mother not to worry. Between Adam's family and all the other guests coming for your wedding, they'll make up for anyone leaving. By the way, I'm going with you to Nate's hotel."

Bella's countenance brightened. "Great. I'll get the van and meet you out front when we're ready to go."

Heather's father asked, "Do you both have time to listen to the report I brought?"

Steve launched into the conversation without answering her father's question. "What did you find out about Skip and Roxy Smith, other than those aren't their names?"

"My source was able to get a copy of their criminal histories. They're not nice people." He placed two stacks of papers in front of Heather. She gave a running narrative. "I'm reading the rap sheet for Roxy. It's five pages. Multiple shoplifting charges, followed by a lengthy career in prostitution. She started out working the streets as a teen but worked her way up to being a call girl, then a madam. One three-year sentence for aggravated assault. She did ten months on it. No wants or warrants on her now."

"Any ties with crime families or gangs?"

Mr. McBlythe answered as Heather thumbed through the report. "I took the liberty of reading the report. There's nothing in the official reports, but the PI's sources discovered Roxy is well connected with some very unsavory characters. They described her places of business as full-service, including a wide range of gambling and drugs."

"Is there anything on why she's not back in New Jersey or New York?"

"The detective wasn't sure. She listed a few possibilities, but nothing definitive."

"What about Skip?"

Heather took over again. "Fights, multiple assaults, one arrest for involuntary manslaughter." She took a breath. "All but the manslaughter dismissed."

Steve nodded. "He was working for someone with money enough to buy his way out of trouble."

Heather added, "He did four years on a five-year sentence. That means he has quite the prison record, too."

"A paid enforcer," said Steve. "Most likely a sociopath or a lapdog doing his master's bidding."

Bella sat up straight. "I say we tell Mom and Dad and get them out of here before someone else gets hurt."

Steve puffed out his cheeks and blew. "They weren't on the property when Nate was killed."

"Rats," said Bella. "I thought we had Nate's murder solved. The Smiths couldn't have killed him if they weren't on the island."

"Think harder before you come to that conclusion."

"What do you mean?" asked Bella.

Steve tapped his head with his index finger. "Use that sharp mind of yours to think of ways they could have come back to the island with no one knowing about it."

"Holy smoke. They could have come by boat and returned to St. Thomas before dawn."

"Now you're thinking like a detective. Let's go to Nate's hotel."

Heather was walking through the lobby when she noticed a taxi parked in front of the hotel. The back door of the cab flew open. Bella squealed with delight. "It's Jack!"

The edges of the scene blurred. All Heather could see was Jack.

Steve took his hand from her arm. "Pass me off to Bella. The prodigal fiancé has returned. You have more important things to take care of today."

23

Heather abandoned Steve and seemed to float toward Jack. Was this a dream? Was it really him? He had his back to her, paying the taxi driver. By the time he turned, she'd passed through the hotel's doorway and skipped down the steps. He turned and she buried her face in his chest.

"Hello, beautiful." They were the words he'd adopted as his standard greeting. This was no dream.

She returned his greeting with, "Hello, handsome." Her universe seemed to fall back in place with the planets aligned. She felt his chest heave and he pushed her away. Was he crying? Surely not. They were together in paradise.

It must have been Steve's sixth sense kicking into high gear. He spoke in measured words. "Hello, Jack. I wish Bella and I could stay and chat, but we have a busy day ahead of us. I suggest you and Heather take a long walk on the beach." He held out his hand for Bella to lead him. "Let's go. We're running late as it is." The tone of his voice didn't invite discussion.

Heather stayed focused on Jack as Steve and Bella slipped from her peripheral vision. She barely heard one of the resort's vans come to life and pull past them.

With the taxi gone and Bella and Steve on their way to Nate's hotel, Heather rested her gaze on the only man she'd ever loved. His shirt looked slept in and he hadn't shaved in at least two days. He hid his brown hair under a Houston Astros baseball cap. Was this a new, rugged look he was going for? No. His bloodshot, sunken eyes told a different story. She looked at the ground beside him. All he brought was a single carry-on bag. She didn't need to be a detective to conclude he didn't plan on staying long. Her heart seemed to shrink in size.

"Steve was right," said Jack as he swiped moisture from his cheeks. "We need to take a long walk."

Heather's muscles contracted until she was rigid as a block of granite. "You didn't bring suitcases. Tell me right now what's going on."

His words came out cold. "Not here."

"You're not staying, are you?"

Jack reached down, picked up his bag, and said again, "Not here. I need to use the restroom before we take that walk Steve recommended." He held up a hand to stop her from speaking. "I'll explain everything."

He didn't give her a chance to respond before motioning her toward the front door. It took him longer to get back to the lobby than it should have. When he returned, it was obvious what delayed him. He'd changed from long pants, a wrinkled white shirt, and black shoes to shorts, a plain short-sleeve shirt, and sandals. Her heart did its impression of butterfly wings upon his return in casual attire. She'd envisioned him looking this way. What she hadn't expected was the hollow feeling in the pit of her stomach.

Jack left his bag with the front desk clerk and said, "I'm ready."

Heather looked at him. His voice sounded like he donned an extra dose of courage along with his change of clothes. How had they gotten to the place of him needing courage to talk to her?

Jack looked toward the bay and took a few tentative steps. Words weren't necessary. Her feet moved on their own. They both came to a halt where a wooden walkway ended and fine white sand began. In unison, they slipped off their sandals and walked on while holding their shoes instead of each other's hand.

Children and their parents splashed and swam in the shallow waters of the bay. Tiny waves kissed the shore and retreated. Jack took in the scene and asked, "Which way is best to find a private spot?"

Heather pointed to the right. It wasn't too long before there were no footprints in the damp sand in front of them. She knew it wasn't necessary to go on for privacy, but they kept walking. She glanced over to take a quick look at him. A tear slid down his cheek. He didn't wipe it away.

They walked until they could go no further. Jagged rocks sprang up out of the sand. A lone palm tree stood at the boundary like a sentinel. Out in the water, a coral reef kept boats from entering. Waves cupped and curled. Heather sensed danger and braced herself as best she could.

Two emotions warred within her. The business side of her wanted Jack to stop delaying. If there was bad news, she wanted him to tear off the bandage in a single, quick movement. Her heart, however, dreaded what he would tell her. Surely, they could work together and fix it, whatever it was.

Her mental jousting ended when he broke the silence. "Would you like to sit on that rock?"

"No. I want you to quit stalling and tell me what's going on."

He looked out at the waves for a moment, then turned back and faced her. "Last month I found out I have a daughter."

Of all the things Jack could have said, this was the one thing she hadn't planned on. Dumbstruck, she felt the sand shift as if it would swallow her. She reached to her right, found the rock he suggested she sit on, and eased herself down. A bevy of questions flooded her mind. She heard herself asking a string of silly questions. "How? Who? When?"

A gust of wind caught the bill of his baseball cap and sent it flying. He didn't retrieve it. "My daughter's name is Briann Lovejoy. She's twelve years old. Her mother's name was Corliss Love-joy. We dated for several months, many years ago. A lifetime before I met you."

"Wait," said Heather as she struggled to take in the broadside of words. "You have a daughter? How long have you known about her?"

"Like I said, only last month."

"And she's twelve years old?"

He nodded.

"And you're just now getting around to telling me about her?"

"I didn't know for sure she was my daughter, and you weren't around to tell."

Anger came alive in her like a sea monster coming out of the depths. "That's the worst excuse I've ever heard."

Jack looked again at the waves. "I waited for the DNA tests to come back. They did, and Briann's my daughter."

Heather puffed out her cheeks. "All right. You have a daughter, and her mother's name is Corliss Lovejoy. Where do they live?"

"It's no longer *they*. Corliss died six weeks ago. They lived in Baton Rouge, Louisiana."

"I assume Briann is now living with Corliss's family."

He shook his head. "No family members are willing to take her in. She's in Conroe with Mom looking after her."

Heather thought back to her early years when she took part in martial arts. She'd received a round-house kick to the midsection that had left her in the fetal position, unable to breathe. This was worse. Never in her wildest dreams had she considered this scenario.

Jack kept talking without her having to prompt him. The words came like blows to her emotions—relentless and vicious. "Corliss was originally from Baton Rouge. She was living in The Woodlands, practicing law. It was a brief relationship. Only two or three months."

The snarky creature inside Heather reared its head. "She must have been something extra-special."

"We were both young and reckless."

"That's obvious."

He looked at her with an expression that told her this was hard for him, and he didn't appreciate her making it more difficult. "Do you want me to continue, or do you want to keep taking cheap shots? If you do, go ahead. You can't make me feel any worse than I already do."

The attorney part of her wanted to attack without mercy. She swallowed her anger and spoke words not in keeping with her feelings. "Keep talking. I need to hear everything."

"There's not much else to tell you. Corliss didn't tell me she was pregnant when she suddenly moved back to Baton Rouge. I tried to keep in touch with her for a while but she ended it. She said it was fun while it lasted, but we needed to go our own ways."

Jack cleared his throat and continued, "I'm sure she knew I'd want to marry her, and that wouldn't make for the type of life she wanted. She was right. I was dating someone else a month after she moved."

"And you didn't have a clue she was expecting?"

"It never crossed my mind."

Anger flared again. "What am I supposed to do with this?"

He shrugged. "All I know is, there's a confused, hurting young lady living at my home that I'm responsible for."

"That explains the travel bag instead of suitcases. You've weighed your options, and I'm no longer at the top of your list."

"I wouldn't put it like that, but I understand why you feel that way. I have new, unexpected responsibilities that I can't shirk."

"When is your flight back to Houston?"

"This afternoon."

The next words sprang from her lips before she could stop them. "Hit-and-run Jack Blackstock strikes again." She hated herself for not taming her tongue but didn't have time to make an apology. Jack had already turned and was walking away. She wanted to go after him, but she couldn't. Her bright-colored dress felt like a rusty boat anchor.

Down the beach, and out of her life, he walked. She watched him through tear-fogged eyes until he shrank and disappeared into the resort. The waves continued their relentless pounding. She was more convinced than ever that they mocked her.

Heather spent the afternoon in the shade of a lonely palm tree. In the distance, beyond any sound but that of the breeze and waves, people played, splashed, and snorkeled. Sailboats cruised past in the deeper blue waters off shore. A couple of boats with divers dropped anchor beyond the breakers and put out flags. Eager men and women donned silver tanks on their backs and explored the reef. One boat came close enough that she recognized the divers. Li Jing, wearing a skimpy bikini, put on her mask, stuck her mouthpiece in, and went over the boat's side backward. Juan Tovar went over the side in like manner a few seconds later.

"Young lovers," whispered Heather, with more than a little edge to her words. "Be careful. It's a dangerous game you're playing."

The palm tree cast long shadows when she spied Bella walking toward her with Max keeping up, step for step. The bride-to-be held his leash wadded in her hand. He was free to roam. Her beloved cat must have caught her scent on the evening breeze. He broke into a run and was soon in her arms. She dampened his fur with her tears.

Bella took her time getting to Heather. She whispered when she arrived, "Steve sent me to get you. You don't need to worry about telling anyone what happened. We know."

She clung to Max. "How?"

"Steve knew Jack wasn't staying when I told him he only brought a small travel bag."

"Did he call Jack?"

Bella shook her head. "Steve called Jack's mother. She told him about Briann."

"Does my father know?"

"Uh-huh. So do Adam and my parents. You don't need to say anything to anyone."

Fresh tears rolled down her cheeks. She should've known Steve would shield her from having to explain.

"He told us not to bother you tonight."

Heather nodded. "I'm not sure how long it will be before I'm fit company."

Bella cast her gaze toward the resort. "Steve told me to bring you back."

Heather rose from the sand. "Come on, Max. You need your supper."

Heather caught the first notes of the band warming up as they neared the resort. To drown out the sound, she asked, "Did you and Steve have a productive day at Nate's hotel?"

"It's hard to say. You know how Steve gets when he's thinking hard. He'll pull his head out from his shell when he's ready to astound us."

Fifteen minutes ago, Heather doubted she'd ever smile again. Bella's good-natured innocence and ability to turn a phrase broke through her grief, if only for a few moments. The chuckle escaped her lips before she knew what happened. Perhaps the sun would come up tomorrow. No, not tomorrow.

24

Heather's eyes felt like someone had come into her bedroom with a pail of sand and spooned it into her eyes. "Jack," she whispered to herself. He was gone. He'd said months ago that nothing could keep him from attending Bella and Adam's wedding. That was before the tectonic plates of their relationship shifted. An emotional earthquake had changed her world, and things would never be the same. New boundary lines had formed.

She rubbed her eyes, dug out the crusties, and blinked until she could focus on the light filtering in around the edges of the curtains. Had she slept at all that first night? Perhaps an hour or two, but no more. When compared to other dreadful nights, that one shot to the top of the charts with flashing lights and bells clanging.

After a full day of hibernating in her room with no contact with the outside world, she'd finally surrendered to a fitful sleep sometime in the wee hours of the morning. The word stepmother bounced around in her head until sleep overtook her. It was the first thing she thought of when she opened the curtains to let in the sunlight.

For the hundredth time, she wondered what she could, or should, do about Jack and their relationship. Nothing came to mind. Her emotions were too raw.

There were problems with the scenario of her becoming a stepmother. To begin with, she and Jack had already decided that children would not be characters in the play of their lives. It was a tremendous stretch to see herself as a mother of any type. The prospect of taking on the responsibility for a twelve-year-old girl sent chills down her spine. It was going to be hard enough for Jack to form a bond with his daughter.

The addition of a stepmother to the mix amounted to cruel and unusual punishment for all three of them. She went down the mental list she'd compiled the day before. Reasons for and against marrying Jack stood like opposing armies. It was a long list for the opposing army.

After all, the livelihood of hundreds, if not thousands, of people depended on her. This number would only increase when her father passed the torch for his empire to her. Also, there was Steve and helping him with the occasional murder case. What was now a welcome respite, a vacation of sorts from the corporate grind, would most likely go by the wayside. And yet Steve needed her.

"Am I the most selfish person in the world?" The question went to her reflection in the patio door. No answer came from the puffy-eyed woman staring back at her, so she tried a different question. "Is it selfish to insist on being married to Jack? His daughter will resent me. Perhaps I need to give him time and space to be a father."

It seemed as if every muscle in her body tightened as yet another remembrance of her conversation with Jack came to her. His priorities had changed. He would do what he considered the right thing and finish the job of raising his daughter. She didn't need to decide anything about marriage. She hadn't been invited to take part.

One hand went involuntarily over her mouth while the second clutched the fabric of her sleepwear between her stomach and her heart. Her mind buzzed as grief somehow mingled with a sense of relief. "I thought this was my one great love affair. How can I feel relieved? Have I been dumped for the first time in my life? If not, how can we move forward?" Too many questions without answers.

The knock on the door cut off any further thoughts or words. She padded her way to the door barefoot and asked, "Who is it?"

"Room service."

"I didn't order."

The familiar voice of her father spoke. "Heather, open the door."

She pulled the door open, and he came in, pushing a cart with a squeaky wheel. A server from the hotel came behind him with a second cart. The train continued with Bella leading Steve. It was Steve who spoke once the circus train arrived. "I thought I heard you talking to someone."

"Myself," said Heather as she went to the closet to retrieve a summer robe.

Bella said, "You look awful. Want to go wash your face before we eat?"

"I'm not hungry."

"Nonsense," said her father. "You'll need your strength when you hear what Steve has to say. It's battle stations with all hands on deck."

Steve issued a firm nod. "Yesterday was an eventful day."

"That's an understatement," said Heather.

"We'll fill you in as soon as you get back from washing your face."

She went into the bathroom. The water felt like cold slaps and brought her to a more level emotional plane. It was nowhere near normal, but at least she didn't long to hibernate. The tease of information and her father's call to battle put curiosity a half-step ahead of heartache.

Back in the room, she found the group filling plates with a wide variety of breakfast dishes. She noticed Steve had limited his breakfast to half a bagel topped with cream cheese. She approached him and asked, "Is that all you're having?"

"I've been up since four thinking. This is breakfast, part two. Eat a full breakfast. There's much to talk about and a lot to do."

Her father spoke next. "The chef recommended the quiche Lorraine. I trust it's still one of your favorites? There are also Scotch eggs if you'd prefer."

After depriving herself for almost two days, Heather had to admit the aromas coming from the carts had her taste buds fully activated. She turned to her father. "Two of my favorites. Thank you."

"What's a Scotch egg?" asked Steve.

Bella gave the answer. "It's a soft-boiled egg wrapped in sausage and fried."

"That sounds delicious. If it's fried, it has to be good."

"I'll give you half of mine," said Heather. "A small slice of quiche and half a Scotch egg is all I need." She paused. "Perhaps a little yogurt and half a bagel to round out the meal."

The gathering sat around the coffee table and balanced plates on their laps. Steve finished his bagel, which allowed the Scotch egg to cool enough so he could pick it up and eat it. Heather waited until everyone was well into the meal before she said, "It's obvious I missed some interesting developments. Who's going first?"

"I will," said her father.

This came as no surprise. After a dab of his mouth with a napkin, her father sat erect. "I received a note under my door when I returned from dinner last night. It warned me about staying on the island any longer. It said, and I quote, 'Leave, or people may die. That includes you.'"

Heather dropped her fork on her plate. She looked for a

reaction from Bella, Steve, and her father. They each kept eating their breakfast like her father had given the daily weather report instead of an ominous threat. "What are we doing about this?"

Steve swallowed his first bite of Scotch egg. "This is really tasty. I hope I'm not getting any on my shorts."

"Your shorts are fine." Impatience filled her voice. "What have you done about this threat?"

Steve lowered the sausage-wrapped egg onto his plate. "The note is in the safe in your father's room. Detective Nohr should be here soon to retrieve it. He's arranged for two plain-clothes officers to stay at the resort until your father leaves."

This was a lot for Heather to take in before she'd finished her first cup of coffee. "I'm confused. Is the threat against Father or someone in the wedding party?"

Her father swallowed before he answered. "You can interpret the note either way. I contacted the private investigator who gave me the report on Skip and Roxy. I sent my plane to fetch her and three associates. They're also skilled bodyguards and will arrive today."

Steve picked up his Scotch egg, but didn't take a bite. "Heather, I'll need you to develop a plan to ensure the safety of everyone. You already have several of the staff keeping tabs on Li Jing. She's spending most all her waking hours with Juan Tovar. I want you to get to know him."

Heather said she would, but added, "Li Jing may think I'm cutting in on her man."

Bella added, "That's Steve's plan. Juan and Li Jing are diving again this morning and this afternoon. I verified it through the owner of the dive boat Juan chartered. They tried to dance the night away on the patio last night. They're with each other almost 24-7."

"What about Skip and Roxy?" asked Heather.

Steve handled this question. "Detective Nohr wants his officers to keep track of them. Hopefully the two people he sent are the only ones armed on the property."

"I'd feel better if I had my pistol," said Heather.

"What's important is that everyone believes you're carrying it."

Heather understood what he was saying. She was glad the purse she brought had a built-in holster. She'd stuff it with something that would make it look believable. Perhaps a couple pieces of wood cobbled together or the receiver of a spare hotel telephone? She'd give that more consideration later. For now, she needed to hear about Steve and Bella's trip to Nate's hotel. That was the last thing she remembered about the case before Jack arrived.

When they were on a case, it sometimes seemed that she and Steve thought the same thoughts at the same time. Once again, he said what was on her mind. "We need to tell you what Bella and I found out at Nate's hotel. When we arrived, Connie was working alone."

"She's exceptional," said Bella. "There isn't anything about running a hotel that she doesn't know or can't do. She's even hired a part-time person to give her a break in the late morning and early afternoon so she can keep the dive certification program going. That's a big part of why the hotel stays full."

Heather thought out loud. "I guess Detective Nohr can't help much."

Steve spoke as a chunk of sausage fell on his napkin. "Not with a murder investigation going on. But, like Bella said, Connie is one of those people who can do six things at once and make it seem easy."

Bella spoke as if sharing a secret. "If Detective Nohr would open his eyes, he'd see Connie is crazy about him. I think all it would take is a little push and he'd admit he has a thing for her, too."

Heather groaned. "Let's keep this discussion limited to solving a murder and keeping people safe, if you don't mind."

"Good idea," said Steve. "Bella and Connie made quick work

of checking the register for familiar names that stayed there during the past six months."

"What did you find?"

"Roxy came by herself five months ago. She stayed four nights. Connie said she was inquisitive and talkative. She wanted to know all about the hotel and the type of people who stayed there. When Connie told her it was mainly people learning to dive or get re-certified, she turned up her nose."

Bella added, "Roxy doesn't go near the pool or the beach here at the resort. If you ask me, I think she and Skip killed Nate."

"They're high on the suspect list," said Steve. "But until we can put them on this island on the night of Nate's murder, they have alibis."

"Speaking of," said Heather. "Has Detective Nohr made any headway in discovering if they could have come by boat at night from St. Thomas and made it back before dawn?"

Steve wiped his hand on his napkin which caused the piece of sausage to fall on the floor. "He has officers on St. Thomas going to all the charter services. Nothing so far, but that may not mean much. There's no shortage of privately owned boats on the islands. All it takes is money to keep people from talking."

A knock on the door brought everyone's head up, except Steve. "Ah," he said. "There's Detective Nohr."

Bella rose to answer the door while Heather made sure her robe hadn't gapped open. Steve's prophecy of Detective Nohr's arrival was spot on.

The ringing of Mr. McBlythe's phone captured the attention of those gathered once again. He answered and asked, "What's your ETA?"

The answer seemed to please him because his next words were, "Come straight to the resort. I'll meet you in the lobby. You'll have twenty minutes to get settled in your rooms and we'll meet downstairs in a small conference room I've secured. My daughter, Mr. Smiley, and a police detective will be there to discuss assignments."

Heather noted how short and cryptic the phone call was. Her father's success hadn't come by wasting time.

Steve was on his feet. "Unless I miss my guess, Heather needs to dress for the day and develop a plan. I hope everyone had time to finish their breakfast."

25

Heather had mascara ready to apply to the lashes of her left eye when she realized what Steve was doing by giving her extra assignments again. She allowed a quick smile and focused on the reflection of herself in the mirror. She applied the charcoal-colored goo first to the top lash, and then the bottom, talking to herself as she did so. "He's filling my time with responsibilities that will take my mind off Jack." Another thought came to her. "I wonder if Father really received a threatening note or if this is another of their conspiracies? It wouldn't be the first time those two cooked up something they believed was for my good."

She leaned away from the mirror. "Nah. They wouldn't go this far unless there was a genuine threat." She paused. "Or, would they? I'd better look at the note to make sure."

While her mind was in the mood for wandering, she let it roam. "Father is so different since Mother died. The cruises he went on changed him, and for the better. He's much more human than he used to be." She brushed the tangles out of her hair and secured it in a ponytail with a scrunchy. Worry lines creased her forehead. "I still don't trust that personal assistant of his. I wonder what angle she's working? Probably after a cut of his fortune." She paused. "Or she could be a Chinese spy, trying to steal proprietary business secrets."

She blinked three times and laughed out loud. "Or she could be from a distant planet, come to earth to capture Father and take him back as her slave."

It was the first time in what seemed like years she'd allowed her mind to take her to the point of absolute absurdity. She didn't know why, but it felt good to stretch her thoughts until they produced play dough wrapped in Silly String. She went to the dresser and pulled out shorts and a sleeveless top. Her feet found their way into white sandals. "Now that I've had my mental play time, I need to switch gears and come up with a plan to keep people safe. Bella and Adam's wedding must go off with no disruptions. I'll make a list of all the people besides Father who could be in danger and run it by Steve. I'm sure he's already made his list and will let me know who I've missed."

She grabbed her laptop and stuffed it into a black satchel. An arm went through her crossbody purse, which held a few essentials and a stapler in the pouch reserved for her pistol. She walked down the hall with a dozen thoughts about Nate's murder competing for supremacy. She felt ill-prepared, but knew Steve had her back.

The resort included a series of rooms with retractable walls allowing for a ballroom with a decent-sized dance floor. Down the hall were a series of rooms designed for break-out sessions or smaller gatherings. Ingrid met Heather in the hall and pointed her to the last room on the left. The directions by Bella's mother came with soft eyes that communicated unspoken sympathy. Heather nodded her head, turned, and walked to the room with her sandals making soft slapping sounds with every step.

The room reminded her of a hundred other conferences and meetings she'd either attended or led. Rows of padded chairs with metal frames stood like soldiers awaiting their commanding officer to arrive. A coffee service and an assortment of snacks waited on a table against the back wall. Facing the front row of chairs was a whiteboard draped with a sheet.

Steve sat in the first chair in the front row. He lifted his head as soon as she entered. "You couldn't sneak up on a glass of water wearing those sandals."

"I didn't realize this meeting required stealth." She eased into the chair beside him. "Did you set up a murder board?"

"I supervised. Bella, Adam, and Detective Nohr taped photos of suspects, the victims, and your father on the board."

She nodded her approval. "Great idea."

"Take a look and see if I missed anyone."

"I'll wait for the unveiling. I know how you love a big reveal and how people gasp in amazement at your foresight."

If Steve had been drinking, he'd have sprayed the room. Instead, he settled for a low chuckle. "Someone is doing better."

"Marginally better," said Heather. Not wishing to sink into a maudlin puddle, she changed the subject. "When will Detective Nohr be here?"

Steve pointed toward to the door. "He's coming down the hall now. Bella and Adam are with him. I like the way they use tile on so many of the floors in the tropics. It makes it easier for us blind guys to tell who's coming and going. Carpet gives me trouble."

Heather looked down. Unlike in the hallway, commercial carpet softened footsteps in the conference rooms. In his own way, Steve had told her he couldn't fully function without her.

Detective Nohr, Bella, and Adam filed in. Steve was the first to speak. "William, any update on Roxy and Skip?"

The response comprised only two words. "Nothing yet."

More approaching footsteps in the hall brought Steve's chin up. "That's the plainclothes officers."

"Good call," said William. "Mr. McBlythe is safe in his room while my officers attend this briefing."

"How do you know he's safe if your officers are here?" asked Heather.

Steve answered the question. "Zhang Min is with him. Among her other qualities, she's a martial arts expert."

Heather leaned into Steve. "Do you trust her?"

He shrugged. "Your father does. That's good enough for me."

After introductions, the two ebony-skinned police officers availed themselves of coffee and a Danish each. It wasn't long before four additional people, all women, arrived. Everyone shared names and handshakes. The leader of the group was a red-haired fireplug of a woman who looked as if she could out-drink and out-fight most men and all women. Her eyes spoke of worldly wisdom earned the hard way. The other three were a mixed bag ranging in ages from one who could pass for a college sophomore to an empty-nester. The woman sandwiched between the other two in age, looked to be in a perpetual state of bore-dom, like she belonged behind a glass screen at a department of motor vehicle registration office.

Heather believed this was a delicious group of spies. If they were half as observant as they were benign-looking, at least one of them could infiltrate any setting and come back with useful information. All four women availed themselves of coffee and something to eat. They must have had an early wake-up call and missed breakfast.

Detective Nohr took over when everyone took a seat. He flipped the sheet covering the murder board, revealing photos with names underneath. The four women hired by Heather's father reached for phones, zoomed in, and took photos while he spoke. "If you didn't catch it, my name is William Nohr. I'm the detective in charge. This is a photo of our victim, Nate Johnson." He pointed to Nate's photo. "This is personal to me. Nate was my best friend."

William's voice failed him, so Steve took over. "I'm Steve Smiley, former Houston homicide detective."

A voice came from the second row. It belonged to the spunky redhead. "Mr. McBlythe briefed me thoroughly on you and

Heather. On behalf of me and my girls, it's a pleasure to be under your supervision."

"Thank you," said Steve, "but make no mistake who's in charge here. Heather and I report to Detective Nohr. He and his officers have the badges, weapons, and authority to detain and arrest."

Heather noted William had composed himself and was ready to take charge again. He squared his shoulders and said, "The weapon used to kill Nate was a garrote. We haven't retrieved it yet, so keep your eyes open for it." Once again, he pointed to a photo. "In case any of you aren't familiar with a garrote, here's a photo of one. You can see how simple it is, but don't let it fool you. In the right hands, it can kill in seconds."

Heather knew Li Jing had hidden the garrote and wondered again why Steve insisted on keeping that vital piece of information from the police. He was up to something, and she needed to find out why he'd allowed the murder weapon to remain undiscovered.

Detective Nohr interrupted her thoughts. "Suspects," he said as she focused on a row of photos. One at a time the names were announced as William pointed to photos. "This is Li Jing. I arrested her for the murder of Nate Johnson and she's currently out on bond. I'll let Steve tell you what we know about her."

Steve stood and turned to face those in chairs. "She surrendered a Chinese passport but the Chinese Consulate refuses to acknowledge that she's a citizen."

Heather stood and added, "I have friends in the State Department and the CIA. They made inquiries and had their hands slapped."

"What does that mean?" asked the youngest of the women from New York.

Steve took one hand from the top of his cane. "There's a chance Li Jing's a spook."

"A what?" asked the female plain-clothes officer.

Heather answered. "It's most likely Li Jing is a CIA operative or something equivalent in another agency. There's also the possibility she hails from another country."

The spunky redhead let out a low whistle. "These are deeper waters than I'm used to swimming in. If she's a spook, she'd know how to use a garrote."

"True," said Steve, "but it's unlikely she'd use it on a civilian like Nate Johnson. There's nothing about him that shows he was involved in any type of international intrigue."

"Then what's the motive?"

"We're getting to that."

William pointed at his late friend's photo. "Nate was a simple, hard-working guy without an enemy in the world. He owned and operated a small hotel in town that catered to tourists who wanted to learn to dive. He'd recently made a deal with Lonnie and Ingrid Swenson, the owners of this resort, to purchase it. Steve believes Nate's murder is likely tied to people wanting to obtain the Swenson property."

Heather realized how far ahead of her Steve had gone. She needed to catch up.

Steve continued, "We're leaving Li Jing on the board as a suspect, even though I don't believe she killed Nate."

"Has anyone been monitoring her since they released her?" asked the redhead.

Bella stood and pointed to a row of photos of the staff. "These are some of my parents' most trustworthy employees. They're keeping tabs on Li Jing and report to me daily. I relay what I learn to Steve. She's spending most of her time with a man named Juan Tovar. Mornings and afternoons are spent scuba diving at the reef guarding the bay. You can find them at night on the patio dancing."

Detective Nohr pointed to another photo taped to the board. "This is Juan Tovar. His mother, Judith Tovar, is also staying at the resort. You can't miss her because she uses a walker to get around."

Bella added, "She likes to take early morning walks and was with me when I discovered Nate's body in the parking lot."

Steve took a step back. "Before we go on, I want to remind you four ladies from New York why you're here, and it's not to solve a murder. It's to prevent another. Your job is to report anything suspicious to Heather. Bella and her fiancé, Adam Webber, will be married this coming Friday. On the board you'll find a copy of the note Mr. McBlythe received threatening him, and possibly others, if he didn't leave the island. Your job is to make sure no one comes to harm."

Detective Nohr pointed at the note. "Before we go on and talk about other suspects, study the note. Let's refuel with coffee and something to eat. The bathrooms are down the hall."

Heather stood by Steve. "Can I get you a fresh cup of coffee?"

Steve shook his head and whispered, "There's something I need to tell you. Pretend I've asked you to lead me to the restroom door, but we'll keep going."

She led him into the hallway, turned left, and kept walking until they were alone in the banquet room with the door shut behind them. "We're all alone."

Steve rested his hands on the top of his cane. "Someone followed me down the hallway from my room this morning. They put the dull side of a knife to my throat and said if you, me, and your father didn't leave the island, one of us would experience the other edge of the knife."

Her heart skipped a beat. Two of the three men she cared about most in the world were in danger. Her question came without thinking. "Have you told William?"

"Not yet. I'll tell everyone when we get back in the room."

"Darn right you will, and you're not going anywhere by yourself until we put an end to this nonsense."

Steve smiled. "Good to have you back."

"I'm back, all right... and plenty mad."

26

Heather stood at the edge of the murder board as Steve took his place beside her. He waited until all talk ceased before he related his story of having a knife to his throat earlier that morning.

Detective Nohr sprang to his feet. "When did this happen?"

"Seven minutes after six, in the hall outside my room. I was on my way to the dining room by myself. The incident unnerved me, so I went back to my room where I dictated a full statement and emailed it to you."

"Man or woman?" asked William.

"A man who knew what he was doing. He grabbed a handful of hair and pulled my head back to expose my throat. He spoke in a harsh whisper to disguise his voice. I smelled the same soap that's provided by the hotel, so it's likely he's a guest."

"I haven't checked my email this morning," said William in a harsh voice.

Heather made no attempt at keeping her feelings in check. "I hope each of you realizes what this means. To begin with, you're looking at a furious woman who refuses to be pushed around. I'm taking these threats to my father and Steve seriously, and if you're not, then you're in the wrong place. No one is to come to harm. We're counting on each of you not to let the beauty of this setting lull you into complacency." She allowed the words to sink in for a few ticks of the clock. "My father, Steve, Bella, and Adam are to be within constant visual contact anytime they're outside their rooms. I'll be with Steve. Be close enough to neutralize any attempt at physical harm."

Steve added, "The weapons used to kill and threaten are a garrote, some sort of stick or club, and a knife. This leads me to believe firearms are not the weapons of choice. I believe we're up against people who prefer to use more silent methods."

"Professionals," said Heather.

Steve nodded. "That's my opinion."

The redhead spoke up. "We each brought a canister of pepper spray, but that's all."

"That should be enough," said Heather. "I also noticed you ladies are each carrying a crossbody bag like mine. If I'm not mistaken, they're designed to carry a pistol."

Four heads nodded.

"If we're dealing with a professional, they'll recognize your purses for what they are and will believe you're packing. Put something in your purse to give the illusion of a weapon."

Detective Nohr added, "Don't anyone leave here without exchanging phone numbers. I'll see if I can get more personnel, but don't count on it."

Steve spoke next. "Now that we're in the right frame of mind, let's look at the remaining people we've identified as suspects in Nate's murder."

Heather led Steve away from the murder board, and Detective Nohr took over again. "These two will interest you ladies from New York. They go by the names Skip and Roxy Smith."

The leader of the New York contingent of private detectives spoke up. "I did the background on them and briefed my girls. Those names are aliases. In reality, they have rap sheets that reach from here to North Jersey. Skip is the muscle and Roxy the brains."

Steve added, "For some reason they've stayed several times over the last months at Nate's hotel. Now, they're staying here. According to Bella and her staff, they spend most of their days and nights in their room swilling gin. It's like they're biding their time, waiting for something to happen."

William took his turn. "They have an alibi for Nate's murder. Hotel records show them on St. Thomas at the time of Nate's murder. We're trying to find out if they paid someone to ferry them to the resort to do the deed and take them back before dawn."

Steve added, "The garrote isn't Skip's M.O., but violence is. He's big, and strong. Both he and Roxy have holes in their consciences like a goat-wire fence. Be careful around those two. They're up to something."

Detective Nohr picked up where Steve left off. "That brings us to the last two. We included them because they have something to gain from Nate's death. The first is Connie, who was Nate's number one employee at his hotel. He left the hotel to me in his will, but Connie gets all the money he saved to make the down payment on this resort. It's a considerable sum."

The redhead asked, "Did you or Connie know what was in his will?"

"I didn't and I don't believe Connie did either. I was with her when we learned. You could have picked both of us up off the floor."

Steve interrupted. "I added Connie to the list because I believe there's a connection between Nate's hotel and the resort. It's possible she knew about the will, which would give her motive." He took a deep breath. "Before you ask, she was on-duty at Nate's Hotel at the time of the murder."

"Finally," said Detective Nohr, "there's a man Heather and her father know fairly well, Jim McCloud."

Heather took this as a cue for her to speak. "Jim comes from big money but has fallen upon hard times because of poor investments. When I say hard times, that's relative. We believe he still has enough to purchase this resort, but claims he's not willing to chance that big of an investment. He may be more interested in Nate's hotel."

Steve said, "Like Connie, Jim is a long shot for killing Nate, but it could make sense because he's looking for bargains in investments. Keep this in mind: each of the suspects has plenty of money to hire someone to kill Nate."

The leader of the women from New York spoke up. "Heather, is your father interested in purchasing this resort or Nate's hotel?"

"He wasn't, but now that someone's threatening him, he may change his mind. I haven't discussed it with him, but I can almost guarantee he's running the numbers today."

"What about you?"

"I haven't given it serious consideration and don't plan to. I'd hate to get into a bidding war with Father, and I have enough to keep me busy with keeping people safe."

Detective Nohr brought the meeting to a close. "This will be the only time we'll meet together. Everyone but Heather and Steve will leave the room separately."

Heather gave her head another firm nod. "From now until we have this case wrapped up, you won't see Steve without me at his side. Send text messages and emails at least twice daily with updates on suspicious activity. Call if it's urgent." Heather turned to face the leader of the women from New York. "You don't need me to tell you how to deploy your women. We're counting on you to observe, report, and protect."

Steve had one more thing to say. "Heather and I plan on inviting Skip and Roxy to dinner. One of you needs to be nearby. We're going to push some buttons and see what happens."

Heather didn't know exactly what he meant, but she nodded in agreement. It was time to quit playing defense and do a little pushing of their own.

As the last of the women from New York and the two plain-clothes officers cleared the room, Heather helped William take down photos while Steve sat in the front row of chairs. He tapped the tip of his cane on the carpet, making soft thudding sounds.

"Do you think your plan to get Skip and Roxy out of their room will work?" asked William.

Steve gave his head a single nod. "They both grew up poor on the streets. Extreme poverty has a way of making people susceptible to altering their routines to get something for free. I spoke to Lonnie and Ingrid yesterday. They're delivering the good news that the Smiths have won first place in a resort giveaway. They're to receive a free meal in the dining room that includes drinks. Also, they've won three days taken off their bill. What they won't tell them is that Heather and I are the second and third place winners and will dine with them."

"Steve's right," said Heather, as she turned to look at William. "You don't know this about me, but my father cut off my money when I graduated from Princeton and refused to join him in the family business. I wanted to become a cop and spent the next ten years living on a cop's salary in Boston, paying my way through law school, and eating Ramen noodles. It wasn't until I turned thirty that my grandparents' trust fund kicked in. Believe me, I would have jumped at free food and I'm just now to where I don't look at the price on the menu before I make a selection."

"Heather lives in a two-bedroom condo right next to mine, even though she could buy the entire complex," said Steve.

"And I would if I thought it was a prudent investment. The point is," said Heather, "I can assure you Steve is reading Skip and Roxy correctly."

"Will the dinner with Skip and Roxy take place tonight?"

Steve stood. "Tomorrow night. I thought we'd give the new troops a day to get acquainted with the resort."

27

Heather and Steve waited in Lonnie and Ingrid's office until Ingrid returned from the dining room. Skip and Roxy had indeed come to dinner and were overjoyed with the basket of Swiss chocolates, cheeses, crackers, and especially the three bottles of gin—one for each day taken off their bill. Ingrid issued the grin of a conspirator and said, "I told the bartender to ply them with stiff drinks. Roxy stopped at two, but Skip's on his third round. Judging from his speech, he spent the afternoon getting a head start."

Steve stood. "We'd better get to them before he's too far gone."

Lonnie walked with Heather while Ingrid led Steve out of the office, down the hallway, and into the dining room. They arrived at the table set for four and Ingrid helped Steve into his chair while Heather waited for Lonnie to pull out hers.

"Hey," said Skip. "What's with da company?" He refocused. "Oh, it's my buddy. Who's da dame?"

Ingrid flashed a wide smile. "Mr. and Mrs. Smith, this is Mr. Steve Smiley and Ms. Heather McBlythe, the second and third place winners of our drawing."

Steve quickly added, "I get a free meal and two days off my bill."

Heather followed with, "I finished third and get a meal and one night's stay. Isn't that great?"

Roxy looked at her through hooded eyelids. "You look like you don't need anyone to give you anything,"

Heather cackled a laugh. "How delightful! I was hoping I'd have interesting people to share the evening with." She turned to Ingrid. "Am I correct that the meal includes drinks?"

"Absolutely. Drain the bar if you wish."

"Oh, good," said Heather. "I was hoping Steve and I wouldn't be stuck with a couple of deadbeats. This will be a wonderful evening of getting to know two interesting people."

Steve chimed in. "Bring me whatever the Smiths are having. I'm dry as Death Valley."

Roxy shifted a suspicious gaze from Heather to Steve and back to Heather. "I take it you two know each other?"

Steve answered. "I've known Heather for years. What a surprise to learn they chose our names to win second and third place."

The server arrived with drinks. It was pre-arranged that Skip and Roxy continued to receive doubles while Heather and Steve received tonic water with a sprig of mint. Heather raised her glass. "To new friends." Both she and Steve drained half their glass while Skip followed their lead. Roxy's glass remained on the table.

Heather noticed Roxy looked around the room and even glanced over her shoulder at the door. She needed to act fast before the woman bolted. "Let's not stand on formality. Steve told me your first names are Roxy and Skip. Is that correct?"

A short nod from Roxy answered her question.

"I can tell by your accent you're from Jersey."

"Yeah," said Skip. "You sound like you come from Bean Town and he sounds like he comes from a place where people wear boots and big hats."

Heather reached out and patted Skip on the forearm. "Well done. I was born in Boston and more or less lived there until I was almost thirty."

Steve took his turn. "You nailed me, except I quit wearing boots when I lost my sight."

"How'd you lose it?"

"A guy high on drugs took a club to the back of my head. He then killed my wife." Steve drained his glass and Heather followed suit.

"Tough break," said Skip. His voice held no hint of compassion.

Heather took her turn. "I'm surprised you two don't already know about me and Steve."

"Why should we?" asked Roxy.

Their server appeared with fresh drinks for four. Once Heather had taken the top inch off hers, she answered Roxy's question. "I wouldn't say Steve and I are famous, but we know tons of influential people." Heather added, "I was a police detective in Boston. Now I'm an attorney and a rather successful entrepreneur."

Steve said, "She's being modest. She and her father are rich as lords and they have friends in every branch of the government. She's also one heck of a private detective. I should know, she's my partner."

"Enough about us," said Heather. "Let's order. I'm blowing my diet and getting the prime rib with prawns. What about you, Steve?"

"I can't decide if I want one lobster or two."

Heather raised her hand. A server was at her side before she could look around. She placed their orders and waited as Skip and Roxy followed with orders of steak and lobster.

Steve tucked his napkin into the top of his shirt and allowed it to flare out, covering his midsection. "Tell me, Skip, what kind of work do you do?"

He spoke before Roxy could stop him. "Collections."

"Ah," said Steve. "I understand that can be quite lucrative."

"It ain't bad."

Roxy took over. "Before you ask, Mr. Smiley, I'm retired."

"That's my goal," said Steve. "I'm getting too old to keep doing what I'm doing. The only reason I help the police solve murders is because Heather needs a break from the corporate grind."

Heather leaned forward. "Don't let him lie to you like that. He's a devil to live next door to when he doesn't have a murder to solve. In fact, we're making good progress on the murder of the man in the parking lot."

Roxy squirmed in her seat while Skip took a large swig from his glass.

Their salads arrived and the four took a break from conversation. After a minute or two of quiet, Heather looked at Roxy. "I guess you know there's going to be a big wedding here on Friday?"

"Oh?"

"That's right," said Heather with an exaggerated nod. "Bella and Adam, the resort owners' daughter and her fiancé. They're to be married on the beach in front of the resort. The ceremony will take place at sunset."

"That's sweet."

"I'm surprised you didn't know. It's the worst kept secret at the resort."

No answer came forth. Steve allowed conversation to die until he had his fill of salad. He asked Heather, "Did I drop much salad on my napkin or the table?"

"Not this time," said Heather.

"That's a relief," said Steve. "I hate to make messes and not realize it." He allowed a dramatic pause. "Speaking of not realizing things." He turned his head to face Skip. "Did you hear about the threats?"

"What threats?" asked Roxy.

"There've been threats against some of the wedding party."

He allowed a dramatic pause. "Nothing to worry about. Heather's father has it covered."

"How?" asked Skip, before a burp escaped his open lips.

Steve ignored the faux pas. "Look around. Fully half the people in this room are bodyguards, private detectives, or plain-clothes police."

Heather looked around. "I'd say more than half, and even more will come as soon as rooms open. That last attack on a guest was a dumb thing to do. Bodyguards of every shape, size, and gender are here with more waiting to come."

At that moment, Steve knocked over his empty glass. Roxy let out a squeal.

"So sorry," said Steve. "It must be the gin. My mouth is running like a broken faucet and I'm clumsy as a blind man trying to thread a needle." He paused. "Wait. I am a blind man."

Heather and Steve shared loud, inappropriate laughs. She followed by saying, "It's a good thing all that spilled was ice. No harm, no foul."

Steve wasted no time in responding. "Speaking of harm, I have a story for you two. A man with a knife threatened me this morning. He came up behind me in the hall outside my room, grabbed me by the hair of my head, and jerked it back. I felt the cold steel of a knife blade on my throat."

Roxy lowered her gaze to the table while Skip smiled and said, "I bet dat scared ya."

Steve flicked his wrist like a fly had landed on his hand. "Naw, I knew he was bluffing. I quit being afraid of death and cheap thugs after one killed my wife. Think about it. What kind of loser picks on a guy who can't fight back?"

Heather held up an index finger and thumb against her forehead to form the letter L. "A complete loser. The guy ensured the resort is crawling with people with guns. I've never seen so many women carrying crossbody bags like mine."

"Did you bring that cute little nine-millimeter with the pink handle?"

"I don't leave home without it. It's easy when you bring your own airplane. No hassle from airport security." Heather followed up with another question for Steve. "How did you describe the guy who attacked you?"

"Strong hands and a rough voice, like he came from one of the big cities on the east coast. He smelled like gin and hotel soap."

Servers arrived with their meals. Roxy rose from her seat. "Skip, get up. I have a headache. We're leaving."

"Please don't go," pleaded Heather. "I thought we could make a night of it."

"What 'bout supper?" asked Skip.

"We'll have it delivered to our room."

Steve fired a last salvo. "Heather hired someone to taste our food, but she always errs on the side of caution. Enjoy your steak and lobster."

Skip grudgingly rose to his feet then wobbled. Roxy was already walking away. He had to hurry to catch up with her.

"That went well," said Heather.

A sly smile lifted the corners of his mouth. "Are all four of the New York women waiting to pass Skip and Roxy on their way back to their rooms?"

"Only two, with one more making noise in the bushes outside their fourplex."

"Let's see what happens next," said Steve.

"Do you really think they'll try something?"

Steve asked, "Do you remember watching old cowboy movies where the bad guys set fire to the settler's cabin, trying to smoke out the good guys?"

"Not really, but I get the idea. Do you think we used enough smoke?"

"We'll find out in the next day or two."

28

Heather called Steve and let him know she'd come to his room in five minutes. They'd go to the dining room for a late breakfast. The generous slab of prime rib and grilled prawns of the previous night meant she'd eat fruit and yogurt this morning.

With handbag draped across her chest, she checked her phone for missed calls or texts from Jack. None existed, so she stepped into the hallway. The youngest of the four women from New York looked up from a sitting position. She'd stationed herself in a chair in the hallway with a view of Heather's room, her father's, Steve's, and Zhang Min's.

"Long night?" asked Heather.

The leggy woman raised her shoulders and let them drop. "Not bad. One of the other girls and I traded shifts. Two of the ladies that came with me kept an eye on Bella's room while the last one roamed the grounds near Adam's bungalow. I don't know about the others, but I have nothing to report."

"That's the way we hope things stay," said Heather.

"I heard how you and Mr. Smiley put a good scare into those two from the wrong side of the Hudson. Sweet move."

"Thanks. Steve and I are going to breakfast. My father and

his personal assistant will join us, in a little while. Steve said he wanted to find a lounge chair and sit under a palm tree most of the morning. I'll be with him all the time and we'll be in plain sight."

"We're all used to getting by on four hours' sleep. I'll follow your father to the dining room and sit close, but out of the way."

Heather retrieved Steve and they made their way downstairs. Jim McCloud's waving hand beckoned them to join him as soon as they arrived at the hostess station. It was a disappointment to see Jim waiting for them, but she tried not to let it show. Of all the people on their list of suspects, she wanted to take his name off but couldn't.

"What's wrong?" asked Steve.

"Jim McCloud wants us to join him."

"Put on your game face."

Heather dredged up a fake smile and waved at Jim to signal they'd join him. She whispered, "I do hope we haven't smoked out a rat from Princeton."

After getting Steve settled in his chair, she turned her attention to Jim. "As late as it is, I thought you'd have finished breakfast by now." She took a good look and realized he'd not shaved in the last two or three days. His hair looked like he needed to change the oil.

"I took your advice to lead a life of leisure for a while. I'm sure you know what they say about working your fingers to the bone."

Steve finished the thought. "You get bony fingers."

It was a horrible cliche, but all three issued what sounded like genuine laughs.

The server came with a carafe of coffee. Heather answered an unasked question with a nod and the young woman turned over two cups and filled them with black stimulant.

Steve lowered his head and sniffed. "One of the biggest joys in life is the smell of freshly brewed coffee at a quality restaurant." He lowered his head even more and inhaled like his cup was a vaporizer. "Ahh. What a perfect way to start the day."

Heather asked, "Have you been here long, Jim?"

"Long enough to have breakfast."

It was a vague answer and made her wonder if he'd been waiting for them to arrive since the restaurant opened hours ago. She was on the verge of seeking clarification when Steve spoke. "Jim, when I was a cop, I used to go to restaurants, a mall, or a park and sit for hours watching people. I found it fascinating and learned much about human behavior. Once you get the feel of a place, you can tell when a particular person or group of people don't fit in. Do you know what I mean?"

"Yeah! That's exactly what I've done this morning. I got here shortly after they opened and I've been studying people."

"What have you noticed?"

"This may sound weird, but there's a high percentage of women carrying crossbody purses."

"Like this one?" asked Heather.

"Uh-huh. I didn't pay attention to it yesterday, but now that I've become aware, I can't help but notice them."

Heather didn't tell him that travel agents often recommend this style purse for tourists. Both hands remained free and the chances of robbery or theft from pickpockets are reduced. Instead, she put her purse on the table. "Do you see this gap in the back?"

Jim leaned down and gazed at her purse.

"This is a built-in holster." She pulled back the flap for only a fraction of a second and revealed a glimpse of black metal.

He sat up straight. "You have a pistol in there?"

"I'll give you three reasons for me wanting to carry a weapon: First, I'm an ex-cop. There are more than a few people I've sent to prison." She held up another finger. "I'm a single woman who happens to be very wealthy. That makes me a double target." She stuck out her thumb to join her index and middle fingers.

"Finally, I'm now a private investigator. Steve and I are still making enemies."

Steve added, "The fourth reason is that she's my bodyguard."

"That makes sense for you," said Jim. He looked around the near-empty room. "I wonder how many of the women I've noticed this morning are carrying pistols?"

Steve answered for her. "That's the beauty of concealed carry. The bad guys don't know who's packing and who isn't. You should see the other holsters they make. Whenever you see a man or woman with their shirttail out, you never know what's in their waistband."

Heather added, "They fit so snug against the body, even trained officers can't tell."

Jim's Adam's apple bobbed up and back down as he swallowed.

The server returned and took orders. Steve behaved himself and ordered a bowl of bran cereal. Heather changed her mind. She'd wait for lunch before breaking her fast. Instead, she remained focused on Jim and changed the subject. "Find any promising leads on investments since we last talked?"

He lowered his gaze and shook his head. "I appreciate what Adam does for a living, but staring at a computer screen all day isn't really my thing. I read people better than charts." He shifted in his chair. "I'm trying to get information about Nate's hotel, but they haven't probated the will. The attorney refuses to give information on who the new owner is."

Steve didn't hesitate. "We can answer that. Detective William Nohr will be the new owner."

Jim's eyes widened. "A police detective? What does he know about running a hotel?"

Both Steve and Heather shrugged to show they didn't know. Heather added, "You and I would be lousy at running a hotel, so we'd hire someone. All Detective Nohr has to do is find the right person to manage it. I understand it's booked solid in the peak months and doesn't slack up much in the windy months or shoulder seasons."

"Do you think this cop would be open to discuss selling it?"

Jim made the mistake of not paying attention to who was coming toward their table. Heather answered his question by saying, "Here's my father. Let's ask him if he thinks Detective Nohr might be interested in selling."

Before Jim could object, her father and Zhang Min were at the table. "Do you mind if we join you?"

"Of course not," said Steve. He gave his nose a quick sniff. "Zhang Min, you're so light on your feet the only way I can tell you're nearby is by that intoxicating scent you wear. What is it?"

"*Spring Bouquet.* Lotus blossom is one of the scents."

"It's so subtle and mesmerizing."

"Thank you, Mr. Smiley. I use it sparingly."

The server came and wrestled two more chairs to fit around a table designed to seat four. Her father told the young woman he'd like coffee and Zhang Min ordered green tea.

Heather wasted no time in getting down to business. "Father, Jim was wondering if you thought Detective Nohr might be interested in selling the hotel he's going to inherit."

Her father fixed his gaze on Jim, who seemed to droop like the petals on a flower left in a hot car.

"I, uh, it's only idle speculation, Mr. McBlythe."

"Nonsense. Some of the most lucrative deals I ever made started with questions that were nothing more than daydreams. Allowing the creative juices to flow and obtaining as much information as you can are prerequisites for any successful investor. I haven't discussed it with Detective Nohr, but I can see where a hotel like Nate's might appeal to you. Of course, that bright detective might not want to sell. With the proper manager, he could supplement his salary and have a built-in retirement plan."

"It seems you've done your homework concerning Nate's hotel."

Her father held up the palm of his right hand and waved it

back and forth. "Nate's hotel is small potatoes. The real jewel is this resort. So much more could be done with this protected cove."

"You sound interested."

"They're both moneymakers and turnkey ready. If I were interested, I'd want both."

Zhang Min added, "I should have the proposal ready for you to review by tomorrow morning."

Her father nodded his approval.

Zhang Min took her crossbody bag off and placed it at her feet. Jim stared at her. Heather smiled at the woman sitting across the table. "Nice purse. I have one that's very similar."

Heather caught Jim's reaction out of the corner of her eye when Zhang Min said, "Better safe than sorry."

Jim rose. "I hear the pool calling my name. If you'll excuse me, there's serious loafing to get to."

Mr. McBlythe shook his head. "You can't fool me, Jim. You wouldn't be here if you weren't sniffing around for a bargain."

"I was, but my feet are feeling very cold. Sometimes the juice isn't worth the squeeze."

Heather turned to her father after Jim made it to the door. "Great job to both of you."

Her father cast his gaze to Steve and his voice lowered to a serious tone. "It grieves me to think Jim McCloud is involved."

"Did you do a deeper dive into his financials?"

Zhang Min responded. "His losses are more considerable than we thought. He invested heavily in the wrong crypto currency. It's still only an educated guess how much of the family fortune he has left. I show around five percent."

Heather's heart sunk. "No wonder he hasn't shaved or bathed. He's getting a head start on being homeless."

Steve rubbed his freshly-shaved chin. "Perhaps not. Let's hold off on suggesting food stamps for him."

Heather puffed out her cheeks. "They don't use food stamps in prison."

The redheaded private investigator took short, quick steps to where they sat. She stood behind Steve and gave her report to the gathering. "All clear last night, Mr. McBlythe."

"Good, but tell it to Heather. She's in charge of security."

"Yes, sir." She shifted her gaze to Heather. "Skip and Roxy Smith stayed in their rooms last night and haven't made a move yet today."

Heather nodded. "What about Juan Tovar and Li Jing?"

"Another day of diving at the same reef. Morning and afternoon sessions booked again."

"Did they stay on the patio last night?"

"No change in pattern."

"Interesting," said Steve under his breath.

Heather told her the highlights of their meeting with Jim McCloud. Steve added, "Don't crowd him, but let Heather know if he tries to leave the resort."

"Why would he do that?" asked Heather.

"He probably won't. Then again, he said he's getting cold feet. That may mean he's contemplating a quick flight off the island, or perhaps he was trying to make your father think he wasn't interested in Nate's hotel."

Zhang Min spoke next. "It's for sure he doesn't have money enough to consider buying this resort, but he still has enough to purchase Nate's."

Heather's father raised a hand. "Everyone needs to know that Zhang Min and I are hopping over to Puerto Rico this morning. I have a meeting there this afternoon. We'll be back before dark."

The redhead lifted her chin. "I'll go with you."

"That's not necessary. Zang Min is more than capable of seeing I come to no harm."

Heather sensed the feisty New York woman wouldn't shirk the responsibility of protecting her father. She also knew her father was fiercely independent. She needed to find a compromise. Without over-thinking it, she said, "Father's pilots are sworn to absolute secrecy, so I'm not concerned for his safety once his plane is in the air. The only place on this island that concerns me is the road to the airport. I'll tell Lonnie or Ingrid that we need to borrow one of the hotel shuttle vans for Father and Zhang Min. You drive, and take one of your women for good measure."

The stubby woman pursed her lips and gave a firm nod. "That works."

Heather looked at Zhang Min, who gave the slightest of nods.

"Thank you, Heather," said her father. "I can't remember a time in my life when two women fought over me. I sort of like it."

Heather and Steve stayed at the table as the three others exited the room. Steve finished his coffee in silence, then stood to leave, but didn't take a single step before she announced, "William and Connie are coming to us."

Once they'd closed the distance, Detective Nohr said, "We need to talk."

29

Heather took a long look at William and Connie. It occurred to her how right they were as a couple, but how much they fought the magnetism that pulled them together. Their sideways glances locked and then broke with amusing effort. It was the same strange courting ritual she'd played with Jack until she finally succumbed to her feelings. Air eked out of her throat causing a soft whimper. New, confusing emotions had formed battle lines in her soul.

Thoughts of William and Connie took flight, replaced by a mental image of Jack. Why did she have to think about him? If only he didn't insist on invading her mind and disrupting her ability to concentrate on the case. Additional thoughts came to her like the wind of an approaching hurricane—irresistible and unrelenting. She wondered what his daughter was like. Pretty or plain? Smart or slow? Self-absorbed or generous and full of grace? How was Jack adjusting to being a father? Was there any chance their relationship could continue sometime in the vast expanse of the future?

Steve's words went to William and Connie and brought her back from the mental trip that reached over a thousand miles to the west. "You two wouldn't be here if you didn't have something important to tell us."

The server's arrival at the table delayed the response. They both declined anything to eat or drink. Connie was the first to speak but only after William gave her a nod. "I found something among Nate's personal papers when I cleaned out his room."

William pulled an evidence bag from a folder he'd carried in. "There're two things. The first is a letter Nate left for me. He told me he had a premonition that something would happen to him. He wasn't sure if I wanted to own the hotel or not and wanted to make sure I understood that I could sell it."

Connie took over. "Show them the document I found."

A second, thicker document lay in front of Heather in a plastic evidence bag. William explained. "It's a tentative contract for the sale of the hotel to Jim McCloud. All the details are worked out and it's an all-cash sale."

Heather asked, "Can I take a look at it? I have gloves in my purse."

"Please do," said William. "Don't forget to sign the chain of custody on the front. I'll sign it and reseal it after you're finished."

Heather took her time reading the document and then announced. "Everything's in order if you decide to execute the sale after probate. Like you said, it's an all-cash sale that transfers ownership to Jim."

Connie asked, "Is the hotel really worth that much?"

Steve answered, "It's worth whatever someone is willing to pay for it."

Heather added, "From my father's research, this is more than he thought it should be, but not too much more. I'd say it's on the high end of fair market value."

"That's interesting," said Steve. "From what we know of Jim McCloud, he's a bargain-hunting kind of guy. It's possible he's using someone else's money."

William's eyebrows pushed together. "Who would that be?"

Heather leaned forward, "I'm leaning toward the theory that Jim's using his own money. Here's why. He's no stranger to making deals. Just because this agreement states a sale price, it doesn't mean that he won't come back and make a lower offer for the hotel. There's nothing in the contract that makes it binding if both parties agree to lower the price. It happens all the time in this type of transaction."

"Ah," said Connie. "Now it makes sense. Get William used to the idea of a quick, easy sale and then go for a bargain."

William leaned back, "I thought this was too good to be true. He's counting on me not being used to negotiating a deal of this size."

Heather noticed Steve had not responded to her theory and wondered what angle she'd missed. She recognized his silence as him fitting the new information into a bigger picture, one that she couldn't see.

Heather slipped the contract back into the plastic sleeve and handed it to William. "Thanks for bringing that to us."

William placed the documents back into a folder and volunteered an additional comment. "There's nothing new on us finding a boat Skip and Roxy could have used to come from St. Thomas on the night Nate was killed."

Steve gave his head a nod, but didn't add anything to the conversation. Had he slipped into his contemplative phase of solving a case? Perhaps, but if he had, it meant he was getting close to untangling a web. All she could see were loose ends poking out in various directions. Perhaps she needed a couple of hours under a palm tree.

William and Connie rose from their seats as if telepathy gave them instructions to do so. He rushed to pull out her chair and she gave him a coy smile for his effort. Connie longingly scanned the room, allowing her gaze to drift out the windows that overlooked the patio bar, pools, and the bay. "Such an amazing place," she whispered. "It's paradise."

"That it is," said William. He turned to Steve. "Keep us

posted if you obtain any new information that might help us. Patience from my supervisors in St. Thomas is running short."

Steve answered with something between a huff and a grunt. Heather put words to her opinion of distant supervisors applying pressure. "We're making steady progress. Inform them of what Connie found and that should buy you a few more days."

Steve broke his silence. "They'll stay awake at night trying to figure out what that contract means. They'll be wrong."

William and Connie both raised their eyebrows. Heather headed off their question by saying. "That's Steve's way of saying he needs to spend some time listening to the waves come to shore." She beamed a smile. "They bring messages from mermaids that help him solve murders."

Laughter came from Connie. She looked up at William and winked. "That's your problem. You're not listening to mermaids. Who knew solving a crime was so easy?"

"Don't underestimate what can happen when you allow yourself to listen to the sea," said Steve. "You and William should try it."

Connie gave him a serious look, then shifted her gaze to William. "What do you think about that?"

He seemed to be summoning up courage to respond before saying, "I'm willing to try if you are."

"Could we come back this evening? The hotel will be covered by the new desk clerk I hired."

"I'd like that very much."

William looked at his watch and the mini-spell broke. He nodded to Heather and escorted Connie from the room. They were soon out of sight, walking with quick steps into their busy lives.

Steve was on his feet and Heather placed his arm on hers to lead him outside. "Let's find a couple of lounge chairs away from everyone. You look like you're in the mood to do some serious thinking."

He agreed. "Lead on. I'll take my sandals off and walk in the sand until we get to a quiet spot. Make sure I'm in the shade. Me and the sun aren't as good of friends as we used to be."

They stepped onto the patio, went down some steps, and past the bar. They skirted a splash pad and shallow pool alive with squealing children and proceeded toward the full-size pool. Unlike many resort pools with curved sides made to resemble a lagoon, this one was a traditional rectangle with black lines painted on the bottom to guide swimmer's laps.

As they approached the largest pool, Heather pulled Steve closer to her and whispered. "Judith Tovar is swimming laps. Do you want to talk to her?"

He nodded. "Let's see what she thinks of her stepson spending so much time with Li Jing."

30

Heather directed their footsteps to the shallow end. She watched as Judith plowed her way toward the opposite end of the pool. Her walker sat several yards away from the steps leading into the water. "I'm surprised. Judith has arms and shoulders that I'd expect on a college-age swimmer. She's not able to kick much, but she swims at a fast clip."

Steve whispered back, "The human body is a remarkable machine. Weakness in one area leads to strengths in others. Any idea what's wrong with her legs?"

"She said something about a spinal cord injury. Do you think it's important?"

"Probably not. Let's focus on Juan and Li Jing."

Heather shielded her eyes from the morning sun and cast her gaze to the far side of the bay where waves broke over the coral reef. "The dive boat is just past the breakers again. Today it's about forty yards north from where they dove yesterday afternoon."

Steve grunted in a way that told her he wasn't going to say anything more. It wasn't long before Judith pulled up at the shallow end, breathing heavily. She raised swimmer's goggles to the top of her head and wiped her face with both hands. Between labored breaths she said, "Well, hello."

"Hello," said Steve in return. "How's the water?"

"Delicious. You should change and swim a few laps."

"I tried it a couple of times. I veer off course and run into walls and other swimmers. Treadmills and stationary bicycles are more my style. I also like walks, but they need to be on trails I'm familiar with."

She gave him a head-to-toe inspection. "You look to be in good shape. You must work out regularly."

"Not as much as I should." He gave a nod to his right. "Heather's the one with the personal trainer."

"It shows. Oh, to be young and fully mobile again." She let out a sigh and added, "Let me get out and dry off. We'll sit and have a proper chat."

With that, Judith half-walked, half-swam to the steps. She reached out her right hand, pulled on a chrome rail, and took stiff-legged steps out of the water. Once out, she walked with short, choppy steps to her walker and grabbed her towel. She dried a little and wrapped the towel around a surprisingly trim midsection. Heather could see in her imagination the figure she must have had before her legs atrophied and her shoulders widened with newfound muscles.

Judith led the way to a cluster of chairs where she motioned for Heather and Steve to join her. Heather formed the chairs into a triangle and settled Steve into his before she lowered herself. She made a point to look relaxed with one leg draped lazily over the other. It wasn't long before Judith asked, "Have you heard anything new about who killed that poor man in the parking lot?"

Steve answered, "We spoke with the detective in charge of the case a few minutes ago. It doesn't seem like he's making much progress, but we're not privy to everything he knows."

Heather added, "There's a general mistrust between the police and private investigators."

"Not to mention that Heather's an attorney."

"Such a shame," said Judith. "I'm so glad Juan wasn't on the island when that man was killed. You know how the cops in the US or their territories always think the worst of men Juan's age who have a Colombian passport. They automatically assume they're involved in some sort of drug activity."

"Silly, isn't it," said Steve. "When I was a homicide detective, I made it a point to allow the evidence to lead me instead of trying to cram square pegs into round holes."

Heather pointed to the diving boat in the distance. "Are Juan and Li Jing diving at the reef again this morning?"

Judith gave a clipped nod. "I think my stepson is part dolphin. He's had an ongoing love affair with the sea since he was a child."

Steve's voice took on a note of concern. "Aren't you worried about him spending so much time with a woman who's awaiting trial for murder?"

It was a tough question that should have elicited a bigger reaction from Judith. Instead, she laughed and said, "You'd have to know Juan to realize his interest in any woman is short-lived. It's a trait passed down from his philandering father, God rest his soul. Besides, he's leaving the island at the end of the week."

"Do you plan on staying?" asked Steve.

"Can you think of a better place to spend the summer? The only thing that can drive me off this island is a hurricane."

Steve took in a full breath through his nose. "Smell that sea air. I believe I'm getting addicted to it."

Judith shifted in her chair. "Tell me, Ms. McBlythe—"

"Please, Judith, call me Heather. I dropped all formalities when the door to my airplane opened after landing."

"Of course, Heather. I was wondering if you, Steve, and your father would like to join me for dinner tonight?"

"I'm afraid my father flew to Puerto Rico for some sort of business meeting and I have no idea when he'll be back. If it runs late, he may not return until tomorrow."

Steve chimed in. "Heather and I are free. Why don't we ask Juan and Li Jing to join us? I'd love to hear about their dives at the reef."

Judith hesitated, but not for long. "That would be fun. I'd like to get to know Li Jing better even though I know Juan will end up breaking her heart."

Steve stood, which was Heather's cue to take him to a quiet place. Salutations were exchanged and a late dinner scheduled. Judith stood by pulling up on the walker and ambled toward the hotel.

"Go ahead and take off your sandals," said Heather. "Past the pool is the boardwalk. We'll be on it until we reach the beach." Steve complied and they walked on concrete, then smooth boards. They reached the sand and traveled to a spot where only distant squeals from children and the waves coming to shore were heard. Heather watched as Steve's cane made contact with a lounge chair.

"Can anyone hear us?" he asked.

"Not unless we scream."

"Good. Tell me what you observed about Judith."

"Nothing physically to indicate anything but a spinal injury. The vertical scar indicates she might have a metal rod in her back. Otherwise, I found it odd that she accepted her stepson's love-'em-and-leave-'em attitude toward women. Too cavalier for my liking."

He took in another long sniff of sea air. "We need more information on Juan. Call your buddies in the government and tell them they still owe you a favor. Since Li Jing is off limits, let's see if we have better luck with her new boyfriend."

Heather slipped her phone out of the pocket of her shorts and placed a call to her friend at the FBI. The conversation with her former college classmate, who was now a mid-level supervisor with the FBI, lasted fewer than six minutes. As usual, they'd buried him in paperwork, but he pounded on the keys of his computer long enough to discover that Juan Tovar was a person of interest. A scheduled meeting prohibited him from doing a deeper dive into Juan's history. He committed to provide more information later that afternoon. She slipped her phone into her bag, and cast her gaze to Steve who looked the picture of contentment on the lounge chair with the sea breeze ruffling his brown hair.

"Success?" asked Steve.

A feeling of partial satisfaction swept over her as she adjusted the back of the lounger to a gentler angle. "He looked deep enough to tell me the feds are interested in him."

"What about his stepmother?"

"He didn't mention her."

"Ah," was Steve's one-word response that only meant he'd taken in and filed the tidbit of information.

It was common for Steve to become a recluse when he was tying together the details of a case. She'd learned over the years not to press him during these times. He'd start the conversation after arranging his thoughts. Then, she'd challenge his theories.

She settled back on the webbing of the lounger, closed her eyes, and listened to the rustle of palm fronds above her head. A deep, cleansing breath was a prelude to concentrating on sounds and not sights. Stress went out with each exhale until she reached a state of semi-consciousness.

31

Time eventually lost its meaning, at least until Steve broke the spell. "Who do you think killed Nate?" he asked.

She kept her eyes closed. "I don't think it was Jim, but it could be. He's sneaky, but doesn't have the guts to use a garrote. I can almost imagine him using poison, but cutting into someone's throat with a metal wire between two sticks? Much too messy and personal."

"He had motive and opportunity."

"Even under extreme duress, the method doesn't fit."

"I think you've eliminated him as a suspect."

Heather knew Steve was testing her resolve on the decision she'd made. She refused to give in to him. Instead, she challenged him. "When was the last time you heard about someone who grew up in the Hamptons and spent summers on Martha's Vineyard using a garrote to commit a murder?"

"There's always the first time, but you make a good point. A brutal, premeditated murder isn't what Jim McCloud would do. What about Skip?"

Heather fought the desire to open her eyes. "He's a likely candidate for hurting someone and he'd do it without a second thought. Still, it's a big step up to intentionally kill someone. I looked into the details of the manslaughter charge. The victim had a bad heart. All Skip did was slap the guy around."

A mental image flashed into Heather's mind. "The same goes for Roxy. She has plenty of strength and comes from a background where life is cheap. But unlike Skip, she's smart and scheming. If she killed someone, we wouldn't find the body."

"They both sit in their room all day drinking liquid courage. What if Roxy distracted Nate in the parking lot and Skip slipped up behind him and did the deed?"

Heather cracked open one eye. "What's the motive?"

"To purchase Nate's hotel cheap and get out of the cold winters of New Jersey."

Heather countered with, "They're born and bred city-dwellers who stay out of the sun all day. They're definitely not sun worshipers. Besides, we still can't place them on the island on the night of the murder. Even if one or both of them did it, they have an excellent alibi. The idea of them coming by boat in the middle of the night was a shot in the dark. The police should have covered that angle by now."

Heather expected Steve to hiss out a breath, expressing his disgust at the duo getting away with the crime. Instead, he moved on. "Juan Tovar. What do we know about him?"

"Not much. Only that he loves to dive and seems to have plenty of money to do so."

When she opened her eyes, Steve was sitting up with legs straddling the lounger, digging his toes into the sand. "Tell me again about where you've seen him diving."

Heather faced the opening to the cove. She raised her hand to point even though it was meaningless. "The dive boat started on the south end of the cove, past the reef before the waves break. Each day he's moved to the north. He's about a quarter of the way to the far side."

"And Li Jing is with him," said Steve.

"Uh-huh, and I'm still miffed that my contacts wouldn't give me any information on her. I think it's possible Juan and Li Jing might have known each other before they came to St. Croix."

Steve pulled his feet out of the sand and leaned back on the webbing. "Of all the things about this case, Li Jing is the most puzzling. I'm looking forward to having dinner with her."

Heather's phone came to life. Instead of it being her friend with the FBI, Bella's name appeared on the screen. She put it on speaker. "What's up?"

"You and Steve need to get back to the hotel on the double. A maid found another guest unconscious in his room. His face is a bloody mess. We've called cops and EMS."

"We're on our way."

Steve was already on his feet. "I was hoping this wouldn't happen."

Heather collected Steve and what little she'd brought, including her sandals, which she carried in her free hand. She led them through the deep, dry sand, then stayed near the water where the footing was firm. Together they jogged all the way to the boardwalk, retracing their way. Bella waited for them poolside.

"How bad?" asked Heather.

"Worse than Jim McCloud."

"Can he talk?"

"I don't know about talking, but he can sure scream."

Misty, the redhaired private investigator, met them as they entered the hotel. "Police and medics are here. What's going on?"

Bella answered. "Another assault."

Muscles in the woman's jaw flexed. "Were they part of the wedding party?"

Bella shook her head to give a negative response. "He's a single guy who has a YouTube travel channel."

Steve said, "Misty, I need you to take me to my room. I'd only be in the way." He turned his head to Heather. "Find out all you can and come tell me."

Heather passed Steve off and quick-walked with Bella until they reached the victim's room. Detective Nohr, a uniformed officer, and EMT's were at work when they arrived. "Let them in," said Nohr to the officer.

A banshee-like scream came from the man when they slid a backboard under him. A radio call gave the attendants permission to administer a shot. The female EMT dug out a vial and a syringe from what looked like a large tackle box. She pulled the plastic top off the syringe with her teeth and thrust the needle into the vial. Once loaded, she thumped the syringe with her left middle finger and administered the shot. "It won't take long for this to take effect, Mr. Rankin."

Heather inspected the man's face. A blood-stained bandage wrapped around his head. The skin around both eyes was red and puffy. The male EMT said, "The cut on the forehead isn't as bad as it looks. It appears to be a single blow that split the skin. He also has bruising to the ribs on both sides."

William spoke up. "There's blood on the edge of the door. It looks to me like he was opening the door to let someone in when the door struck him in the head and sent him to the floor."

"Where are you taking him?"

The EMT spoke while keeping his gaze on the patient. "St. Thomas. We don't have the facilities here to do the advanced diagnostic tests he needs. His vitals are good, but there could be internal injuries. We'll send him over by air."

Detective Nohr asked, "Can I ask him a few questions?"

"You can try. The doctor ordered a full dose of feel-better juice. As soon as it hits him, you'll have better luck talking to the wall."

Right on cue, the man's head lolled to one side. Any chance of questioning him about who'd done so much damage was gone for the time being.

Additional first responders entered with an ambulance gurney. It wasn't long before only William, Heather, and Bella remained in the room with an officer standing in the hall. William looked at Heather. "Any ideas?"

Heather gave a somewhat guarded response. "By the injuries he sustained and the condition of the blood on the floor, I'd say the assault took place within the last two to three hours. This type of beating fits what Skip Smith would do, but I expect Roxy to give him an alibi. If it were me, I'd have a talk with Skip as soon as possible. Try to get a search warrant for their room. That might be tricky, but try anyway."

"I need to process this crime scene first. I'm the only one with the training here on St. Croix."

Heather looked toward the door. "Bella and I are going back to Steve's room."

Bella added, "Let me know when we can clean the room. No rush, but my parents will want it done as soon as possible."

The trip to Steve's room passed without words until Bella said, "I don't get it. Mr. Rankin seems like a nice, harmless guy. Why would someone do that to him?"

Without thinking Heather said, "Follow the money."

"What money?"

Heather realized what she'd said. "I was parroting one of Steve's go-to lines, and he's usually right. People do all kinds of cruel things for money."

"I wish they wouldn't do them so close to my wedding."

She hooked her arm in Bella's and allowed a smile to seep out. "Let's tell Steve he's not doing enough to solve the murder and this is the second victim of an assault. That should light a fire under him."

Bella's smile turned crooked with doubt. "I'll let you tell Steve that."

"It might be fun to see his reaction."

Bella waved her hands like a football referee signaling an incomplete pass. "If you want to have a battle of wits with Steve, do it without me. He plays chess and I play checkers."

"Good analogy, but the only way you learn chess is to dive in and lose a few hundred games." Heather sucked in a full breath. "You give him the report of what we saw and heard. It will be good practice. Listen closely to his follow-up questions. You'll learn a lot."

"Back me up."

They reached Steve's door and knocked. Misty answered and let them in. Once they'd gathered in the seating area, Bella did an excellent job of relaying what she'd seen and heard. Steve nodded his approval and asked, "Did you smell anything unusual?"

"Uh..."

Heather took over. "There was a fairly large puddle of blood on the floor. Other than the distinctive metallic smell, all I noticed was medical supplies until I went in the bathroom. Mr. Rankin uses a cloying body spray. It's something none of our other suspects use."

Bella rolled her eyes. "I didn't even think about unusual smells."

"Most people don't," said Steve. "Once you get in the habit, you'll be surprised how much you'll pick up on." He took in a breath. "Let's review. The injuries that Mr. Rankin sustained are consistent with the MO of Skip Smith. Right?"

"Right," said Heather.

"Why was he beaten more severely than Jim McCloud?"

Misty answered, "That's what they do in Jersey to people who owe money. First they warn, then they up the ante to a hospital visit. The third time it's concrete shoes and into the river."

Steve asked, "Does it have to be money?"

"Not necessarily, but ninety-nine out of a hundred times, money's involved."

He pulled his hand down his face. "I agree it's related to money, but perhaps not directly."

Heather's mind kicked into gear.

Steve leaned forward in his chair. "Misty, for your benefit, I'll tell you something that Heather and I found out about Nate's hotel. Jim McCloud signed a tentative contract to purchase it from the person named as the owner in Nate's will. Nate had a buyer lined up in case he died, and the new owner wanted a quick sale."

Misty tilted her head. It made her look like a confused puppy. "I don't understand how the sale of either property has anything to do with the assaults."

Steve answered. "Follow the money. Someone's trying to make this resort drop in value before Lonnie and Ingrid can sell it."

32

S teve leaned his head back and inhaled deeply through his nose. Heather cheeped a muted laugh. "Every night we come to this dining room and you do the same thing. Your love affair with food is on display for all the world to see."

"Let them look," said Steve, without a hint of regret. "And for your information, I'm taking in more than the smells."

"Like what?"

"Like the thump of the bass guitar playing on the patio and the murmur of dozens of conversations taking place at the same time punctuated by guffaws of laughter. There's also the clink of silverware on plates, the quick steps of servers set against the slower, faltering steps of diners weaving their way to and from tables. Combine those with the teasing smells of exotic spices, and I'm in one of my happy places."

She took steps forward. Because of the late hour, the dining room was half empty. Heather continued the conversation. "I knew missing lunch was a bad idea. Now you're starving. You'll eat way too much and go into a food coma instead of concentrating on the case. Don't forget that we're here to pump Juan and Li Jing for information."

Steve swept a narrow path in front of him with his cane as he held on to her arm. "I'll behave myself and not order the escargot."

"You wouldn't eat snails if they came wrapped in bacon, were beer-battered, and deep fried."

"I call it dining with discretion."

"Call it whatever you want. This restaurant is making your clothes shrink."

"They're supposed to when you're on vacation. You've watched me cook when I'm puttering around my condo. There's not much in the way of quality, quantity, or variety. I also hit the gym almost daily as long as we don't have a case to work on."

"True, but that doesn't give you carte blanche to gorge yourself."

Heather wondered how many times they'd bantered back and forth like this. The subjects of their pretend bouts of contention changed but the game was always the same: each staked out their position and dug in. She'd discovered a long time ago that he did this for her benefit much more than his. She needed to keep her mind sharp to help solve a murder... a skill set unique from her normal grind. The stakes in business boiled down to profits and losses. Not so in a murder investigation; the result of failure or success could lead to more deaths. Yes, money was often involved, but losing freedom and living in a concrete and steel cage meant more than money for the perpetrator. For society, it was peace of mind that justice had been served.

She whispered, "Shh. We're almost there." Greetings were exchanged as Juan sat sandwiched between his mother and Li Jing. Judith sat with shoulders square. She toyed with the stem of a wine glass half filled with a rose-colored liquid. Juan had drained most all the dark liquid in a highball glass, while Li Jing lowered a glass of what looked like white wine.

Judith acted as master of ceremonies. "There you are, right on time. Have a seat and we'll get the server to see what magic potions the bartender can conjure up."

Steve found the back of his chair and spoke before he pulled it out. "I'll have whatever local beer they have on tap. I'm prone to knock over bottles and the server might as well tip over my wineglass and save me the effort."

Heather made sure he was settled with his collapsible cane folded and stored under his chair. "White wine for me." She cast her gaze to Judith. "I hope we didn't keep you waiting."

"Not at all. We're still on our first round of the evening."

The server arrived to take drink orders. Juan was the only one of the early arrivals who wanted a replacement. He ordered a Cuba libra.

Heather noted his selection and said, "I only drink Cuba libra when I travel to Havana." She leaned forward and finished her thought. "I also dip the end of a genuine Cuban cigar in the rum and cola and puff on something that doesn't taste like tree bark. There's nothing like a hand-rolled cigar in Havana."

The confession had the desired effect on Juan. He leaned forward and offered a toothy smile. "I'll have to remember that trick the next time I'm there." His lecherous gaze said more than his words.

Heather leaned back. She'd already scored an imaginary point by learning that Juan had ties in Cuba.

Judith flashed a glance in her stepson's direction but quickly refocused on Steve. "Tell me, Steve, why were the police and ambulance here this morning?"

He spoke in a matter-of-fact tone. "Someone assaulted another guest."

Judith's eyebrows raised. "How dreadful. A murder in the parking lot and now two assaults. I hope the injuries weren't too serious."

"They think he'll survive and take home a nice scar as a souvenir."

Juan asked, "He's still unconscious?"

Heather nodded a positive response while Steve said, "Whoever did it got carried away."

"What do you mean?" asked Juan.

"The blow to his head caused significant damage."

It wasn't true, but they didn't need to know that.

Heather added, "One thing's for sure, he'll never be able to identify who attacked him."

Judith and Li Jing's faces showed no emotion while Juan covered the inkling of a smile by draining his glass of all the liquid that remained. Heather gave herself another half-point for extracting what she thought was a reaction from Juan. She couldn't make it a full point because she wasn't positive that he'd actually smiled.

The server returned with the drink orders, which gave a welcome break to the grim conversation.

It came as a surprise to Heather when Li Jing winked with the eye away from Judith and Juan. She asked, "Are you and Mr. Smiley really private detectives?"

Steve tilted his head as he reached for his beer. "Who told you that?"

"I read the book about how you two reunited Bella with her parents and caught the killer of her kidnapper."

Judith added, "I read it, too. And to think that wicked man took her from the very beach past the pool I was swimming in this morning."

"We were lucky," said Steve.

Li Jing dove back into the conversation. "One method you use to catch the killer VERY smart. You discover who had skill to kill Mr. Brumley."

Steve played along. "Motive, means, and opportunity. Those are the three pillars of any investigation. If you don't have all three, the investigation falls apart. We had to consider who had the skill to kill from such a long distance."

Li Jing's voice took on a playful tone. "Let's play game. Pretend police say we attack man this morning. How many have alibi?" She rushed her next sentence. "I'll go first."

Steve held up his hand as a stop sign. "Before we can

proceed, you need to know something about the crime. The assault took place between seven and nine this morning."

"How do you know that?" asked Juan.

"Two things. Someone spray painted several security cameras starting at seven. That established the first time. The end time is more complicated. It has to do with the rate of blood coagulation. The longer it's outside the body, the more it hardens and changes color."

Heather bobbed her head in agreement. "So, Li Jing, where were you between seven and nine this morning?"

Her eyes opened wider than normal. "My room. Juan and I dance very late. Diving and dancing make me tired. I need rest."

Steve asked, "Did you eat breakfast?"

"I eat protein bar and fruit in my room."

"Did you order coffee or juice from room service?"

"I make tea in room."

Heather jumped in. "That's not much of an alibi."

Steve shook his head. "Sorry, Li Jing. We'll have to leave you on our suspect list."

Heather spoke in a teasing tone. "What about you, Mr. Smiley?"

"Like Li Jing, I was in my room alone."

Heather clucked a series of tsks. He interrupted and said, "Wait. A private detective your father hired stayed in the hall outside our doors all night. You and I have air-tight alibis."

"That's right," said Heather. "You and I are in the clear." She turned to Juan. "What about you, Mr. Tovar?"

"Not guilty," he said with a wide smile. "Like Li Jing, I needed sleep and was dead to the world until eight."

Heather spoke in a teasing manner. "Not good enough. You'll need a witness."

His black eyebrows knitted together over deep brown eyes. He flashed a smile. "There's a security camera that covers the hall outside my room. It will show that I didn't leave my room until after nine."

Steve said, "We'll have to verify that it wasn't spray painted."

"It wasn't," said Juan. "I have a habit of looking at security cameras."

Heather quickly added, "I thought I was the only one who did that. It drives me crazy every time I go to London. Cameras are everywhere, and I'm forever running into people because I'm looking up at those intrusive one-eyed monsters."

Once again, Juan had let something slip that he didn't need to. Heather concluded he might be a skilled diver, but keeping secrets wasn't his forte.

Steve ran a finger down his sweating mug of beer. "We'll give Juan a pass unless he's wrong about the security camera. That only leaves Judith." He spoke in a menacing tone. "Where were you between the hours of seven and nine this morning?"

"Oh dear," said Judith with pretend fear in her voice. "Bella and I took our normal walk at daybreak. I went back to my room and ordered breakfast. I placed the tray outside my door about seven forty-five and watched news on television until I went to swim laps at nine-thirty."

Steve tilted his head. "And isn't your room down the hall from the victim's?"

"It is."

Steve rubbed his chin. "I hate to tell you, but you and Li Jing are still on our list of suspects. You'd both better call an attorney."

Judith leaned her head back and laughed. "What a lark this has been. I'm certainly glad I fail the other criteria. Crippled middle-aged women without a motive don't make for convincing suspects."

Steve snapped his fingers. "Darn. I thought we had the case solved." He raised his mug in a salute. "To unsolved crimes."

Everyone followed his lead with Juan repeating the words with gusto.

From behind her, Heather sensed someone. She turned to see

her father sweeping the table guests with his gaze. "Is this a private party or can anyone join?"

She stood, received a hug, and stated the obvious. "You're back. I thought you were going to stay the night in San Juan.

Zhang Min dipped her chin. "We don't want to interrupt your dinner."

"Nonsense," said Steve. "I can tell by the size of this table there's plenty of room for two more."

"Yes," said Judith. "Please join us, Mr. McBlythe."

"Have we met?"

"No, but I assume your last name is the same as your daughter's since she wears an engagement ring without a wedding band."

Heather overcame the flip of her stomach and passed out introductions as her father and Zhang Min nodded greetings. Heather cast a lingering gaze at Li Jing and introduced Zhang Min to her in Cantonese. A broad smile pulled up at the corners of Li Jing's mouth. Zhang Min dipped her head and tried to cover a chuckle.

Steve was quick to cut in. "Watch out for Heather if you speak a language other than English. There's a good chance she knows enough to get by."

Juan tested her by speaking in rushed Spanish. He asked if she'd like to join him on the patio after dinner. She asked about his diving partner. He replied that she'd told him she needed a break from dancing tonight.

The wink from Li Jing signaled she also was multilingual and had hidden her ability to speak Spanish from Juan.

Judith lifted her chin to look down on her stepson. "I don't know about anyone else, but I'd like to order. Unlike some people, I can't dance the night away."

Steve laughed a little too hard and then explained. "I was imagining what it would look like if you and I tried. I've danced with children and all shapes and sizes of women, but never with someone pushing a walker. At least I wouldn't step on your feet with your walker between us."

Conversation remained light until most of the way through the meal. It was then Heather's father dropped his bombshell. In a matter-of-fact voice, he said, "Heather, I didn't tell you why I went to San Juan today. I secured funding with three other investors to purchase this property and Nate's hotel."

Juan jerked his head up as Judith and Li Jing looked on with wide eyes. Li Jing recovered the quickest while Judith patted her lips with a napkin. Juan laid his fork on his plate along with what remained of his meal and pushed it away.

Heather turned to her father. "I thought you were lying low and waiting until the economy showed signs of recovery."

"Timidity is the stepfather of failure."

"That's good. Did you make it up?"

"No, but I wish I had."

It wasn't long before Juan turned to his stepmother. "Tomorrow will be another full day of diving. Are you ready for me to see you to your room?"

"Are you sure you don't want to enjoy the music again?"

"Not tonight."

Heather cut another bite of steak. "No dessert? I splurged and had the *tres leches* cake last night. It was to die for."

Judith was already on her feet with Juan holding loosely to her arm. "Either my swimsuit is shrinking or the wonderful food is taking its toll on my figure. I'd better pass on dessert."

Judith, Juan, and Li Jing excused themselves. When they were a safe distance away, Heather turned to her left. "That was a very convincing performance. Why did you really go to San Juan today?"

He gave her a look of pretend hurt feelings. "I only bent the truth a little. I was checking out property in Old San Juan that's coming on the market soon."

"Is it a promising deal?"

"Not really, but we had a nice day walking around the city."

Steve raised his water glass in a pretend toast. "Here's to deception."

Zhang Min asked, "Are the latest victim's injuries serious?"

Heather leaned forward to look around her father. "His head injury was superficial and there are two broken ribs. No internal injuries. The biggest damage is to the reputation of the resort."

Steve folded his hands in front of him. "One more loose end and we'll put a bow on this and give Detective Nohr a nice present."

Zhang Min spoke in low tones. "I'm not comfortable with your father staying in his room."

"What do you suggest?" asked Steve.

"That he and I switch rooms until you, Heather, and Detective Nohr conclude your investigation and people go to jail."

Heather turned to her father. "I think it's a wise thing to do. Are you willing to trade rooms, Father?"

"I'm not an expert on security. I'll go where I'm told."

"That settles it. We'll play musical rooms."

33

The ringing of the hotel phone on Heather's nightstand woke her from a dreamless sleep. She looked at the green digits on the clock beside the phone and sat up. What mischief necessitated a call at 3:45 a.m.? Her mind went immediately to her father's safety as she jerked the receiver from its cradle.

"What's wrong?"

Instead of receiving an answer to the question, a voice spoke in Cantonese. She wasn't expecting to hear the sing-song of the exotic language, but she tuned in as Li Jing gave her name and said, "I need to see you. May I come to your room?"

Heather responded in the same language, but with an accent she knew blended Boston with Texas. "I'll call Steve. Let's meet in his room. I assume you know which one it is."

"Yes. Please tell the woman in the hall to allow me to pass."

"We'll expect you in ten minutes."

No additional words were required. Heather phoned Steve, who was already awake. Being blind, daylight and dark meant little to him, especially when he neared the end of an investigation. She sensed that time was drawing near.

"I'm coming to your room," said Heather. "Li Jing will follow me by five minutes."

"Good. That will save us from having to hunt for her today."

Heather had time to brush her teeth, change out of her sleepwear, and tell the woman in the hall to allow Li Jing to pass. Steve must have heard her footfalls, and pulled the door open. His first words were, "I'm making you a cup of coffee."

"You're a prince among men. I was enjoying the best night's sleep in days when she called."

Her flip-flops slapped against her heels as she made her way to the tiny coffee maker capable of producing only one cup of stimulant at a time. It finished with a final sputter and hiss as she approached it.

"You didn't seem surprised that Li Jing called me."

Steve's head didn't budge. "It was a matter of time."

"Do you know what she wants to discuss?"

"I have a good guess."

Heather spoke through a yawn. "Do you mind letting me in on it?"

"That would spoil the surprise."

She put the thin paper cup on the small table in front of the couch. "This coffee is too hot to drink and my mind is still in sleep mode. You'll have to carry the conversation."

Tentative taps on the door sounded. Heather abandoned her steaming cup to let the visitor in. Li Jing wasted no time in traversing the short distance to the couch where she sat on the edge of a cushion. She was short of stature, but her self-confidence shone through and made her seem larger.

Steve bid her a good morning and asked if she wanted a cup of tea. She refused. "I apologize for the early hour, but I came to tell you what I know about Juan Tovar's activities."

Steve, seated in a club chair, folded his hands on his lap. "I think I already know."

"Oh?"

"He's mapping the reef."

"Correct."

"Do you know why?"

"I only have speculation."

"Tell me what he's done so far."

Li Jing bobbed her head. "He started diving at the south end of the mouth of the bay. With each dive he completed about twenty-five yards of measurements, including the distance from the bottom to the top of the reef. It's dangerous, but he'd swim over the reef and take the same measurements from the bay side."

Steve asked, "Did he also measure the width of the reef?"

"He used a laser to measure from multiple angles. It's a sophisticated instrument that records measurements and downloads them into a computer that produces 3D images."

"Do you think he intends to map the entire reef?"

"If we can believe him, he's leaving the island in three more days."

"How much of the reef will he have mapped by that time?"

"Approximately one third. Perhaps a little more."

"Interesting," Steve allowed a few seconds to pass before he continued. "Heather couldn't help but notice you two have been spending your nights dancing. Did you learn anything valuable there?"

A breath of air huffed from her nose. "He treats women like he's choosing vegetables in an open-air market."

"I expected that," said Heather. "The things we go through to glean information."

A look of commiseration and mutual respect crossed Li Jing's countenance before she turned her attention back to Steve. "Otherwise, he's guarded with his words. It was only by overhearing a conversation in Spanish that I learned when he plans to leave the island."

"Do you know who he was speaking to?"

Her black hair swayed from left to right. "It was a man's voice."

"Do you know where he's going when he leaves the island?"

"His first stop is Miami. That's all I heard." Li Jing tilted her head. "Does this help you?"

Steve smiled. "Things are coming together nicely. One or two more days and we'll give Detective Nohr someone besides you to arrest."

This earned a smile from Li Jing. "You're living up to your reputation."

"Let's not celebrate yet. There's still a lot that can go wrong."

A look of genuine concern came across Li Jing's countenance. "Is the guest injured as bad as you told Juan?"

Heather took this question. "We stretched the truth a little, to get a reaction."

"Clever. You also made him believe every woman with a crossover purse is carrying a weapon."

"The art of deception," said Steve.

At that moment, all sources of light blinked off. Heather sprung from her place on the couch. "Father!"

"What's wrong?" asked Steve.

Heather fielded his question. "No electricity." She groped her way to the drawn curtains and jerked them back. A cloudy, moonless night ensured no slivers of light shone in from the outside. She reported her findings.

"I don't like it," said Steve. "Go check on your father. Don't use the light on your phone when you open the door. Put your back to the wall and feel your way. His room isn't far."

Li Jing's voice pierced the darkness. "I'll stay here with Steve."

With purse strapped against her, Heather made it into the hallway and moved toward the young private investigator. Using the same senses Steve used, she found the woman lying in a heap with her chair overturned. She was breathing, but motionless. The smell of chloroform hung in the air. A door opened from halfway down the hall. A bleary-eyed guest came out of his room with the light from his cell phone punching a hole in the darkness. He shone it in Heather's direction. "Are the lights out all over?"

"They seem to be. It's a good morning to sleep in."

"What's wrong with her?" the man asked.

"Too many shots of tequila. She almost made it to her room, but not quite. I'll wake her and get her in bed."

"Need help?"

"Thanks, but no. She's getting over an abusive boyfriend and may become violent if a man touches her."

The man gave a wave of surrender and went back into his room.

Heather took her phone from her purse and turned on the light. She made it to her father's room at the same time Misty did. Heather used a series of knocks that she and her father had worked out as their password. He cracked the door open and asked, "Is everything all right?"

"Someone chloroformed the woman assigned to guard the hall. Misty will stay with you. You don't leave this room."

She turned to leave and her father asked, "Where are you going?"

"To check on Zhang Min."

"Wait," said her father. "You'll need the key. It's a good thing this hotel still uses metal ones. Bella gave us an extra."

Heather took the key and quick-walked to the room her father traded with Zhang Min. She slipped the key in the door and turned the lock. Cat-like steps brought her into a room as dark as a dungeon. The light of the phone imitated the beacon of a lighthouse as it shone into the room. Once again, the pungent smell of chloroform hung in the air.

She took three steps into the room before a blow sent her reeling. Muscle memory kicked in and she broke her fall with outstretched hands. Stunned, she lay face-down on the carpet. The door slammed. By the time she cleared her head enough to rise to her feet and stumble to the door, the hallway was empty except for the unconscious guard.

Furious with herself for not keeping her back to a wall when she burst into the room, she went to the bed to check on Zhang Min. The woman was coming around and speaking Cantonese. The gist of her words was a self-loathing rant seasoned with creative expletives. She blamed herself for sleeping so deeply while on assignment.

Heather again used what she believed was the woman's native language. "We both failed, and we'll pay for it with terrific headaches."

Zhang Min rubbed her eyes. "Is your father safe?"

"He's in your room safe and sound with Misty."

"Did you get a description?"

Heather shook her head. "Whoever it was knows their business. They almost knocked me out with a blow to the back of my neck."

"We must go to your father and report our failures."

Heather already had her cell phone in hand and took care to keep the light out of Zhang Min's eyes. Instead, she conducted a quick search of the floor. The light stopped moving when the beam passed over an object that sent a chill down Heather's back.

"I'm luckier than I thought," said Zhang Min.

Heather nodded. "Another garrote. Someone is serious about wanting to kill my father." She reached for Zhang Min's hand. "If we have to confess our incompetence, let's get it over with."

"I'm not used to doing this. I don't like it."

"Me either," said Heather.

Once reunited with her father, Heather said, "Let's go to Steve's room. That will save me and Zhang Min from having to tell our tale twice."

The trip to Steve's room took about thirty steps. The hallway guard had partially regained consciousness. They helped her back into her chair. The eldest of her co-workers came running down the hall with a small flashlight throwing beams of light in front of her. The younger woman wasn't one-hundred percent, but good enough to wave help away and give an assurance she was all right.

The gaggle of visitors arrived at Steve's room. He was the only one not wearing sleepwear. After a full accounting of actions and mistakes made, Steve and her father took turns brushing aside confessions of ineptitude.

After assurances of no permanent damage, Steve got down to business. "Man or woman?"

Heather said, "Either, but whoever it was knew how to punch. The smell of chloroform was too strong to pick up any other scents."

Zhang Min added, "I'm not a heavy sleeper. The person was very light on their feet, but strong." They continued to discuss the minute details of the attacks until there was nothing more to say.

A knock on the door caused everyone's head to jerk upward. Heather looked through a peephole and said, "It's Detective Nohr."

In a matter of seconds, the detective stood in their midst and gave a partial report. "This isn't a random power failure. The electricity is off on a quarter of the island."

Steve asked, "Have you done a thorough search of the room Zhang Min was in?"

"Not thorough, but I bagged and tagged the garrote. An officer is posted at the door."

"I have a favor to ask you."

William looked at Heather and raised his eyebrows to ask if she knew what it was. She shrugged and shook her head.

Steve continued, "Heather will give you a list of people who shouldn't leave the island. Can you make sure no one on the list flies out?"

"It's a small island and I know everyone who works at the airport. It's not uncommon for tickets to get lost and their computers to lose reservations."

"Perfect."

William's radio crackled to life. He left the room to respond to the transmission.

Steve spoke with conviction. "We'll wrap this case up tomorrow morning."

"That soon?" asked Heather.

"The wedding rehearsal and rehearsal dinner are fast approaching. We don't want this spoiling Bella and Adam's celebration."

Heather couldn't believe she'd pushed the wedding out of her mind.

Steve then asked, "Is it daylight yet?"

"First light," said Misty.

Heather moved to the curtains and opened them. As soon as she did, the lights came on.

"Good," said Steve. "I hear air conditioners and refrigerators running. Who's going with me to breakfast? Nothing will be ready for a while, but it beats sitting in this room."

"Perhaps we should all go," said Heather. "Unless I miss my guess, there are a lot of loose ends that will need to be tied up today."

Steve asked, "You mentioned last night, you might fly to St. Thomas to check on Mr. Rankin. Are you still planning to go?"

"Unless I need to stay here."

Heather's father broke in. "I want to go with you."

Zhang Min chimed in, "I go where he goes."

Misty spoke next. "Me, too."

Heather asked, "Anyone else?"

Steve rubbed his chin. "Take Bella, Adam, and one more of Misty's crew to guard the bride and groom. The happy couple should have the jitters about now. A quick trip away will do them good."

It amazed Heather how many details Steve could cram into his mind at one time.

Steve's phone announced he had a call from William Nohr. He froze in place with the phone pressed hard against his ear. "I understand. Heather's on her way."

He held the now silent phone in his hand. "Get to Jim McCloud's room. Another beating."

34

That afternoon Heather and her father looked down on Jim McCloud as he worried the tape securing an IV. Steri-Strips closed a gash on his forehead, and looked like lines of white out, the poor speller's best friend. She thought how appropriate it was to think of Jim as a mistake maker. After all, he'd squandered away most of the family fortune and had involved himself in something that resulted in him lying in a hospital bed.

The beating had also delayed Steve's timeline to solve the case by a full day.

Not wanting to make Jim feel worse, she pulled a pretend smile from a supply, slapped it on, and said, "The cut on your forehead isn't bad at all. I was afraid it was farther down your forehead and you'd be out of luck with the ladies. From all the blood, I thought it was much more serious."

Jim spoke in a voice painted with regret. "It's my fault for trying to back out of a deal."

"Business deals are civil matters. I emphasize the word civil, which doesn't involve violence."

"I must have skipped that lecture at Princeton." Jim tried to come up with a convincing smile and failed. "You didn't have to come see me. I'll be all right once I get this leg fixed."

Heather's father asked, "Is that the opinion of the orthopedists, or your own wishful thinking?"

"A little of both. The bruising to my ribs hurts like crazy, but they only cracked one. As for my leg, the knee cap is a mess. They say I'll have a limp to remind me of my time in St. Croix. I'm hoping a specialist back home might have a better prognosis."

Heather took his hand. "I know you don't think so, but you were lucky."

Jim averted his gaze. "I guess you're right. It could have been much worse." He paused. "And it still might be."

Heather squeezed his hand. "Nothing more is going to happen to you. We'll see to that."

He fixed his gaze on her. "Who's we?"

"Me, Steve, the police, Bella and Adam—we have a small army helping us."

"Include me on that list," said Heather's father.

"I appreciate what you're saying, but you can't watch over me all the time. I'm a marked man if I don't do what I'm told."

Heather spoke with unflinching certainty. "Not if the people who did this to you are behind bars where they belong. They're counting on the fear they've put into you to be stronger than your character."

Jim spoke through a ragged breath. "They'll kill me if I don't do what they say."

Heather hovered over him and looked into his eyes. "Look at me, Jim. If you live in constant fear, your life is already over. I don't mean to preach, but it's time you quit looking for shortcuts to get your money back."

"Things look different when you're on a hospital bed, unable to move without pain shooting through you. When was the last time someone laid you out on the floor?"

She responded without hesitation. "Same as you, yesterday morning. While you were getting beat to a pulp, someone caught me in the back of the neck and drove me to the floor."

Heather's father chimed in, "Their plan to kill me failed because Heather and Steve's crew didn't let it happen."

Jim's eyes widened. "They tried to kill you?"

"We found a garrote on the floor by his bed. If Father's personal assistant hadn't suggested the two of them trade rooms, he might be dead now. But that's not what's important. How we react to someone coming against us is all that matters now. We're fighting back."

Jim's confused gaze preceded his eyes darting from left to right. "How can I fight back? Look what they did to me. This was only a sample of what they're capable of."

Heather held up her right hand with her forefinger and thumb separated by only a quarter inch of distance. "We're this close to putting a pack of people in jail." She took a step away from the bed and folded her arms to communicate a challenge. "What happened to that smart, fearless guy I knew in college? You're the one who broke into the dean's office and stole his Mont Blanc pen."

A smile spread and brightened Jim's face, but only for a moment. "That was on a dare and I mailed it back to him. Anonymously, of course." He issued a weak chuckle. "I also made two hundred bucks for taking it."

Heather gave him a nod of affirmation. "You've never been a coward, Jim. This is no time to start. With you or without you, we'll solve this case. It will be sooner if you help us."

From some unknown place, he dredged up a small dose of character. "What do you want me to do?"

Heather pulled out her phone. "Give me a full and accurate statement of everything leading up to your assault." She gave him a piercing stare and repeated a word that caused him to swallow. "Everything."

Jim looked down in shame. "Does your father have to hear this?"

"You've hidden things from the police and from me. I want a reliable witness to hear what you're going to tell me. Besides, it will be good practice for when you tell Detective Nohr the same thing."

Jim remained quiet except for his shallow breaths. When his shoulders dropped half an inch, Heather knew he'd decided. He reached out his hand for her to take. "You're just like you were in college, moving forward with absolute confidence. You knew I'd break and tell you how I got into this mess."

Heather's father gave a different angle to her confidence. "Sometimes it's difficult to distinguish confidence from mule-headed stubbornness."

She tented her hands on her hips. "Are you saying I'm stubborn as a mule?"

"If the bridle fits..." He left the rest unsaid as Jim's belly bounced up and down and he pulled his arms tight against himself to still the movement.

"The ribs! Don't do that," he squawked. "Don't torture me. I'll tell you everything."

It took over thirty minutes to complete. Questions and clarifications volleyed back and forth before Heather had wrung everything out of Jim. He'd danced around the edges of crime. Not a safe place to play, but, as she saw things, there wasn't enough to convict him of anything warranting a prison sentence. A skilled lawyer could wrangle a misdemeanor probation.

The thought of a good defense attorney brought up a mental picture of Jack. She tried to push his face out of her mind, back to where he belonged with his daughter.

A TAXI TOOK HEATHER, HER FATHER, MISTY, AND ZHANG MIN to the old warehouse district of St. Thomas. It was a multi-block area of renovated warehouses dating back hundreds of years. Centuries ago, they housed all manner of goods, especially those related to the rum trade. Thick-planked doors from ancient timbers gripped brick walls with the aid of hand-forged hinges.

The bricks, first used as ballast in the bottom of merchant ships, came from a smattering of European countries, primarily Holland. The buildings once held sugar, rum, and the plunder of pirates' raids. Rooms that once kept the spoils of slave traders were now shops, boutiques, and restaurants. The ghost of the pirate Blackbeard seemed to inhabit the narrow alleys.

They met up with the rest of the crew that had made the short flight in Heather's corporate jet after lunch. They relaxed and enjoyed a meal amid a throng of tourists from docked cruise ships.

Bella and Adam became the focal point as Heather suggested everyone buy a small gift for them to celebrate the next day's rehearsal and the dinner to follow. Bella agreed, but put a twenty-dollar limit on the gifts and added that they couldn't be any larger than a twelve-ounce glass.

Since the day started early, and the return flight took mere minutes, they were back at the resort by nightfall. Steve hadn't been idle.

Her phone rang the minute she walked through the hotel's front door. She could tell by the tone of his voice that he was in full detective mode. "I'm in the same conference room we used before. Come see me. There's work to be done."

When Heather arrived, Bella's father was moving a white-board into place at the front of the room. The chairs were in the same rows as they had been for the original meeting. She asked, "Do you want the photos back on the board?"

"Leave it blank for now. Tell me about your visit with Jim. Did he agree to tell you about his assault?"

"Mission accomplished."

Lonnie excused himself to attend to other duties, which left Steve alone with her. "Who did Jim say attacked him?"

"It's the person you named." She tilted her head. "Was that a lucky guess?"

He over-exaggerated his response. "Of course not. I simply took in all the evidence, filtered it through my brilliant mind, used inductive and deductive reasoning, and came to the only possible answer."

Heather snorted. "You guessed."

"Let's just say I'm lucky at flipping coins... for a blind guy, that is." He kept talking as she chuckled. "Give me details of your visit with Jim."

Heather launched into the tale of Jim's injuries and what led to them. She concluded with, "Detective Nohr should have a formal statement by now. How do you want to use the whiteboard?"

Steve explained his plan for bringing the case to a conclusion. Heather chose her words with care. "Isn't that risky? What if any of the suspects don't respond the way you think they will?"

He placed both hands on the top of his cane. "Everything was muddy until I realized the motive behind Nate's murder. Now it all makes sense."

"Agreed, but all the pieces need to fall into place in the right order or the whole thing could fall apart."

Steve grinned. "That means we can't make any mistakes."

"Have you run this by Detective Nohr?"

"I sent him a text telling him I need his help in gathering suspects tomorrow morning. Everything hinged on you getting Jim to talk. The dominoes are set up now for a little push." Steve ran a hand over his face that needed a shave. "It would be a real plus if Jim could make a surprise appearance at tomorrow's meeting. Do you think you could bust him out of the hospital?"

Heather puffed out her cheeks and released the air while she considered. "He's in a lot of pain, and his leg is in a cast. If he's released, he'll need a wheelchair and pain pills. We'll also need a private-duty nurse."

"All we need is for him to show his face. Call his doctor and see what you can do."

Heather wasn't sure she could bring home another blue ribbon with this challenge. "I'll call as soon as I get to my room. Are you ready to go upstairs?"

Steve held out his hand for Heather to take. "Lead on."

They almost made it to the end of the hall when Steve slowed and whispered, "Who's working the front desk?"

She walked on a few yards by herself and then returned. "It's Frank and Mary Jones."

Steve used his cane to feel his way forward. "Hello, Frank and Mary. How are my two fellow Texans?"

Mary's words didn't match her downcast gaze. "Excellent, Mr. Smiley. How can I serve you?"

"Could I get one of you to lock the door to the room I've reserved for tomorrow morning?"

"Certainly," said Mary.

Heather issued a word of thanks and took Steve's hand again. She turned and spied the resort's van delivering passengers. Her stomach worked its way up her throat and back down. Weak-kneed, she spread her feet to gain a firmer footing, then blinked three times to make sure her eyes hadn't deceived her. They hadn't. Under the awning, waiting for luggage, stood Jack with a gangly, brown-haired girl holding a pink cell phone.

Panic covered her like a bird caught in an oil slick. Turning to Steve, she said, "Jack and his daughter are here. I can't face them. You're on your own."

She ran for the elevator. The door refused to open, no matter how many times she pushed the button. Giving up, she sprinted for the stairs and didn't stop until a shaking hand fit the key into the lock of her room. The door flew open. She slammed it shut behind her and threw herself on the bed.

After half a box of tissues lay scattered on the duvet, she rose and went to wash her face. She spoke to the pathetic visage that looked back at her in the mirror. "So much for bringing my A game tomorrow morning."

An audible gasp came forth when her phone rang. It rang ten times before it quieted, leaving only the sound of cool air whispering through the room's vents. With trepidation, she moved to her purse and took out the device she'd spent so many hours talking to Jack on. The identification of the last caller flashed on the screen. She then manipulated the phone to replay the message.

"It's me. I talked to Jack and told him not to bother you until tomorrow afternoon. I'll stop by after you've pulled yourself together."

35

The knock came at 8:00 p.m. and froze Heather in place. She gathered what little courage she could dredge up and went to the door. Her lungs pushed out a huff of relief-filled air when she saw Steve standing alone.

The door clicked shut after she allowed him to pass. As if he could read her thoughts, he said, "Don't worry, Jack's not skulking behind me."

She took him by the hand and gave a gentle tug. Questions sprayed the room. "What did Jack say? Did you meet Briann? What's she like?"

"Do you mind if I sit down?"

She led him to the chair, which was a sister to the one in his room. "Sorry. I'm flummoxed."

He settled in the chair. "Good word. It fits, and to answer your question—yes, I spoke with Jack and Briann. She still goes by her mother's last name, which is Lovejoy."

"Briann Lovejoy. Tell me about her. Does she seem happy to be here?"

"How would you feel if the only parent you ever knew died? Add to that you had no choice but to live with people who didn't know you existed two months ago."

It was like a knife twisted in Heather's gut, but Steve kept talking. "I told Jack you were busy helping me wrap up this case and he should give you space until after it's over."

Steve folded his hands together on his lap. "The timing of this is lousy, but the only way you're going to make it through is to take things one at a time. From now until handcuffs click shut you need to focus on the case. I need your sharp mind and keen instincts. You know how much is riding on us doing our job. It's literally a matter of life and death, and the person they want dead is your father."

She hung her head. "I know, but—"

"But, nothing," said Steve with a whip's crack in his voice. "This is not a simple murder case. It's not a crime of passion, but a carefully orchestrated plan." He took a deep breath and let it out before he lowered the intensity to his words. "Have you looked at the file since you fled to your room?"

A sheepish negative answer confirmed she hadn't.

"Take a shower, order a nice salad, open the file, and go over every detail. Examine the plan for flaws. If you think of a better way to wrap this up, call me."

"You don't want to go over the file together?"

Steve shook his head. "I have a dinner date with a young lady and her father. She agreed to be my guide if I introduced her to Bella. She read Bella's book on the airplane and thinks the future bride may be the coolest woman in the world." Steve grinned. "Her vote is still out on you."

"As well it should be."

Steve rose faster than expected. "Enough talk. It's time for you to get to work and me to carry the conversation between Jack and his daughter. They're not used to each other yet."

She walked him to the door. "Do you want me to take you back to your room?"

"No need. This place is crawling with people protecting your father."

LIGHT POURED THROUGH THE PATIO DOOR AS HEATHER AWOKE with a start. She'd convinced herself sleep wouldn't come, but she'd proved the voice in her head wrong. Was it the warm shower or the reading and re-reading of notes in the case file that allowed slumber? Perhaps listening to ocean waves on noise-canceling headphones did the trick. Probably a combination of it all temporarily blocked out the trauma of seeing Jack and being judged by his daughter.

The photos and pages that she'd spread across half the king-size bed went neatly back into the file. Steve's plan seemed risky, but sound. She dressed in no time, put on a modest amount of makeup, and was ready to face the day. Breakfast first. She thought about going to the dining room but decided against it and ordered room service. No need taking the chance of running into Jack and Briann. She had to stay focused.

Her phone rang and as expected, it was Steve. "Any problems getting Jim sprung from the hospital?"

"My pilots flew Detective Nohr over this morning and picked him up. It was a chore getting him loaded and unloaded on the plane, but they're on the way to the resort now."

"Excellent. Meet me in the room downstairs. We'll put Jim in the room next to the one we're using."

Taking no chances of getting on the elevator with Jack and Briann, Heather took the stairs and walked with head down going to the last room in the hallway. She sneaked a peek at the ballroom. A lone worker scurried about, setting up tables.

Heather made it to the room where Steve and Detective Nohr waited. After giving William the opportunity to wish her a good morning, Steve asked, "Did you bring tape for the photos?"

"In my purse."

She made her first mistake of the day when she asked, "How was your dinner last night?"

Steve's posture stiffened. "We'll play twenty questions later. Get focused."

She swallowed her regret for asking. "You're right, and you both have permission to remind me not to let my mind drift." She looked around the room. "Is Jim in the room next door?"

Steve nodded. "One of Misty's body guards is keeping him company."

"Which one?"

Detective Nohr fielded her question. "The young, tall one." He added, "The pills they gave Jim for pain have the side effect of lowering inhibitions. He took one look at his guardian angel and proposed marriage."

Heather rolled her eyes. "Jim always was impulsive."

The conversation ping-ponged back to Detective Nohr. "Your father is on his way."

"Good. He'd be disappointed if he didn't have a role to play in this drama."

The wait wasn't long until Misty stuck her head in the door, scanned the room, then looked over her shoulder and motioned with her head. In walked Heather's father, flanked front, back, and sides by female body guards and Zhang Min. He gave greetings and moved to the back row of chairs. Heather earned a father's wink as they traded glances. She couldn't remember him ever winking at anyone.

Steve stood at the far end of the whiteboard; Heather, on the side nearest the door. Detective Nohr stood between them at the halfway point. She placed the file containing photos and the roll of tape on the chair beside her, but kept her purse draped across her chest.

Steve plowed ahead. "We can get started by identifying the victims. Heather, tape the photos of everyone assaulted and your father in a single row along the top. On a row under them, tape the other photos. Use the marker to write names under each photo."

She completed the assignment a few seconds before a loud

voice in the hallway pierced the quiet. In walked Roxy Smith with a uniformed officer on each side. Her face glowed red with defiance. "You clowns got no right to detain me."

Detective Nohr looked at the officer on each side of her and then at the woman. "Did she resist?"

"A little," said the beefy uniformed man on her left.

The detective's gaze shifted to Roxy. "Is your name Roxy Smith?"

"Go fly a kite."

"You're now under arrest for lying to an officer, hampering a police investigation, and resisting arrest." He shifted his gaze. "Cuff her."

Steve held up a hand. "Hold on a minute. That might not be necessary."

Detective Nohr ran a hand over his chin. "This isn't the mainland US. We do things different here on the islands."

Heather knew the detective's words were mostly a bluff, but not entirely. It's legal for police to use deception to gain information and confessions from suspects. Still, suspects have rights that when infringed upon could sink their case if abused.

William played his part well. "We know who she is and what she did in New Jersey. Her rap sheet gave me eyestrain from reading so much."

Steve's voice held a plea for mercy in it. "I know what she's done, but that doesn't mean she killed Nate or knee-capped Jim McCloud."

Roxy looked at Steve with approval. "Darn right it doesn't."

Steve motioned to Heather. "You'd better explain the photos to Roxy."

Heather took a step toward the board. "The police know what businesses you ran back in Jersey. You're a tough woman with a history of associating with people who like to hurt others. They also know you came here to purchase Nate's hotel, but there's a small problem. You don't have the cash it will take to buy it."

Detective Nohr thrust out his chin. "I believe we can convince a jury you hired a boat to bring you to St. Croix and return you to St. Thomas with plenty of time to spare." He took in a deep breath and pointed a finger at her. "You researched Nate's hotel when you came several months ago and again this trip until you received new instructions to research this hotel. It's simple. You wanted to run a hotel like the ones you did back in New Jersey—one that played fast and loose with the law. You even brought your enforcer with you to make sure you got it. You distracted Nate in the resort parking lot late at night while Skip killed him."

Steve pulled a hand down the left side of his face. "It's an excellent theory, and might be true, but I think there's a lot more to this story."

"Are you saying she's innocent?"

"Roxy? Innocent? That's a hoot. She's guilty of plenty, but killing Nate may not be one of her crimes." Steve put cold steel in his next words. "Like Detective Nohr said, they do things different here on the islands. There's an ever-growing pile of circumstantial evidence against you. There's also the simple fact that you'll go before a local judge and jury. Plotting to get the property of a well-loved and respected native of the islands was a really stupid thing to do. Almost as stupid as participating in his murder."

Heather walked in front of the whiteboard with the line of photos on full display. "This reminds me of a case I studied in law school." She pointed at the photos. "The police had three murders. They knew several gang members committed the crimes. The problem they had was getting any of the gang members to testify. They offered leniency to the first person who would tell the truth."

Heather pointed to the photos on the board one at a time. "Nate Johnson... murder." She moved down the line of photos. "Jim McCloud... attempted murder and aggravated assault with a weapon."

Detective Nohr interrupted, "I believe we can get a conviction on attempted murder the second time he was assaulted."

"Very possible," said Steve.

Heather moved on. "Zhang Min and the private detective in the hotel hall... attempted murder with chloroform, not to mention that Roxy left behind the same type of weapon as the one used to kill Nate. To paraphrase Mr. Smiley, 'How stupid can criminals get?'"

"You can't hang that on me. I was asleep in my room."

Detective Nohr spoke up. "We have footage from a security camera outside your fourplex that tells a different story. You didn't notice that we put up additional cameras around the resort, did you? That's another lie you've told."

Heather continued pointing at photos. "Mr. McBlythe, my father... attempted murder because he was the intended victim when Zhang Min was attacked." She kept talking when Roxy opened her mouth, presumably to protest. "We know Father was the target because he was looking into purchasing Nate's hotel. That would have left Roxy without her dream of living in St. Croix."

Detective Nohr spoke with mocking sympathy. "More evidence is piling up against you, Roxy. I can see the scales of justice tipping, and the prison door slamming shut behind you."

Heather moved to the next image on the board. It was a photo of a series of electric transformers. "The last crime was against property. Specifically, someone broke into a substation and cut the power to a quarter of the island. That power didn't cut itself off."

Steve took his turn. "I don't know why, but I think the reason Roxy wasn't in bed when the botched attempt on Mr. McBlythe happened is because she was a few miles away, turning off the lights."

Heather added, "There's also the matter of Mr. Rankin being beaten in his room. Someone has to account for that. It might as well be Roxy."

Steve let the accusation have its effect before saying, "Tell me, Detective Nohr, would your people be willing to do a deal?"

"What kind of deal?"

"Let's say Roxy pleads guilty to breaking into the substation and turning off the lights. For this good deed, she tells all she knows about the assaults and Nate's murder."

"I'll have to check, and the information would need to be something that convinced me she could help prove who killed Nate." He tilted his head like an inquisitive kitten. "Heather, what happened to the gang members in your law school story?"

She drew a sweeping imaginary line with her finger under every photo. "They were all charged under laws pertaining to organized crime. Every one of them went to prison on life sentences. Most people don't realize you don't have to actually kill someone to be charged and convicted of murder. If you're involved in the planning or commission of it, you can be held responsible. It's called the felony-murder rule."

Detective Nohr gave a conspiratorial grin. "That's music to my ears." He turned to the officers. "I'm sick of looking at her. Cuff her, and take her to the room down the hall."

Steve spoke as the officers grabbed her by the arms, applied the handcuffs, and turned her toward the door. "I'm trying to help you, Roxy, but I need something to bargain with. Think about how old you'll be if you finally make parole in thirty or forty years."

Roxy struggled against the hold the two officers had on her arms as they escorted her from the room.

Once the room cleared, Steve said, "That went well. Tape Roxy's photo under the one of the electricity transformers and draw a line between them. Bring Skip in next. Let's see how loyal he is."

36

Heather watched as two burly officers returned with Skip Smith in handcuffs,

Detective Nohr gave a loud command. "Put him in the front row so he can see the nice pictures."

"These bracelets are too tight."

"Get used to them."

Steve moved a step closer to Skip and asked, "If I talk Detective Nohr into allowing you to wear the handcuffs in front of you, do you promise to behave yourself?"

Skip didn't have to think long. "Sure. I'm here on vacation. Besides, I ain't never hurt nobody."

Heather countered his last statement. "That's not what your rap sheet says."

"All dat was a long time ago. I'm reformed."

Heather fought to keep a straight face as Steve moved on. "Let's give Skip the benefit of the doubt."

Detective Nohr motioned for the officers to unfasten one side of the handcuffs and reattach them in front of Skip. Once completed, he moved closer to the man with thick, tattooed forearms and a head that seemed a couple of sizes too small for his body. "You won't like what happens if you try anything. I'm instructing these two officers to sit behind you. They're both carrying Tasers. Your records show you know what it's like to be on the wrong end of the metal barbs. Imagine what it's like to have two jolts of electricity hit you at the same time."

Skip tried to put on a good front, but a bead of perspiration clung to the tip of his nose and refused to drop. "Is any of youse guys going to tell me what's goin' on?"

"Great question," said Heather. "I'll explain." She pointed to the top row of photos. "You're involved in Nate Johnson's murder and in assaults on everyone else on this board."

"No way. I ain't killed no one."

Detective Nohr's response cracked like a massive tree limb breaking. "She didn't say you killed Nate. Only that you're involved."

Steve spoke, which caused Skip to shift his gaze. "You really need to listen more carefully, Skip. If you don't, you may get confused."

Heather took her turn. "Look at the photos in the top row. Do you recognize all these people?"

Skip's gaze parked on each photo until he got to the last one. "The one on the end ain't a person. You trying to trick me?"

"I'm glad you noticed that. Whose picture is underneath the photo?"

"That's Roxy. What's with the line connectin' 'em?"

Steve broke in. "Tell me about your room here at the resort. How is it set up?"

"Huh? What's dat got to do with Nate gettin' bumped off?"

"You have to answer the question to find out."

"Oh. It's older, but not bad. A small kitchen and bathroom. There's a dining table and a couple of chairs. The TV is big, and the patio ain't bad. It's got a lounge chair and a plastic one."

"Does Roxy ever let you relax in the lounge chair?"

"If she ain't out there."

"How many beds?"

"Two. One for Roxy and one for me."

Heather said, "One for each of you. That tells me you and Roxy aren't married."

"Roxy ain't the marrying kind."

"You drink a bottle of gin every day by yourself." It wasn't a question, but a statement of fact.

"Roxy gets it for me. She says it's so I won't get any ideas about me and her. I do a lot of pushups and sit ups in the mornings. Someday she'll notice me."

"That must be frustrating," said Steve. "I bet you'd do anything Roxy asked."

He pushed out his lips in defiance. "I got my limits."

Steve's voice remained calm as he said, "In regard to your question about the line connecting Roxy's photo and the power station... Roxy went to the power station and cut off the lights." Steve's hand went up to block any denial. "She was in here before you and made it clear she left your room in the wee hours of the morning."

Heather didn't give him a chance to speak. "You've worked for Roxy a long time. That means you know her very well. She makes special deals to get out of trouble with the police."

"Yeah. She's smart."

Heather pointed to the photos on the top line as Steve said, "Take a good look. One person is dead and several hurt. Now look at the last photo and Roxy's picture below it. What does that tell you?"

He lifted his shoulders and let them fall. "I dunno."

Heather helped him with the answer. "You've already told us that Roxy makes deals with cops. That means it wouldn't surprise you if she made a deal for herself. Right?"

Hesitation filled his response. "I... I dunno 'bout that."

"Now look again at the last photo. There's no line between Roxy and any of the other pictures. Put everything together and tell Steve what you see."

The dim light of revelation flashed in his eyes as a scowl

furrowed his brow. "She's made another deal. She'll cop to turning off the lights if she don't get busted for nothin' else."

Steve, Heather, and Detective Nohr all nodded in agreement. Steve asked, "How does that make you feel?"

"Mad." His hands clenched into fists.

"Have you ever considered making a deal of your own, like Roxy does?"

"She makes 'em for me. All I do is keep my mouth shut."

"Not this time," said Heather.

"Why not?"

Steve answered. "It's murder and it comes with a life sentence."

"I ain't killed no one in my life."

"That's not true," said Heather.

Skip's eyebrows pinched together in concentration. His eyes opened wide. "That guy don't count. He had a bum heart." His head shook side to side. "No way I killed that guy named Nate."

It occurred to Heather how much Roxy had taken advantage of the weak-minded man. He'd blindly do what she said.

"I believe you," said Steve, "but people got hurt bad and one is dead. I know you're not a snitch, so we've come up with a way that you don't have to say anything."

Heather explained, "Like Steve said, you don't have to say a word. All we want you to do is nod or shake your head when I point at a picture. If you in any way hurt any of these people, nod your head. If you didn't, shake your head like this." She demonstrated as she gave him the instructions.

Steve interrupted. "Heather, draw a line between Skip and Jim McCloud. We know he gave Jim a bloody nose."

Heather moved on before he could deny or confirm it. "What about the power station. Did you do something to turn off the lights?"

Skip shook his head.

"I didn't think so," said Heather. "That means Roxy did." Heather turned to Steve. "Skip's nodding his head."

Down the list she went. Time after time he non-verbally denied harming any of the victims until he got to the private investigator who was rendered unconscious in the hall outside her father's room.

Skip must have forgotten not to speak. "I missed one. Can I go back?"

"Sure," said Heather as she started with the first photo which was Nate's. Skip shook his head. She moved on to Jim's. Skip gave his head a firm nod, but said, "Only the time on the path. He stood still and let me pop him in the snoz. Roxy set it up for me."

Steve broke in. "What about the assault of Mr. Rankin in his room?"

Heather pointed at Rankin's photo. She narrated for Steve. "He's nodding his head."

Heather looked at Skip who turned from her gaze. "Roxy sent you to rough him up, didn't she?"

"She told me to give him a little extra to put on his YouTube channel."

Now it made sense. Rankin was singled out to be bad publicity for the resort. His YouTube channel would guarantee it. They were on a roll. If they could just keep Skip going.

Heather moved back to her own photo and pointed. "Are you sure you didn't strike me when I came through the door of the hotel room my father was supposed to be in? It smelled like the chloroform you used on the woman in the hallway."

"Roxy told me all I had to do was pour that smelly stuff on a rag and put it over the mouth and nose of the dame in the hall. I left quick and went back to our room when she went to sleep. I left the bottle and rag in the hall."

"Was Roxy in your room when you got back?"

"Naw. She came back later."

Steve took a step forward. "That's enough for now. Let's give Skip some time to think, drink a cup of coffee, and have an eclair or two."

Detective Nohr gave his officers a nod of approval. "Take him out and make sure he doesn't talk to anyone."

The door closed as the officers took him away. Detective Nohr took steps toward Steve. "Do you think he's telling the truth? I had him pegged as the one who did the serious damage to Jim McCloud and killed Nate."

Steve walked to the front row of seats with his cane sweeping a path in front of him until he turned and settled in a chair. "Someone wants us to believe he beat Jim the second time." He lifted his chin and changed the business-like tone of his voice to something more casual. "I like your idea of coffee and a snack. Unless my nose is lying, both are on the table near Heather's father."

For the first time, Mr. McBlythe spoke. "I'll bring you a cup. Would you prefer a muffin or a scone? They cleaned out the eclairs."

"Scone, please. Are you enjoying the show?"

"I'm learning a lot. If you ever give up solving murders, I could use you negotiating with labor unions."

"I'll leave that dangerous work to people like you and Heather."

Steve was halfway through his cup of coffee and scone when Detective Nohr sat beside him and asked, "Who do you want next?"

"Roxy's had enough time to think. Let's take another run at her."

Officers placed Roxy in the front row again, away from Steve. He hadn't finished his scone and purposefully made her wait. The quiet room had the desired effect of causing her to fidget and dry wash her hands.

Steve stood and walked back to his spot at the end of the whiteboard. "Heather, draw an arrow between Roxy's picture and Jim McCloud's."

Heather drew the line as Roxy demanded, "Why are you doing that? I didn't touch him."

Steve shook his head. "You should have taken the first deal." His voice rose several decibels. "We now have confirmation you're responsible for breaking into the power station and cutting off the lights. We also know you had plenty of time to get back. Because you plunged the resort into darkness, most security cameras became useless. Multiple assaults took place during the blackout."

Roxy looked on through narrowed eyelids. "That's a shame, but I was in bed."

Instead of erupting, Steve mocked her claim. "Do you think we don't know you're trying to pin as much as you can on Skip? He's been your useful fool for years. The only reason you keep him around is to do some of your dirty work and give you alibis."

He turned to Heather. "Add more lines to the board."

Heather nodded. "You'll notice I've put Skip's photo on the board and now there's a solid line between him and the bodyguard he chloroformed in the hallway. Also notice there's a line connecting you and Skip to Jim McCloud for the bloody nose."

Steve interrupted. "The one thing we didn't ask him was whose room you went to when you came back from the power station. That was an oversight but one that we'll soon remedy. Skip is quite the conversationalist after he starts talking."

Heather took the marker in her hand. "I might as well draw another line between your photo and Jim McCloud's for the second assault."

"Don't forget the other assaults," said Steve.

"Right," said Heather. "There's Mr. Rankin, Zhang Min, me, and the attempt on my father. Either you or Skip assaulted all of us."

"Not true," said Roxy with vigor. "Skip may have gotten a little carried away with Mr. Rankin, but that's all he did. I didn't touch a soul."

Detective Nohr shouted, "You're lying. I want a dotted line between her photo and the one of Nate. I still say we can get a conviction based on circumstantial evidence."

Steve changed the tone of his voice again to something with a few flecks of sympathy. "Think about this, Roxy. We know why you keep Skip around and get him a bottle of gin every day. You two sleep in separate beds and you keep him out on the patio most of the time like he's your pet bulldog. Now that he's realized you've used him for years, we found him to be quite cooperative. In fact, he's already admitted to several of the assaults on the board and he's tired of the way you've treated him."

Heather gave a firm nod of her head. "Very tired of it."

Steve followed Heather's words with, "The irony of all this is that you're being played the same way you play Skip."

"Nobody plays me," growled Roxy.

"No? Think about it. Do you really believe they would ever allow a woman like you to run Nate's hotel or this resort? They'd already changed their mind and found someone with an Ivy League education to fill that position. He tried to back out of the deal and paid the price. They don't want a washed up madame from the wrong side of the Hudson. Face it, you're completely out of your league and they've set you up to take the big fall. As soon as they feel heat, your name will be in the papers for killing Nate."

Roxy's darting eyes told Heather Steve's words had struck home. Heather looked at Detective Nohr and gave the slightest of nods.

"Take her out again," said the detective.

Steve put an exclamation mark on the conversation by saying. "When we bring you back, it will be your last chance to save yourself."

Officers had Roxy halfway to the door when she turned. "What kind of deal?"

Steve gave a slight nod. "That's a smart move, Roxy."

37

An officer moved Roxy to a chair in the third row after Steve, Detective Nohr, and Heather had plumbed the depths of her knowledge about the crimes. As a reward, the officer allowed her to bring her hands in front of her to put on the handcuffs.

Next, officers brought in Skip and placed him on the opposite end of the row from Roxy. She tried to shrink him with her stare until he responded by sticking his tongue out at her.

At Detective Nohr's nod, officers retrieved two more individuals. Like Roxy and Skip, Juan and Li Jing sported chrome handcuffs. Li Jing kept quiet, but Juan had no intention of doing so. "Someone's going to lose their job over this."

Steve was quick with a comeback. "You're right, but it won't be who you think."

Juan and Li Jing sat side-by-side in the front row. They examined the whiteboard until the door opened and Bella, Adam, and Lonnie walked in. Bella spoke first, "Juan's stepmom is coming. She looks mad as a hungry shark with a toothache."

Detective Nohr turned toward the door and spoke over his shoulder, "I'll head her off."

The speed of Judith's approach told Heather the woman with

the spinal injury made exceptionally good time when she wanted to. Her voice blasted through the partially open door. "Where's Juan? Why was he led from the beach in handcuffs?"

"You can't come in," said Detective Nohr in a soft but firm voice.

"I demand to see Juan Tovar and to know why you've arrested him."

"He's being detained for questioning."

Steve raised a hand. "I don't see why she can't come in. She might help us with a few details."

The detective gave Judith a firm stare. "I'll make an exception this time, but it comes with the condition that you're not to speak unless I tell you to. Also, you're to sit at the back of the room."

"I'm not promising anything."

"Then you're not coming in. Go back to your room, or wherever else you want to go."

She let out a huff of disgust. "All right. Have it your way for now, but expect a formal complaint followed by a lawsuit."

It was the same response Steve had told Heather to expect. She lost that side bet. Much to her chagrin, it happened more often than not with Steve.

Judith scowled, gave her stepson an assurance that all would soon pass, and pushed her walker to the end seat in the back row.

Heather opened her file folder, took out a photo of Juan, and taped it to the whiteboard under the photos of all the victims. She then drew a solid line between Juan and Jim McCloud and a dotted line from Juan to Nate Johnson. "Your turn, Steve."

He faced the room with both hands on the top of his cane. "As you can see, we now have proof that Juan committed the assault on Jim McCloud."

"What proof?" demanded Judith from near the back of the room.

Detective Nohr barked out, "I warned you, Mrs. Tovar. One more word and you're out of here."

Steve took the lead again. "Even though Judith's question is out of line, it's one that merits an answer. Two witnesses are prepared to testify that they have firsthand knowledge that Juan Tovar broke into Mr. McCloud's room and assaulted him."

"Impossible," said Juan. "I was asleep in my room."

"Not much of an alibi. You're staying in a room whose balcony is directly above Jim McCloud's. You dive twice a day and you're in excellent physical condition. How easy would it be for you to tie a rope on the railing of your balcony and use it to climb a few feet down?"

"I don't even know that guy," protested Juan.

"But you know Roxy Smith, and she knows Jim quite well." He paused. "Please don't insult Detective Nohr's intelligence by trying to deny it."

"Phone records," said the detective before Juan could speak.

"So what? I heard Nate wanted to sell the hotel. Roxy wanted out of New Jersey and I told her about it."

Judith spoke from the back of the room. "Say nothing else, Juan."

Steve ignored the voice and plowed on. "Like I was saying, Juan, you climbed down from your room, onto Jim's balcony, went into his room and worked him over."

Juan challenged the claim with a smirk while saying, "And why would I do a thing like that?"

"I'll let someone else tell you."

"Who?"

Roxy raised her handcuffed hands. "It's all over for you, Juan." She looked to the end of her row. "Ain't that right, Skip?"

"Yeah. I never did like him."

"Those two will say anything to save their skin. You couldn't find two more unconvincing witnesses," Juan sneered.

"Thank you," said Heather, "for confirming you know these two."

Judith seethed but had the good sense to clamp her mouth shut.

Juan asked, "What reason would I have to harm Jim McCloud?"

"We'll get to that in due time," said Steve. "What's important is that you're going to be arrested for the attempted murder of Jim McCloud and for the murder of Nate Johnson."

Judith's mouth came unclamped. "Now you've made complete fools of yourselves. Juan was in Colombia when that man died."

Heather took her turn. "Cartagena, Colombia, to be exact. That doesn't mean he didn't hire someone to kill Nate or help plan the crime. It's a good thing we have people who can corroborate that was his plan."

"That's impossible," said Judith with absolute certainty. "If you want the person who killed Nate Johnson, look no farther than that woman sitting next to my son. The police know she did it and they have plenty of proof."

The corner of Steve's mouth quirked up in a smile. "Has anyone noticed that we haven't talked about who has a motive for killing Nate Johnson?"

The question hung in the air. Finally, Steve said, "Li Jing, Mrs. Tovar thinks you murdered Nate Johnson. Can you tell us what you're doing on the island and what you know?"

Li Jing stood, took a few steps toward the board, turned, and faced the room. "I work with an international organization that's dedicated to the preservation and protection of marine environments. Our agency received a tip some time ago that someone wanted to destroy the reef that protects the resort's bay."

Bella gasped with a hand over her mouth.

Adam asked, "Who would want to destroy the reef?" He put a hand around Bella's shoulders and drew her close. "Sorry. I didn't mean to interrupt."

"All the same," said Steve, "that was an excellent question

Adam, because it goes to the heart of the motive for killing Nate."

Before Steve could explain, a knock on the door sounded. In walked a police officer wearing gloves and carrying a plastic bag containing a laptop. Detective Nohr took it from him and went to a side table. He turned to Li Jing.

She complied with the pre-arranged signal. The handcuffs came off and he handed her a pair of gloves. "Can you identify this lap top?"

"It belongs to Juan Tovar. He took it on the diving boat each day and kept it in his room. It's easily identified by the stickers."

"Do you know the password to get in it?"

Li Jing gave her head a nod.

"That's illegal!" shouted Juan. "You can't take my computer without a search warrant."

Detective Nohr reached into his pocket and pulled out a tri-folded document. "Ask and you will receive. A judge signed it yesterday and officers searched your room while you were being detained."

While William was talking, Li Jing powered up the computer. "No need for me to give you the password. It's already unlocked."

Heather and William moved to where they could see the screen. Li Jing gave a running narrative. "Every day Juan added to the topographical map he made of the reef." She dragged the mouse and clicked. "This one is the most complete."

"What do all the X marks represent?" asked Detective Nohr.

"That's where the holes are to be drilled into the reef. There's a separate chart that tells the type of explosive they intend to use and the quantity required for each blast."

Bella's words were filled with dismay. "I can't believe anyone would want to destroy the reef. Why?"

"It's simple," said Steve. "Money. It's a lovely resort, but how much more would it be worth if the new owners could fill the bay with blue-water sailboats? Blow a hole through the reef and you have a channel for them to pass through."

"Over my dead body," said Lonnie.

Steve shook his head. "No. Over Nate's dead body."

Bella's blue eyes flashed. "Juan Tovar killed Nate."

Judith erupted in a full-throated denial of Juan's guilt. Fingers pointed and voices raised.

Heather moved to Steve. "You'd better cut to the chase."

38

Detective Nohr held up both hands as a signal for everyone to stop. "Before we go on, I need to speak to those who are being detained."

"Good idea," said Heather. "You don't want to blow everything because of a silly mistake."

The detective took in a full breath and spoke rapidly. "Everyone wearing handcuffs, you're officially under arrest. You have the right to remain silent..."

He kept talking as Judith rose to her feet without using her walker. "I'll not tolerate this. Juan will not go to jail for things he couldn't have done."

Detective Nohr rested his hands on his hips. "Mrs. Tovar, I gave you multiple warnings about interrupting this investigation. You're under arrest, too. I'll start over on the warning I'm required to give all suspects."

"On what charge?"

"Interfering with a police investigation."

After the detective finished the formalities, Steve took his place in front of the whiteboard. Heather moved to Steve's side. "Mr. Smiley will now relate the events that happened in the hotel when the lights went out."

Steve waited until the room was quiet. "Roxy, did you cut the power off at the substation?"

She dipped her head. "Yeah. But I never touched nobody."

Steve spoke to her as if she were a third grader. "Come on, Roxy. You can do better than that. Who approached you and paid your way to come to St. Croix and stay at Nate's hotel? Who's paying for you and Skip to stay at this resort?"

She dipped her head and said, "Juan Tovar. He paid us in cash. Skip and I are here to scout out the hotel and the resort, report back to him, and rough up a few people."

"Why harm Mr. Rankin?"

"The same reason Skip gave Jim McCloud a bloody nose. We were to give the resort a bad reputation to get the owners to sell cheap."

"Skip," said Steve. "Did you assault a woman in the hotel's hallway when the lights went out?"

He looked a little confused and said, "I put a rag over her face till she went beddy-bye. That's all."

"Thanks Skip. Did you kill Nate Johnson?"

"Nope."

"Did Roxy?"

"We were in St. Thomas that night."

"Did you accidentally push Mr. Rankin too hard and kick him a few times when he was down?"

"Yeah. He started cussin' me."

"Thanks Skip."

Steve paused and scratched his chin. "Roxy. Who told you to spend the night in St. Thomas?"

"Juan called me. He paid, and I didn't ask questions."

"You can't prove that," said Juan with too much confidence.

Steve came back at him with, "It was a mistake to tell them to go to St. Thomas. If they'd been here, you might have been able to pin Nate's murder on them."

"That was the original plan," said Roxy. "He wanted Skip to take care of Nate. I told him Skip wouldn't do it."

Heather asked, "How did Juan react?"

"He got mad." She cast her gaze to Juan, eyes blazing. "You shouldn't have told me I wasn't good enough to run Nate's hotel."

Steve took over. "Let's talk about what happened when the lights went out." He directed his question to Roxy. "I know you took a key to Mr. McBlythe's room by bribing one of the desk clerks. You gave that key to someone, didn't you?"

Her gaze shifted to the carpet. "Yeah."

"It was Juan, wasn't it?"

"Ain't no use in denying it. You got all the right answers."

"More lies," shouted Judith.

Heather knew what was coming next from Steve. He loved to keep suspects off balance and go back and forth between separate story lines, only to bring them back together and tie up the loose ends.

"Bear with me as I explain the entire plan. Nate owned a small but successful hotel in town. When he learned the Swensons wanted to sell their resort, he wanted to purchase it. Jim McCloud heard through the grapevine a money-making hotel was coming on the market and he flew to St. Croix to check out Nate's hotel. Jim had made a series of horrible business decisions and wanted a silent partner to back the deal. It wasn't an enormous deal to Juan and his associates, but hotels are a good place to launder money. Juan agreed but at a price. Jim would be the purchasing agent, but would have no input into the running of the hotel. Juan chose Roxy to run the hotel and sent her and Skip to check it out. After she arrived on the island, Roxy told Juan about the Swenson resort, and he realized this could be a landslide, two-for-one deal."

"This is nothing but lies," said Judith from the back of the room. "You can add slander to the charges I'll bring against you."

Steve went on like he hadn't heard her. "All it took was one look at this resort, and Juan and his people were licking their lips. If one hotel was a good place to wash dirty money, how much better if it were two? The first task was to get Nate out of the way. That was easy. Kill him. But that wasn't enough for Juan and his associates. They wanted to lower the value of this property. Their plan began with a fake assault against Jim. They escalated it when they waylaid Rankin, who produces travel and resort videos. Jim's second beating was a warning to stay in line with the plan and had the added benefit of devaluing the resort."

Heather interrupted, "When Juan and his associates heard my father was putting together investors to make a bid, they saw their plan crumbling."

Steve nodded. "Surely the murder of Mr. McBlythe would scare off anyone else, and they'd get the resort at a fraction of its worth."

Heather took up the story where Steve left off. "Once they obtained this resort, they planned to increase the value of the property by blasting a channel through the reef. Visions of yachts and multi-million-dollar sailboats in the bay danced in their heads. They were undone by greed and caught the attention of people who don't take kindly to destroying marine wildlife habitat."

Heather gave Detective Nohr a nod. He walked to the door, opened it, and motioned with his hand.

Steve spoke with confidence. "We have a special guest who would like to hear the rest of the story."

An officer pushed a wheelchair carrying Jim McCloud through the door.

Heather watched as Juan Tovar's eyes widened and jerked against the handcuffs. An officer pushed him back into his seat.

"Good morning, Jim."

Jim looked at Juan. "He's the one who attacked me in my room. Is he going to jail?"

Heather answered for Steve. "For a long time."

"Glad to hear it."

Steve pressed on. "Here's what else happened in the hotel when the lights went out. Roxy has already told us she bribed a desk clerk for the key to Mr. McBlythe's room and Skip stated he rendered the guard in the hall unconscious. With no one in the hall to hear, Juan attached a rope to his balcony and climbed down onto Jim's balcony. He entered Jim's room through an unlocked patio door and attacked him."

"Now I remember," said Jim. "I heard a noise and turned on the light on my phone and saw him come in. He told me I'd be food for the fish if I didn't go through with acting as the buyer. He hit me in the head with a short wooden bat, and I went to the floor. I remember him laughing when he started kicking me. That was bad, but nothing compared to when he took the bat to my knee. Over and over, he kept hitting the same spot."

Juan was on his feet. "He couldn't identify me. It was pitch black."

"Don't worry, Juan," said Judith. "I'll get you the best lawyer money can buy."

Detective Nohr spoke. "I received a text from officers in Juan's room. They found rope fibers on the railing of his balcony."

Steve turned to Juan. "Perhaps you should follow your mother's advice and not say anything else."

Bella raised her hand.

Heather leaned into Steve. "Bella has a question."

"Yes, Bella," said Steve.

"Who tried to kill Mr. McBlythe?"

"Well done," said Steve. "You remember details that are left hanging. The person who tried to kill Mr. McBlythe is the same person who killed Nate Johnson."

A dramatic pause followed. Every pair of eyes in the room locked on Steve. Time slowed as people leaned forward. Finally, he said, "Judith Tovar."

A riotous laugh came from the back of the room. Anger replaced mirth as Judith spoke through clenched teeth. "Look at me, Mr. Smiley." An evil, taunting laugh burst forth from her. "That's right, you can't see me because you're blind. If you could, you'd know I'm physically impaired and struggle to walk. That makes it impossible to kill a healthy man in his prime."

The corners of Steve's mouth pulled up. He tuned to Heather. "Describe Mrs. Tovar's physical condition."

"Her legs are moderately impaired, but she's capable of walking short distances without aid. She exercises daily by taking early morning walks and swimming laps. Her shoulders are broad and her upper body is firm and strong, as you'd expect from a habitual swimmer."

"Would you say she's capable of walking ten to twenty yards without the aid of her walker?"

"I saw her do so at the pool."

"Are you saying she's physically able to kill someone?"

"Absolutely."

"It's all a lie," shouted Judith.

"Let's move on.

"Roxy came back from the power station and used the key she got from the desk clerk to unlock Mr. McBlythe's door." Steve raised his chin. "Take it from there, Roxy."

"I went in the room with the chloroform Skip had waiting for me in the hall." She nodded toward Zhang Min. "Juan never said nothin' 'bout there being a man or a woman in the bed. Only that I was to knock 'em out, and that's what I did."

Juan shifted and glared at Roxy. "Expect a late-night visit from some friends of mine."

Roxy shot back. "They'll be on my turf if they come to Jersey. It ain't a healthy place for people who don't live there."

Steve took up the chain of events, cutting off the threat and counter-threat. "Roxy then exited the room. Right, Roxy?"

"It's like you was there, Steve."

"Thanks. You're doing a lot to help yourself by telling the truth." Steve took a step back and continued, "Roxy left the room and put the key in the lock for Judith, who came with a garrote. She hovered over the sleeping body and realized it wasn't Mr. McBlythe. While she considered what to do, she heard Heather unlocking the door with the spare key. In her panic, she dropped the garrote, and moved against a wall. Heather walked in to check on Zhang Min and was knocked to the ground. Judith made her escape into the hallway. We've already established she's not as physically impaired as she pretends to be."

"Good luck proving any of this," snarled Judith.

A knock on the door preceded an officer entering with an evidence bag in her hand. She handed it to Detective Nohr and spoke in a volume so muted only he could hear. He walked to where Heather stood beside Steve and held up the bag for her to inspect. He then faced the room and spoke to the woman near the back. "Mrs. Tovar, I believe this to be the garrote used to kill Nate Johnson. We found it under the mattress in your bedroom. It matches the materials used to make the one you left on the floor of Mr. McBlythe's room. Don't worry about trying to explain how it got there. You'll have plenty of time to do so after we get you to jail."

Detective Nohr nodded to his officers. "Take them all away."

The train of suspects was led out of the room accompanied by threats and shouts of injustice from Juan and Judith Tovar.

Steve said, "That's my cue to stop talking. There's a lounge chair under a palm tree calling my name."

With the case wrapped up, Heather allowed herself to think about the long-delayed talk she needed to have with Jack and his daughter.

39

The morning sun was four hours into its ascent when Heather walked past the pool. She was fifteen minutes early for her appointment, still practicing what she'd say. She moved to the boardwalk and sought encouragement from the small waves washing to shore. Her eyes were closed when a voice belonging to a preteen made the reality of the moment all too clear. "Jack said I had to talk to you."

Heather turned and tried to look into averted eyes. The rigidity of Briann's body spoke the language of defiance. She said the first thing that came to mind. "Let's get away from everyone. What we have to talk about is private."

It surprised Heather that she and Briann were the same height and build. The girl's mostly brown hair had light hues of red.

"Where are we going?"

Heather pointed. "All the way down the beach."

The preteen lifted a sulky shoulder and let it fall. They took off their sandals and turned when they reached damp sand. Neither spoke until they reached the mouth of the bay where waves curled over the reef.

Heather's young companion plopped down under a palm tree

and hugged her knees. Heather settled beside her and allowed her gaze to lock onto the surf. "What did you and your dad do last night?"

"We had supper and listened to music on the patio."

"That sounds nice."

"Not really. Life pretty well sucks for both of us."

Heather cast her gaze to Briann, but the preteen focused on the waves. "I'm sorry to hear about your mother."

"Yeah, I bet."

"No, really. My mother died suddenly last year and it still hurts."

"She must've been old. My mom was thirty-five."

Heather knew it was a losing proposition to compare grief with an adolescent, so she backed off and changed the subject. "What do you think about the resort?"

A light shrug rolled across Briann's shoulders. "It's okay."

"Did you meet Bella and Adam?"

"Yeah. She's cool, and he's a major hunk." She cut her gaze to Heather then back to the water. "Maybe I'll get married soon. That would leave you and Jack to get on with your lives."

"Don't be a dolt."

Briann might as well have been a threatened porcupine. "You're engaged. That means it won't be long until you're my stepmother."

Heather shook her head. "You're wrong." She let the words float away in the wind.

Fire glittered in Briann's eyes when she turned her gaze to Heather. "What do you mean, I'm wrong?"

"Didn't Jack tell you?"

"Tell me what?"

"Your father and I met after you were asleep last night. We came to an agreement."

A frown cut across Briann's face. "What sort of agreement?"

Instead of giving a direct answer, Heather asked, "What do you know about me?"

The girl's gaze returned to the waves. "Steve told me some stuff last night."

Heather raised her eyebrows in surprise. "When?"

"While you and Jack were talking on the beach, I went out to the pool and Steve was there. He told me you're a rich business-woman, an attorney like my mom, and you help him solve murders."

"Anything else?"

The girl lifted her chin in challenge and turned her gaze on Heather. "Yeah. He said you're afraid to get married, and the thought of being a stepmother is more than you can stand."

Anger flashed until Heather realized how right Briann was. She leaned her head back and let loose with a hearty laugh.

Briann stiffened. "What's so funny?"

"Steve knows me better than I know myself. He's absolutely right. I've never wanted children because I know I'd be a lousy mother." She took in a fresh breath of sea air. "That's why your father and I agreed to take a giant step back from our relationship."

"Oh, great. I'll get the blame for breaking you up."

Heather shook her head slowly. "The only thing you did was make us both realize that we enjoy being single. We get along fine the way things are."

Confusion passed across the young face. "That's weird."

"Why? Your mom never married."

A light of hope shone in Briann's eyes. "Are you saying you and Jack won't see each other again?"

"Not at all. We'll keep on like we are."

"Are you engaged or not?" she snapped.

"Not. I gave the ring back to him last night."

Briann turned her full gaze on Heather.

"I still have strong feelings for your father, but this is the right path for us. We're in agreement."

"Will you and Jack ever get married?"

"No time soon. Probably not until you're grown and out on

your own. Until then, your father and I will continue to see each other, but we'll lead separate lives. You two need time by yourselves. You also have a grandmother you need to get acquainted with. If you'll allow yourself to get to know her, I think you'll really like her."

Heather saw Briann's stiff shoulders ease somewhat.

"Right now, she's the best part of the deal. She's quitting as his secretary so she can be home any time I need her."

Heather issued a half-smile. "You're the grandchild she wanted and I wasn't willing to give her."

Briann tilted her head and asked, "Do you really have your own jet?"

Heather nodded. "After the wedding you and Jack are flying back to Texas with me and Steve."

Briann lifted her chin. "No offense, but I'm glad you're not going to be my stepmother."

A small smile lifted Heather's lips. "Believe me, I'm somewhat relieved myself."

The two stood at the same time. Heather asked, "Are you hungry?"

"I will be by the time we walk back to the resort."

Heather breathed a silent sigh of relief. All that was left to do now was forge a friendship of sorts with this stubborn young girl who could care less. She fervently hoped she hadn't used up all her miracles.

40

Heather stepped off the elevator the following morning humming a tune. Steve stood with his back to a wall, near the lobby, waiting for her. "You sound chipper."

"I am. All the bad guys are in jail and my relational planets are back in their proper orbits."

Steve whispered to her that they needed to stop at the front desk. Heather recognized Frank Jones as he stepped from a back room. "Good morning, Mr. Smiley." He shifted his gaze. "Ms. McBlythe. What can I do for you?"

Steve spoke before Heather could, which was a good thing. She had no idea what Steve wanted or needed.

"Your wife's not working with you today?"

His gaze shifted to look at some distant spot as his shoulders dropped a full inch. "She returned to Texas for a family emergency."

"That's a shame," said Steve. "When did she leave?"

"Today. On the first flight out. She's in the air now."

"Back to Houston, I assume."

"That's right."

Heather came on point. That wasn't the right answer. Frank

and Mary Jones came from Dallas. Perhaps her family lived in Houston.

"Have all the groom's family arrived?"

"The shuttle has gone to pick up the last of the family members."

"Thanks, Frank. We'll keep Mary in our thoughts and prayers."

Heather led Steve and whispered, "What was that about?"

He whispered back, "You're about to find out. Let's go to breakfast."

"Only coffee for me. I'm still full from the rehearsal dinner. Lonnie and Ingrid went all out."

The trip through the dining room took longer than usual as most of Adam's family had arrived the day before and wanted to know the details of the previous morning's arrests. Steve spoke in a nonchalant manner, minimizing the events of the previous two weeks. He gave assurances that the resort was safer than any other in the world, which wasn't a lie. Appreciative police and judicial officials were scheduled to come and go all day. In addition, her father gave his New York bodyguards the bonus of staying extra days.

They joined Jack and Briann at their table where the preteen sat entranced by the images on her pink phone and Jack looking relieved that she was.

After a casual greeting and coffee cups filled, Steve leaned her direction. "Heather, I'm sure you picked up on this, but Connie and William Nohr are on the verge of being a serious item. The wedding this evening should push them over the edge."

"It didn't take a detective to figure that out."

"Did you know they're making a deal with Lonnie and Ingrid to buy the resort?"

"So, it's moving forward. That puts William running Nate's hotel and her here at the resort?"

Steve spoke as if he was a prophet of the unseen future. "He'll turn in his badge, and they'll run both. Mark my word."

"I knew Father wasn't interested in purchasing the resort. It makes sense that they would own both, at least for a while. If they ever get in a financial bind, they can sell Nate's Hotel."

Heather sensed Steve had more on his mind than William and Connie. She tried to beat him to the punch.

"I hate to spoil your surprise, but I know the reason you spoke with Frank Jones at the front desk. He sold the hotel key to my father's room to Roxy. I'm surprised you and Detective Nohr missed that when you rounded up everyone."

Steve spoke in a matter-of-fact tone. "I asked William to delay arresting him."

Heather reeled back in her chair. "Why did you do that?"

"Frank's at a crossroads in his life and needs a break."

"How do you know?"

"I talked to Mary this morning before she left." He located his glass of water but didn't take a drink. "By the way, her name isn't Mary Jones, and Frank Jones is an alias, too."

Heather sat with her mouth hinged open. Jack took over and asked, "Do you know Frank's real name?"

"I do, and so does Heather. It's Quinton Rush."

Heather shook her head to show she didn't recognize the name. Seconds passed, then she gasped as a bolt of revelation hit her.

Steve chuckled. "It's so much fun to hear the gears in your mind turn until everything falls in place."

Heather turned to face Jack. "Leo needed help the day before we flew here. It was a possible homicide. It didn't take Steve long to discover that the man had faked his death. Bella called us that very day and told us about Nate's murder here at the resort. I put the case out of my mind after that. The man that faked his murder is working the front desk."

Steve added, "Without the woman who left him today to fly back to Houston."

Heather didn't hide the concern in her voice. "Do Lonnie and Ingrid know he sold a copy of the hotel key?"

"They know. So does Detective Nohr."

"Will he arrest him?" asked Jack.

Steve placed both hands on the tablecloth. "I talked them into letting him stay. The insurance company will never pay on the policy, and his girlfriend left him today with what little money they had. He's stuck on this small island with no way to leave." He took a sip of coffee. "Besides, Lonnie and Ingrid need him to work double shifts today and tomorrow. All the staff wants to be at Bella's wedding, then it will be all hands on deck to get everyone checked out the next day."

Heather and Jack traded knowing glances. Steve had been two steps ahead of her again. Instead of anger or self-loathing, her emotions kicked up their heels. One more planet back in its proper orbit.

———

HEATHER THOUGHT HOW PERFECT IT WAS THAT BELLA HAD chosen a harpist to play at her wedding. The notes rang out clear, clean, and pure... just like Bella.

She peeked out from behind a muslin screen that had been erected where the pool met the boardwalk. A light tropical breeze caused it to billow softly. Beyond the boardwalk sat guests in chairs looking like soldiers in formation. Adam ran one finger nervously around the collar of his white shirt, then clasped both hands in front of him. In his black tuxedo and Bermuda shorts, he stood out from his groomsmen who wore white tuxedo coats and white Bermuda shorts. Their bare feet dug into the sand.

Briann joined Heather to take a look. She whispered. "Are you sure about this? What if he bolts away from me?"

"Just hold on to the leash. Max loves to be the center of attention."

"This is goofy. Whoever heard of a cat as ring bearer?"

"There's a first time for everything. Remember, after the best man unties the ribbon holding the wedding bands to the harness, your job is finished. Rejoin Jack and Steve. If Max balks, I'll come back up the aisle and pick him up."

The notes changed and the other bridesmaids moved into position. "That's the processional. Remember to wait until I'm in position. You and Max will be the last ones down the aisle before Bella and her father."

"All right, but if this turns into a dumpster fire, it's your fault."

As maid of honor, Heather would be the last bridesmaid to walk on the runner of white carpet. The procession was slow, with each of the four women waiting until the one before them took their place and faced the crowd. Finally, it was her turn.

She stepped onto the boardwalk, took halting steps and reached the carpet. An arbor stood behind the pastor with sheer white fabric billowing around it. Tulle and flowers in shades of purple covered the wooden frame, giving the perfect stage for the event that would forever change Bella and Adam's lives. It set a boundary but allowed a view of the sea beyond it. In the distance, the setting sun kissed the waves breaking over the reef.

Heather took her place in front of the arbor, turned, and awaited Briann and Max's arrival. Chuckles and the sound of cameras clicking joined the notes of the harp. Max walked with chin raised and tether slack. Her furry son acted like a veteran thespian. A kitty treat awaited him when he arrived at her feet. The best man joined her and they traded winks as the bride and groom's rings were set free from Max's flower-bedecked harness.

The only hiccup in Max's performance came when he let his feelings be known that he had no intention of leaving the play that was about to unfold.

Heather whispered to Briann. "Leave him with me. He'll be fine."

Briann handed the leash over without complaint or comment and retreated to her seat. With a quick glance to Jack, Heather signaled all was well.

The harpist swept her fingers up and down the strings, signaling a change in volume and music. Heads turned and the crowd of over two hundred stood. From behind the barrier Bella and Lonnie appeared. Seeing the two of them brought tears to Heather's eyes. She wondered if anyone would remember anything but how gorgeous Bella looked.

Her strapless gown, the long skirt flowing softly from a ruched bodice, made her look like a goddess. Two narrow braids held her long white-blonde hair off her face, clasped together in the back with a purple orchid and baby's breath. Her softly curled hair fell to her waist. Simple. Breathtaking.

Heather saw Adam's shoulders relax as he took his bride's hand and turned to face the pastor. The wedding progressed with all the pomp and solemnity of one held in a cathedral until they were pronounced husband and wife. Solemnity fell away and joy erupted when Bella took Adam, bowed him backward, his arm flailing, and kissed him. Shouts and whistles of approval came from the crowd when Adam stopped resisting and enjoyed the moment. With a wide smile, Bella grasped Adam's hand and took her bouquet from Heather.

Holding her flowers in the air, Bella shouted, "Reception in the ballroom. Let's celebrate!"

Bella and Adam ran down the white carpet with youthful abandon. Amidst thunderous clapping, the guests rose and began to follow the bride and groom. Heather, the bridesmaids, and the groomsmen gave up any idea of making an orderly exit.

As the crowd dispersed, Heather made her way to Jack, Steve, her father, and Briann.

She turned to Briann. "I have a favor to ask you."

Young arms folded across her chest. "What?"

Steve answered for her. "Bella wants Max at the reception.

Could you take him? I need to talk to Heather, Mr. McBlythe, and Jack for a few minutes. You'd be doing Bella a big favor."

Briann reached for the leash. "Come on, Max. Let's see if they have caviar."

Once his daughter was out sight, Jack said, "She's nuts about Max. Don't be surprised if she asks to sleep with him tonight."

Heather rubbed her chin. "We might be able to come to some sort of agreement, counselor."

Jack's left eyebrow raised. "You realize I'm a tough negotiator."

"You'll need to be."

Steve cleared his throat, interrupting the private conversation.

Heather and Jack turned to face him. She asked, "Do you have something to say?"

"To quote something said during the wedding, 'I do.' After I tell you what it is, our investigation is complete. Bella has asked me to dance with her after she takes Adam and her father for a spin around the floor."

"Then we'd better hurry. I thought all the loose ends were tied up."

"Not quite. Did you notice anyone missing at the wedding?"

Heather searched her memory. She was about to give up when Steve blurted out, "Zhang Min and Li Jing."

Heather's eyes widened in revelation. "That's right, I haven't seen them since yesterday morning. Did they leave the resort?"

Her father took a step forward and spoke in a loud whisper. "A little mother-daughter time together on the government's dime."

Heather looked at her father for clarification. Receiving none, she looked at Jack.

He shrugged and said, "Don't look at me. I'm on the fast track to learning how to deal with a hard-headed daughter."

Her father placed a hand on her shoulder and looked her in

the eye. "You're not the only person who has contacts in the CIA."

Heather's voice croaked as she asked, "Do you mean they're Spooks?"

Steve grinned. "Both mother and daughter. You didn't see that one coming, did you?"

FROM THE AUTHOR

Thank you for reading *A Beach To Die For*. I hope you enjoyed your escape to the Caribbean as you turned the pages to find out whodunit! If you loved it, please consider leaving a review at your favorite retailer, Bookbub or Goodreads. Your reviews help other readers discover their next great mystery!

To stay abreast of Smiley and McBlythe's latest adventure, and all my book news, join my Mystery Insiders community. As a thank you, I'll send you a *reader exclusive* Smiley and McBlythe mystery novella, plus you'll be among the first to know about new releases, discounts and recommendations.

You can also follow me on Amazon, Bookbub and Goodreads to receive notification of my latest release.

Happy reading!
Bruce

Scan the image to sign up or go to brucehammack.com/the-smiley-and-mcblythe-mysteries-reader-gift/

Dig Deep For Murder

It was the perfect murder... until the truth refused to stay buried.

With no active murder case to solve, blind private investigator Steve Smiley is enjoying a week of peace and quiet. Meanwhile, his partner is preoccupied with her latest real estate project. However, their tranquility is short-lived when a dead body is unearthed at the construction site.

Suspicion falls on a young construction worker and brings the project to a standstill. When the boy's lawyer hires them to prove his innocence, Smiley must navigate the complicated dynamics of high school friendships and broken relationships.

Tight-knit loyalty and deception among the teenagers challenge Smiley's investigative skills. He'll have to dig deep to uncover the truth and set an innocent young man free while stopping a killer from getting away with murder.

Scan above image or go to brucehammack.com/books/dig-deep-for-murder/

About The Author

Drawing from his extensive background in criminal justice, Bruce Hammack writes contemporary, clean read detective and crime mysteries. He is the author of the Smiley and McBlythe Mysteries, the Fen Maguire Mysteries, the Star of Justice series and the Detective Steve Smiley Mysteries. Having lived in eighteen cities around the world, he now lives in the Texas hill country with his wife of thirty-plus years.

Follow Bruce on Bookbub and Goodreads for the latest new release info and recommendations. Learn more at brucehammack.com.

www.ingramcontent.com/pod-product-compliance
Lightning Source LLC
LaVergne TN
LVHW042130270325
807131LV00031B/644